The Old Girl

THE OLD GIRL

A novel by

Joshua Gidding

HOLT, RINEHART AND WINSTON
New York

Library of Congress Cataloging in Publication Data

Gidding, Joshua.
The old girl.
I. Title.
PZ4.G453501   [PS3557.I24]   813'.54   79-26850
ISBN Hardbound: 0-03-052196-3
ISBN Paperback: 0-03-057998-8

FIRST EDITION

DESIGNER: *Lucy Castelluccio*
Printed in the United States of America
2 4 6 8 10 9 7 5 3 1

To my grandmothers Cissie and Dodo;
to my mother, in deepest gratitude, and
my father, in continuance,
this book is dedicated.

I believe that my days and my nights, in their poverty and their riches, are the equal of God's and of all men's.

—Borges

The Old Girl

Prologue

My grandmother, a woman of eighty-one, divorced, widowed, transplanted in her time, will be married again next month. Though it would hardly be appropriate, considering her morals (which ostensibly are the strictest) to term it a "shotgun wedding" (besides which this description would suggest, for her, a biological impossibility), it is no secret that she has known the gentleman in question for some time less than a year. Barely three months, in fact.

The wedding has been set for Sunday, May 11. My grandmother insisted on a Sunday, as she also insisted on a Jewish ceremony. Mr. di Barnaba, the groom-to-be, accepted her insistences with characteristic magnanimity. From what I understand, his first wife was Jewish (he wears the wedding band still in altered position on his left middle finger). The idea of a Jewish ceremony seemed to him an indifferent detail; and seeing how important it was to my grandmother he went right along with her—although it is apparent, to me at least, that he is not, nor most likely was he ever, "a believer." But he certainly seems to believe in my grandmother. This is not difficult to understand—as you will see.

There is a story behind the wedding, of course—I suppose there is behind most weddings of any interest, especially when

1

the couple are, respectively, eighty-one and seventy (or so he says), and not exactly what one would call intimate in every sense. (Here I am only presuming; pardon me, Grandma.) But this story is not one of loneliness—not at all. That would be my story, if I should ever want to tell it, if anyone should ever want to hear the mildly misadventurous confessions of a prig. . . . The story of my grandmother's wedding is actually a bit more involved. It depends on, or rather it includes, other stories: the story of my uncle—his greed; his delusions; his divine improvidence if you will; I might even say, his fate. For character is fate, is it not? (At any rate, his is a fated one.)

And the story, the many stories, of Mr. Tullio di Barnaba, the last of Old Europe.

But what am I saying? The last of Old Europe—my uncle's fate? Too dramatic, almost absurd. If you only knew the characters, you would see how really absurd it is! Yet here we are, there is no changing it now: Grandmother remains to be married. I must say the Old Girl is pretty shrewd. Not only did she snag a charming continental gentleman ten years her junior (at least), but she did so with a minimum of effort on her part. She made it seem as if he were pursuing her, when I suspect that really the opposite was the case.

I have been charged with the wedding arrangements. She has decided she wants to be married in the biggest, brashest temple in Los Angeles—Temple Beth Israel, Wilshire Boulevard, Beverly Hills. Now please understand that my grandmother is not a vulgar woman. I would even call her overrefined, in some ways. She appears slightly eccentric. Born in New York City, she speaks nevertheless with a mild British accent, which she claims was forced on her by English nuns in a convent school in Japan. (Explanation in due course.) She is given to afternoon tea, bonnets with veils, calling a raincoat a "macintosh" and galoshes "rubbers," and an inveterate love of potatoes. She owns not a single fur coat, or any article of fur-lined clothing. In fact the only coat I can ever remember seeing her wear is my father's ancient riding coat, bought when he was ten, and passed on soon afterward to his mother. So unvulgar is she that she had the brown velvet lapels changed to black. In matters of religion she describes herself as a "Jewess of the Reform school," and refers to those of her religion as "of the Jewish persuasion."

Is it not, then, peculiar that a woman such as this should want to be married in the Temple Beth Israel? I tried to dissuade her, pointing out that she knows very few people in Los Angeles—certainly no more than would make a mere drop in that Dead Sea. But Grandma held fast. She wanted "nice music," and she had heard they had a wonderful organ.

Tomorrow, then, I go to talk to the senior rabbi. And today I am preparing my story. . .

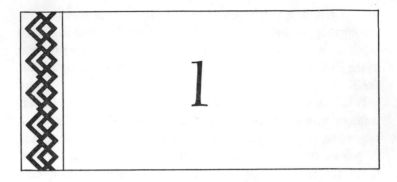

1

In this story there is a city—*"urbs antiqua fuit,"* Vergil wrote, though at ours no doubt he would have shuddered. Hardly ancient, anarchically modern—City of the Angels, city built on dreams, spanning the desert basin from the mountains to the sea—vast, expanding, amoebic, planting its pseudopods in parched canyons, hillsides, scrubland, grasping the land as it lies, furrowing it with freeways, bypasses, growing cloverleafs, overpasses, underpasses, access and exit ramps.

Divine machinery! Before the freeway, I am sure, there was naught. Darkness reigned over the land. Not a sidewalk, not a street, not a soul. Yes, there were fields: orchards, groves, wide plantations, so they say. But this was not life as we know it. Life as we know it came later, under the Freeway Commission, which commanded, "Let there be lanes!" And there were. Only one set at the very first, the Pasadena Freeway, leading from Pasadena, through Glendale, Burbank, skirting Hollywood and on into Downtown. A silver streamlined Appian Way through the golden land of the West. But soon there were others—had to be others, for this single artery was already feeding a growing body. And so they laid down the Harbor, the Hollywood, the Golden State, the Santa Ana, the San Diego, the Santa Monica. And where these met, they created intricate crossovers, soaring skyways, graded ramps on graceful pillars. Such constructions won architectural awards for their safety as well as their beauty (for if there were accidents, they were the fault of men not of roads). All lane markings had gentle bumps to rouse or remind the wandering driver. Central dividers were built of wire mesh and cable, designed to stop and entangle the careening violator before he could crash through into oncoming traffic. Shoulders (both inside and outside) were ample. Electric billboards governing traffic control, placed at regular intervals, warned the motorist of congestion or detours. Helicopters were used to scout out future adversities, such as roadblocks, accidents or breakdowns. The Highway Patrol was alert and ubiquitous. Numbered call boxes were systematically positioned along the outer shoulder for anyone who needed help; these were connected by radio to the Highway Patrol. And for the weary or uncomfortable, there were rest areas set off to the side, with washrooms, vending machines and picnic tables.

It was, for those on the roads—which is to say for everyone, sooner or later—the most convenient, the most sensible, the best of all possible worlds.

And into this world I was born. . . .

The city of course is Los Angeles, my city. Not my grandmother's, although it appears she has finally settled here. Not my uncle's, who always insisted he was staying merely "to set things up," and then moving on. Not even my parents' city, while they were alive, for they, like many here, were transplanted Easterners. No, this is my city, I possessively assert: because I am a native, and live here still, will live here always; because I feel that I alone understand it. I have a particular feeling for its emptiness, its gratuitous artificiality, its insane eclecticism, its gracelessness (in spite of graceful freeway pillars), its proverbial and often real mediocrity, its vulgarity—of a grade more pretentious, more vigorous than the usual American sort—its hopeless lack of curiosity and, really, anything worthy of curiosity, its horror of age and aging, its banal worship of youth. . . .

5

Yes, its beauty. The dun starkness of its hills and cliffs, the shoreline vistas, the moist smell of the sea. Its feckless seasons: fog in June, fires in September. Its vanity, its barrenness, its boredom . . .

I know all this, yet I am not being merely willful when I confess that I care for my city, when I own an affectionate tolerance, nay, a grudging love for it in all its insipidity. I am aware that certain critics of our city, especially New Yorkers, find it unlivable for the very reasons I have just enumerated. But what really offends them about Los Angeles is its most obvious fault: its lack of "culture." We are trendy, we are shallow, we are fanciful, we are socially undignified, we are misguided, we are laughably *unserious*; we are Boeotians in their Attic eyes. We are, in a word, uncultured.

But Boeotians, just as Greeks, will propagate themselves; and I was born into an uncultured world. . . .

A world, however, not lacking in many of culture's trappings. My mother had an ear for music, my father a mouth for . . . a number of things. He started out as a stand-up comedian with a taste for the obscene and, from various reports, a repertoire to match. I imagine his impact on his audiences as something like that of Joseph Pujol, the professional French farter (1857–1945). If one can believe what one reads in the only known biography of this man, Pujol could reportedly fart out nearly anything he pleased: a candle (from a distance of one meter), the "Marseillaise," the sound of a cannon's roar or of a piccolo's peep. Nurses were on hand in the audience in the event of fainting or stroke from excessive hilarity. I doubt that my father was ever so harmfully ribald, though he did tend to be flatulent. I do know, from the various clippings I have saved, and from my uncle's accounts (if these have any validity), that much of his humor was indulgently dirty and foolish—"bathroom humor" would put it about right. I was never present at any of his performances. I was not even born by the time he began to sell his cleaner material to Bob Hope, left the stage forever and moved to Hollywood, where he met my

6

mother in 1940, although they were not married until after the war.

My mother was a Scranton girl, born and bred in Scranton, Pennsylvania. Her father, Aloysius Corrigan, worked for the Scranton Anthracite Authority as a mining engineer and consultant. That is to say, he built strip mines. Attacked by those who opposed this defacing of the land, he nevertheless defended his enterprise until the very end. They were safer for the men, he argued, and cut extraction costs. But my mother claimed that in private, with his family, he was always ambivalent about the job; he was a bit of a nature lover.

He was also a music lover, and gave his daughter an early feeling for it. He played the piano more than adequately, from her accounts, and composed song-and-dance numbers, some of which were once performed at the Scranton Music Hall, with the composer at the piano. Countless times in my childhood, I heard the story of this performance, when Scranton discovered that Corrigan the miner was also a composer. It made a lasting impression, and most of all on my grandfather himself, although in later years he would always play it down, for he was a modest man.

But of his daughter he was unconcealably proud. He sat her at the piano at age six, and didn't let her get up until—well, he never let her get up, really, as long as he lived. Did you practice today, Snooksie? How long? New material? Benignantly solicitous he was, but if the wrong answer came—hell's bells pealed forth. His dedication to music—or rather, his idea of what his daughter's should be—was tyrannical. It was not until she was nineteen that she could find the courage to stand up from the piano stool while he was in the room. And when she did, she never sat down again. He took it as a renunciation.

Remarkably enough, in spite of all this, my mother loved to play, and she played well—just how well I can judge only on the flimsy authority of vague recollection. To my child's ears it sounded fine enough. She played Debussy, some Bach, even some Rachmaninoff. (This I know from the annotated sheet

7

music still inside the piano bench.) I have a hunch she was better than her father, although she was never so recognized. I seem to remember her remarking to me once, "They always used to say, 'Bunny plays well, but not like her father.'" And I remember being very upset by this criticism.

By the way, that was my mother's name—Bunny. Beatrice, actually. One wonders about the nickname. It is quite a ridiculous one, especially for a serious woman. And my mother was a very serious woman—which was probably why she received such a ridiculous nickname.

My mother was a serious woman, and she married a funny man. This in itself should not seem unusual. For we marry, I suppose, in order to be rescued from ourselves. This is why the meeting of opposites is so prevalent, even necessary; and yet it is curious that people are always surprised at such combinations. "He's so funny, and she's so serious," they say, or: "She's smart as a whip, but he's no mental giant," or: "She's so sweet, and he's such an unfeeling clod." But these choices are sensible, part of the instinct for self-preservation; and they reveal also our secret, inexpressible yearning for self-oblivion.

Let me tell how my parents came to meet. I must repeat the story secondhand, for I heard it only recently from my grandmother. For this reason I cannot promise that it is an entirely faithful account, or free from senile lacunae, or even invidious interpolation. . . .

Yet even from Grandma's jagged telling, the tale seems to be one of—parent pick-up! Yes! A bar, a serious, stunning brunette, working as a celebrity correspondent for a Philadelphia-based service called NewsBank (thus Grandma)—the prey of a fast-talking, disarming, little-boy-at-heart comedian. The wisecracks must have flown like airplane propellors into seagulls. (Perhaps that is too harsh; like a glider, then, into starlings.) At any rate, he swooped; I imagine she even swerved, but too late. He left his mark. They were married in 1946.

I was born in 1948. At the time my parents were living in the Garden of Allah Hotel, on Sunset Boulevard. On the Strip, as a

8

matter of fact. I was born on the Sunset Strip. The Garden was a residential hotel, and fairly fashionable at the time, though falling into an atmospheric disrepair. Long grass and mustard flower were growing between the bungalows; poppies had spread from the central patio along the paths. We were separated from the Strip, and the Strippers, by a low, curving, yellow tile wall, barely higher or more protective than a curb. I remember inching along beside this wall, hearing the rumble and swish of the traffic on the Strip. Not long afterward I somehow managed to tilt a small rocking chair (my own) over the wall and onto the sidewalk. A brown man kindly returned it.

The precious few years I spent with my parents as their only child seem to have been unmarred; I see them in my mind as sun-filled. Soon we moved to a house; my parents were becoming Californians.

We lived near the top of a winding drive called Tigertail Road. The back yard gave a view out over a canyon below—a drop of several hundred feet. I was growing bigger every day, and soon managed to get rid of the ill-starred rocking chair by pushing it over the edge and out of my life forever. Looking back on this, and over the sheer drop that abruptly ended our back yard, it occurs to me that I was tremendously lucky not to have followed my rocking chair. I believe I was punished in some way or other for this act of wasteful daring.

I don't remember having had any playmates at this time. We were up on the hill, away from playgrounds and such, and I was still too young for school. Los Angeles is a private city. We did not meet our neighbors for years; I was never aware of the existence of any coevals. Besides, Tigertail Road was not appropriate for children and children's games. It was narrow and winding, the surface hard concrete, and the traffic constant. Often, at night, there were accidents around the bends. It is natural that even in my young mind this road should be associated with danger—especially after my father ran over a tortoise in the driveway. The affair as I remember it was shockingly bloody. He gathered the bloody chips in a newspaper, and my mother exclaimed, "Eeegads!" Even now, on the infrequent occasions when I still hear this expression, it is painful to me.

If I didn't yet have any playmates, I did have a brown towel, and a dog, Billy. Billy was a hyperactive Dalmatian, bought at a dog show, who liked to nuzzle my ears, wetly. The sensation was excruciating, and even the dog's intriguing spots could not finally compensate for this repulsive habit of his. I soon became bored and disgusted with him, and harried him with a garden hoe until he ran away forever.

The brown towel was another thing altogether. I could not sleep without it. For some reason, at the time possessing the child's impeccable (and now inscrutable) logic, I had to enwrap my head so that both ears were covered. If even one ear was left exposed, I could not fall asleep. This arrangement would be disrupted during sleep, but if I happened to awake sometime during the night and find that my brown towel was not covering both ears, I would immediately have to rearrange things in the dark. Otherwise, I somehow instinctively knew, the forces of darkness (imagined as air-breathing sea monsters) would close over my head.

I seem to have had a certain way of folding the towel, which I cannot now remember. My mother, coming in later to say goodnight or to check up on me, would sometimes pull aside the towel to kiss me. And these kisses, welcome as they were, were also disconcerting—for as long as the vulnerable ear lay exposed. It was never even a question of preferring the towel to my mother (who was certainly as good a protection against the forces of darkness), but simply that the towel would be with me all night, and my mother, I knew, would not.

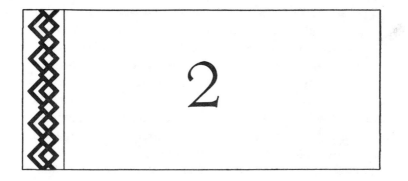

2

I was, even as a child, and as if in anticipation of my uncle, a darling of waitresses. What was it that endeared me to them? Was it my earnestness that conquered their hearts? My speech impediment? (I was by this point talking, though for a while I couldn't manage my *r*'s.) "Excuse me," I would venture, stepping up rather boldly to the counter of Wil Wright's Old Fashioned Ice Cream Shop, "excuse me, but may I t*w*ouble you for a maca*w*oon?" Invariably this brought disarmed sighs, titters of delight, and a flood of the delicious cookies in question. No matter that, as a rule, a single macaroon was served only with an order of ice cream; for me the gates of paradise were always open, and my waitresses the complaisant keepers. I had only to utter the magic word, without an *r,* and the prizes would pour forth.

First there was Blossom. A sweet, chunky, middle-aged lady with an enormous face in which rugged pores were visible, and a wreath of red hair. She carried her weight lightly, her small feet deftly maneuvering around the treacherously twisted wrought-iron chair legs on the checkered parlor floor. Blossom was loving, Blossom was attentive. From her I had only to ask and I received, in abundance. Knowing Blossom, giving Blossom: she was my first.

I believe Blossom was originally my father's friend—a friendship cultivated when he came to Wil Wright's for strawberry water-ice. She packed and weighed it for him; he never bought less than two quarts. I remember, the times I went with him, his eagerly watchful eyes and fretful mustache as he bent over the counter, just to see how tight she was packing the ice. The action behind the counter was invisible to me. Stepping up onto the polished brass rung, I could barely see over the top. But I did see Blossom's large face, shining with loyal effort.

In those days, macaroons were still as yet unknown to me. I gazed at the shelves of candy jars—parti-colored, abundant, sealed, inaccessible—and the glass decanters of clear pastel liquid gracing the top shelves and display window. ("Just colored water," Blossom explained. For some reason this explanation was always insufficient.)

Soon my mother was bringing me to Wil Wright's every day for lunch. We took the daily sandwich special; Blossom liked to prepare a half-special for me. "Half-pint special," she called it. One day there was a strange cookie on my plate. I immediately bit into it; the consistency was spongy, the taste rhapsodic: my first macaroon.

I cannot begin to explain the significance of this confection in my early years. The taste holds the secret: definite, persistent, declarative, yet always elusive. Was it an exotic flavor? I had certainly never tasted anything like it, but I think it was more bluntly desirable than exotic. Because unlike most exotic things, it was, for me, easily attainable. The trick was that it was never there for very long—which is why, I suppose, I desired it so. It was individual, not only because unusual, but also simply because the cookies came never more than one at a time. Not that I didn't consume several at a sitting; but I did so one at a time. No box, no can, no assorted platter, but a single macaroon in a wax paper sleeve depicting an angel in red, and the inscription: "It's Heavenly."

So my world had opened up a little. I was getting out, getting known; I had made my first good impression on restaurant society. Things were changing at home, too: we had acquired a household helper.

His name was Paul. He was from Germany. But he had been in this country a very long time, he said. Paul walked with a limp. There was something very disturbing about this limp; with it came a creaking sound, the sound of a twisted old chair when you sat down. I remember it intrigued me because the sound actually came from his leg, was part of his leg. I believe it was the right one.

Paul had moved in with us, and slept in my room. I was used to sleeping alone, and although I'm sure my parents felt that Paul's presence would in the long run be comforting to me, it wasn't. For in the bedroom also there were sounds. The sounds of Paul undressing in the dark; the strange, mysterious preparations and tossings that ensued; and finally the sounds of Paul asleep. He made smackings and squeakings with his lips. I drew the brown towel tightly around my head, trying to block out the sounds.

And in the daytime also, Paul had his odd habits. One of them was goose fat. The refrigerator was full of it. Paul said it was good for the skin, good for health. "Try once some goose fat nice on a slice of bread, you'll see what I mean."

He liked to tell stories about his boyhood in his hometown, Solingen:

"I took once a shortcut through the woods. I was to visit a friend in a village next to Solingen. There was a lot of fog, like walking through clouds, so thick. There was a road in these woods, where I walked on so many times. So I kept walking, but I did not come to the village. I knew this road led to the village, but the fog made me lose my way. I begun to be scared, like I was trapped here in these woods, with no one to help me. Even though there was a road, no one was coming. I said to me, Paul, soon it would get dark, and cold. It was already cold. Not like here—this Los Angeles is a tropical city. But in Germany you have always the north wind. With the north wind comes snow and fog, even in summer. And I was not dressed warm—only a jacket and tie. What a dumb kid, ya."

Paul paused. He pinched his nose, and picked it; then he continued his story.

"If there wasn't an angel I would have been a goner. There was an angel in the treetops. The fog burned off and there she was, sitting in the treetops. Just in the nick of time. I was very scared, ya, sure, but finally I got courage to talk. I asked which was the way to the village. The angel pointed, and I went that way and pretty soon I arrived in the village. There, nobody could believe my story. Even my friend said it must be a dream. Then why did it take me so long to get to the village? That's what I still say. If there was no angel, why did it take so long? And how did the fog disappear?"

Paul hated artichokes. "Once I was with a fancy lady, a real wealthy customer in a fancy restaurant. She ordered artichokes, and when it came it was all thorns and needles. I put this in my mouth and spat it out, and had to wash my mouth once out good with soap and water."

Similarly, Paul hated fat, the fat of meat—all fat except goose fat. "I have to spit that fat meat out when I chew it. It makes my whole body sick to taste it. I will never cook fat here," he promised.

Paul was a fan of wrestling, American-style. He sat in front of the television and encouraged the wrestlers: "Give him once a good crack, ya. Oh, you dirty player. What was that? On his nose, in his eyes, you dirty guy! Referee should kick him out, the good-for-nothing bum. Ach, that's not a sport, that's dirty play." In his excitement, a cowlick of dark hair hung awry on his forehead. Tonguing a toothpick, he smacked his lips and groaned with delight. "Dirty play, dummy!"

Paul's father had been an engineer for one of the surgical instrument companies in Solingen. Solingen, Paul said, was the world capital of surgical instruments. The engineering of the instruments required hair-splitting precision, steady hands and fine eyes. These skills were also what made Paul's father an expert billiards player. He played in the private clubs, where he always won. He had the technique of a surgeon, which he taught to his son—but to no one else.

"Pretty soon I was beating everybody too. We was a real team, my father and me. I was dressed nice, fresh jacket and tie, shaved smooth, with a sprinkle cologne water. The ladies liked me the way I looked." He made the squeaking sound with his lips, like a kiss. "I was a dandy young man. Lady-friends I had lots of. They like to see a man dressed nice and smell nice, not like these California 'gimme's,' these cowboys without a razor. I was a classy customer."

Indeed, Paul still wore a jacket and tie most of the time. He used Old Spice after-shave and cologne, and combed a thick white pomade called Fifth Avenue through his hair. He disliked what he called "crazy professor hair." And he disliked pool, which he saw them playing one night on "Gunsmoke."

"Nach, that's no game, not like billiards. That's like a toy—too easy. You just knocking the balls into the holes—pow pow pow. Like cowboys. Not like billiards, where you got to have every angle just set up and all right. If you scratch the felt, the owner he kicks you out and never lets you in again. I never scratched the felt."

But in spite of the pool, Paul liked "Gunsmoke"; he especially liked the character Chester, who was humorous and had a limp. Besides, Paul had worked for James Arness, and appreciated the way his former employer delivered certain lines. "He used to talk to me like that," Paul chuckled. He was delighted when Marshal Matt Dillon got into fights. "Crack him once good, Mr. Arness!" he would cheer. "That's a real he-man." Then he would limp to the set and turn up the sound.

I spent many hours alone with Paul. He was devoted to my father, whom I often heard him call "a prince"; and when, now and then, my parents would go away for a short weekend trip,

Paul felt it his duty to take their place as best he could. He was very careful with me; in fact I am afraid he was too careful. He was especially concerned about what I ate.

Paul knew many cases of children dying from eating poisonous combinations of foods. "Pickles and ice cream is death," he would say. "This food forms a deadly gas which explodes inside. In Solingen was a young boy, son of my father's business friend—I knew him too. One day at a party the boy ate such a mixture of pickles and ice cream, even when they told him not to. He was so sick, then he died. Another is beans and chocolate. Ya, terrible." Paul shook his head and smacked his lips. "This is why you should not eat so fast. The stomach is not so big, you know. It breathes like a lungs; you cannot stuff it too full. If you hurt your stomach it will not forgive you—soon you will be belching like a crazy man."

Paul believed in the enema. "An enema once and I feel great for days," he claimed. "It shoots through like butter. Put in once a little mineral oil and you got clear sailing. Many great men had the enema—Mr. Gandhi special. There is no shame in this."

Whenever I was constipated, or Paul thought I might be, an enema was administered. The red rubber bag, filled with warm water and a tablespoonful of mineral oil, was hung above my head; the black nozzle was inserted "upstream"; a not unpleasant, warm heaviness began to fill my belly; soon I was shooting out water.

"Nach, not yet," scolded Paul. "Let it loosen," he coaxed. "Then you will feel good."

Sometimes I remarked to my parents on Paul's strange ways, but they would reply, "Paul is a good soul." With all due respect to the memory of my parents, I feel I was somewhat misled about this matter of a "good soul." I could only picture for myself a definition in terms of goose fat, enemas, sudden-death combinations of foods, and grotesque wrestling matches.

In some ways my parents were right, though; Paul did have a good soul. He certainly had a frugal one.

16

Once, when my parents returned from a longer trip, Paul, who as usual had been keeping house and me during their absence, presented my father with a bill for all his expenses—food, gasoline, cleaning and painting supplies. The bill was ridiculously low. According to his records, one week Paul had spent $7.46 on food; another week $9.16. The cost of gasoline worked out to under ten dollars a month for three months. My father wondered how this was possible.

"You don't need much supplies," Paul said casually. "Too many people is overspending. If you eat the pure food you end up spending less and getting more for your money. You got to watch for bargains, too. Every week I see ladies with their shopping cars piled like mountains. Are they going to eat this all? I think mostly it is waste.

"You want to know what I do, Mr. Lorditch? I take once a nice veal bone, boil it nice with some vegetables and salt, boil it down so you have a soup that lasts a week. I'm no chef, but I sure know what I like. Other times, I might take a chicken and boil it."

"Yes, but you didn't have to spend so little," said my father. "You know us, Paul; we wanted you and Peter to eat whatever you like. Such economy was not . . . necessary."

"I'm no cheapskate," Paul defended himself.

"I'm not saying that. But you practically . . . starved yourself. How can you eat on seven dollars a week? And you hardly ever went out—you spent about thirty dollars in all on gas. I don't understand it." My father looked pained, as if he were guilty of having forced us both to live like hermits. But Paul set him straight.

"Listen here, Mr. Lorditch," he began. "You're a real fine man—in my book, a prince. But you don't know how to live thrifty. Maybe that's not bad, maybe you have some fun. But that's something I noticed in America special. Waste, waste—too much garbage cans everywhere. People rushing everywhere with their foot on the pedal." ("Foot on the pedal" was a favorite expression of Paul's. "Take the foot off the pedal," he would say, meaning "slow down." And of people who were nervous, aggressive or disorganized: "She's a baby always with her foot on the pedal.") "Soon," he continued, "the stomach has pain, the bowels has trouble, you're a sick man, you will see I am right. 'That old Paul,' you will say, 'he told me to take the foot off the pedal.' "

By this time I had entered elementary school, but it made little impression on me, aside from the upsetting observation that my classmates already knew each other—since in this school the elementary division was a continuation of the kindergarten, which I hadn't attended.

So I was apart from them, for a while at least, yet they did not tease me. I had even made a little friend, Cindy—a very special name to me, since it was the same as my new dog's (we had bought a chow to replace Billy). Cindy—the human—was a tidy little girl. Her sums and rounded letters stood in perfectly ordered rank and file; the creases she made in her paper were perfectly straight, as were the crayons arrayed before her in prismatic, chromatic gradations. She always received a gold or silver star for her work—and I of course received none. For Paul had brought disorder into my life.

But the worst was yet to come. . . .

Sometime during this period, my father bought my mother a new car. It was a huge brown Buick, with fins and electric windows, a radio in the front and back, and a swivel mirror that read, in script: *Buick is a beauty, too.* To celebrate the car, we drove it up to a restaurant in the Palisades, where we parked it so that we could look out at it from the window. The waitresses admired it too. They said it was as big as an ocean liner. The waitresses, I remember, were wearing orange shorts, and orange caps that hung precariously on the sides of their heads.

Later we decided to pick up some ice cream at Wil Wright's. Blossom was working that evening, and we showed her the car.

18

She was very pleased with it. Then she looked at me and re-marked, "How you are growing. Soon you'll be able to drive this car. If your mother lets you," she added, laughing. She took the new car to mean that my father would soon be fa-mous; then, she told him, his name would be printed on the back of the Wil Wright's menu, along with the names of all the other celebrities.

"I usually don't make predictions, but . . ." said Blossom. And who knows, perhaps the good woman's hunch might even have come true. . . .

Dis, alas, *aliter visum.* . . .

I should say something about this now, even if it means skip-ping five years of early autobiography, and a comparable num-ber of waitresses who filled those latent formative years with their tender ministrations. . . .

My parents were killed in an Indian restaurant in New York City. The circumstances of their death were flukish. They were in New York in the winter of 1960, on business with one of the television networks, and went to dinner one evening at a res-taurant with the infelicitous name of Paradiz. My grandmother was not with them that night, having been (providentially) re-placed by a network executive. The story, carried on the front page of the New York papers, is brutally ridiculous.

A penthouse apartment in the building next door to Paradiz was being renovated. The penthouse was on the twenty-eighth floor, Paradiz on the twenty-second. The workers had broken off for the day, leaving—God knows why— a massive load of broken stone hanging suspended over the side of the building. Why suspended? Or one may as well ask, why my parents? But I have been over this terrain countless times since, and have learned to chalk it up to the vindictive leveling interplay—Vedic in inspiration, if you will—of construction and destruction. Sus-pended then, I gather, because they were bringing the stone in through the windows, and some lazy manslaughterer had simply been too tired to lower the cable for the night. The stones were just hanging there when the winch snapped or gave way, and down plummeted the murderous load, down through the frail skylight of a Paradiz now turned Hell. . . .

Not only my parents, but also the network executive and a visiting rajah were killed. The restaurant soon moved to another location, where it has been thriving ever since.

This incredible news reached us—Paul and me—only hours before my grandmother did. She came out to California to accompany us back East for the funeral, so that we would not have to travel alone—so that she could ease my grief on that unbearable plane ride. But I think the real reason, and one of which she was perhaps not conscious, was that she felt the news would lack reality if she was not there to affirm it; that the words describing such a tragedy, lacking her sensibility, her voice, her mouth to form and re-form them for us, would be hideous, empty, laughable perhaps, conveying nothing more than the terrifying delirium of an absurd accident.

I have never gotten over that impression of New York. Or perhaps more truly, I have never been able to see it otherwise. The world was gray; the snow, the sky, the people, the trees, all were gray. Of course, this is what I was disposed to see at the time. But that was the way it really looked, to any recent orphan who was looking. Most of the time I could not understand what I saw. People's actions, their words, even inanimate objects, were scrambled by a common code of misery that I could not break—and, as far as that sepulchral city is concerned, have never been able to break. I realize that this code is entirely of my own making; I put it together, and I should be able to take it apart. But for the life of me I cannot. . . .

My parents, then, were buried in the family plot, in a cemetery in Brooklyn under the gray snow, inside the gray earth. My sorrow, too, was a general, permanent gray.

My grandmother came back to California to live with us. There had at first been some talk of our moving to New York, but it was decided that I should not be uprooted at this difficult time. And besides, Paul couldn't stand New York. He described the New Yorkers as "war babies." Precisely what he meant by this was at the time unclear to me; but it would later become apparent when I better understood his dialect, and could appreciate the odd sensibility it expressed.

Thus began my first prolonged encounter with my grandmother. I had met her once or twice before, on the few short trips back East I had taken with my parents, and I had stayed in her ample town house—my father's home throughout his younger years. This house, built to hold a larger family, was now much too big for my grandmother and uncle alone, especially as the latter was often abroad on "business" trips, leaving his mother to oversee four empty floors. Even Gazelle, the live-in maid, cook, companion and confidante, now spent nights and weekends in her own apartment in the Bronx. I think she secretly moonlighted on my grandmother—and who could blame her? I don't think Grandma had ever raised her starting salary, generous in the thirties, but increasingly inadequate through the years. And in addition, Gazelle found that she had less and less to do around the house. A household that had at one time included my grandfather, my grandmother, my great-grandmother, my uncle and my father had now dwindled to two, and often one. Gazelle would remark frequently on the need for "another man" in the house, but Grandma would only frown and, inwardly, I am sure, deem her "vulgar."

And so my grandmother's departure for the West, taking into account the tragic and trying circumstances, probably came as something of a relief to her. The old house could only seem emptier in view of the recent calamity. There was my uncle urging her to get away, to take a vacation (because of the tragedy, he had had to cut short his own). And besides, now there was an orphan to take care of. Grandma was not about to entrust me exclusively to Paul, whom I don't think she had ever met before the disaster. She recalled that my parents had given him a sterling recommendation; still, she had to see for herself.

At any rate she didn't plan to be out here for long—certainly not nearly as long as it finally turned out. Her chief concern at that time was that I be set back onto the normal course of my life. My grandmother, you see, has incredible powers of abstraction—I mean that in a moral, not an intellectual sense. It never occurred to her—or if it did, she chose to ignore it, in that maddeningly oblivious nonchalant way she has—that her son's, my uncle's, life had long since deviated irrevocably from such a course; yet she determined to set the same for me.

No, she did not expect to be out on the Coast for very long at all. Although at first she allowed that she liked it. She remarked at once on our garden. It is a very pretty one, and shows that my mother was a consummate gardener. I would almost say "landscaper," for in her lifetime she designed the garden as it now stands. She cultivated the tropical plants that now flourish rifely; she set the orchids hanging from the tall tree stump by the pond, knowing that they would gather extra moisture from the water; she somehow abolished all moles, even to this day; she battened the hedgerows into a towering wall of green; she balanced bushes with trees, envisioning behind their beginning inchoate sparseness a full (but posthumous) maturity. So that now we barely have to touch the garden—not that I would really know what to do if it ever came to that. Fortunately it hasn't. Eddie, the Japanese gardener, comes twice a week to water the whole place, sometimes to fertilize. His friend Joe comes once a month to spray. (Aphids, mildew and whitefly are three of our plagues.) And I sprinkle desultorily.

Indeed, it might be said of me in some greater sense: I sprinkle desultorily.

Anyway, Grandma was impressed with our garden. But she could not have fully appreciated it then, for it was still taking shape. Paul was at that time strong and working. He handled much of the transplanting and bracing of limbs—which I suppose is ironic, since I suspect one of his own was artificial. I never got a good look at it, though.

Paul, unsurprisingly, had strange work habits. He worked in a clean white shirt, dark slacks, and black leather shoes—hardly work clothes. Perhaps this is because he wanted to be "ready" at a moment's notice. Ready for what? Important visitors, perhaps. I have mentioned that Paul had formerly worked for celebrities—perhaps he even included my father among these. And who is to say whether he did not secretly expect, hope, dream that Jack Holt or James Arness might come walking through the garden and ask for him back? In that case he wanted to look ready, and his best.

A more practical question now occurs to me. I wonder how Paul was making a living. My parents, it transpired, had died intestate; but even if they had made a will, I doubt that it would have provided for Paul. There must have been generous annuities from the two life insurance policies devolving on my grandmother, which enabled her to support me, and the house, and keep Paul on. The settling of the estate was another reason why she was out in California; and also to make sure, in her own practical way, that Paul was worth the expense.

He certainly was. I don't know what she paid him—although if it was anywhere near as low as the figure she was unashamed to pay Gazelle, he was certainly worth more. Most likely his salary had been raised in accordance with his increased responsibilities.

For if Paul had been devoted to my father, he was now devoted to the memory of him, and transferred the active part of that devotion to me. He drove me to and from school, made my lunches, supervised my homework. (A man with no formal education above the elementary level, but with all the compensatory disciplinary fervor, Paul was a grim believer in arduous exercises, often making them out to be more arduous than they were. The result was that I took trivial assignments more seriously than was necessary.) I remember an art scrapbook I was assembling for a junior high school project: a long but simple affair of mounted reproductions and short reports on the artists. Paul first suggested, then insisted that I include an index. Perhaps he had heard somewhere that the greatest tradition in that discipline came from his own country, so that the issue of an index was to him a matter of chauvinistic pride. But I couldn't complain; it earned me an A, and an early exposure to scholarship—admittedly elementary, but of the same dreary sort, I now see, that carried me through college with a Classics degree.

Throughout this time I was observing my grandmother with curiosity, and a certain amount of awe; she was now the self-appointed lady of the household. I soon found that even my curiosity could not keep pace with the continual revelation of her various peculiarities.

She was, even then, the most eccentric person I had ever known. Let me reiterate the salient oddities: English accent, tea at four-thirty, bonnets, sentences opening with the declarative "I say," the use of "macintosh" for "raincoat," "rubbers" for "galoshes," and—best of all—the word "motor" for the verb "to drive." Some of her sentences I have committed to memory:

"I say, we may have to motor out to the Valley this afternoon."

"No, I suppose there really is no need for rubbers in this weather."

(Or, of someone quite demonstrably evil, in this case Madame Nhu:) "I don't think she is a very *nice* person."

My grandmother understood character—and the world, really—as comprised of two camps: the "nice"—including the virtuous, the brave, the honest, the worthy; and the "not very nice"—criminals, tyrants, liars, adulterers, insurance agencies, most women, and the non-white races, excepting the Japanese, for whom she had a special feeling, which I will later explain. Her concepts of "nice" and "not nice" described a wide range of attributes, which seemed homogeneous at first, but which I gradually learned to distinguish in context. Thus her appraisal of a woman as "not a very nice person" meant that the woman was thought either to be scheming, of vulgar character, or a downright whore or adulteress. (Men, however, were not described in equivalent terms.) Hitler as "not a very nice person" meant that he was a tyrant, and a German anti-Semitic one at that (Grandmother being a Jewess of German extraction). The insurance people as "not very nice people" meant that they had underappraised her policy and were withholding full claims. (This however was not true; we were now richer, or becoming richer, through these monies.) And, much later, girls I would bring to the house were so described to indicate that they were probably not Jewish and that she did not approve; but she was always careful not to reveal the real grounds of her disapproval.

Of course, I did not understand all these subtle distinctions at first, although I did have a feeling for them. But the more obvious idiosyncrasies grabbed me right away. She was disturbed to find that we had no formal tea service. "Earthenware pots?" she demurred. "Well, I don't think they are very *nice*." (Meaning elegant.) But she learned to coexist with them. After all, at that point she couldn't very well send for her New York service if she planned to be out here only temporarily.

Or did she? At times she would show signs of grudging approval, or at least tolerance, of certain aspects of our bucolic suburbia. "So green, like a bower," I once overheard her remark in the garden. "Your mother had a gift with plants, didn't she?" And she loved our California fruit. "I so much feel like a nice fruit compote right now. Oh, if only Gazelle were here," she would sigh, for she was utterly helpless in the kitchen.

This soon became a problem, as she did not think much of Paul's cooking, yet was herself sublimely ignorant of culinary mechanics. But she knew what she liked—and it was seldom prepared. The hints in that direction were subtle, often too subtle for Paul's Teutonic ear, which in any case was not trained to pick up the English inflection. Paul was no fool, however, and was terribly sensitive about his cooking.

One evening there were snarls over the boiled veal in butter sauce.

It began, "I say, perhaps we might have some lemon."

(Paul defended himself.) "Lemon? How come lemon? You got some butter sauce there spread nice over the top. I made it special—" (His supererogatory effort clearly precluded any adjustments.)

"Oh, it's very nice," Grandma sniffed. "I simply think that a little lemon on my plate might be nice . . . brings out the flavor."

"It's got plenty flavor for me," clipped Paul. "Mr. Lorditch always asked for this special." Paul appealed to me. "Remember so much how he liked it, Peter?"

"Yes, it's very good, Paul," I said. Actually, it tasted a bit bland, but I never would have told him that.

"Mr. Lorditch was a prince of a man," Paul continued wistfully, "a real old-fashioned genuine"—he pronounced this word with a long *i*—"one-of-a-kind prince of a man. Ya, he sure did like his food, didn't he? I used to tell him, Mr. Lorditch, don't you eat so fast, you'll do your stomach hurt. He didn't have no respect for his stomach. I used to tell him, take it from Paul, the stomach is a fancy machine, you got to treat it nice and easy. I know so many people what had bad stomachs trouble—"

"I say, is there any lemon, or have we none?" Grandma broke in. "Excuse me, Paul—" Meaning that she was terribly sorry, but if he would just get up and bring her some lemon. . . .

"Ya, we sure got some lemon, if you want it," Paul said grudgingly, with a sour look on his face as he rose.

"Yes, I would, if you don't *mind*." Grandma also had a sour look on her face. While Paul was in the kitchen, she grumbled something unintelligible including the word "rude." I could tell

26

from her expression that Paul was not being a very nice person, and that her self-sacrificing powers of discretion were being taxed to their very limits. . . .

How can I explain this extraordinary woman? Who was she, really, and how did she get to be that way? I was just beginning to wonder myself, and at the time I was very confused. I still am, though I have since done a good bit of thinking and my share of research into the matter. I suppose I wouldn't be writing this if I had found the answers. . . . But I have found only more questions. And poor Grandma, she couldn't possibly answer them all. But she has other things on her mind now. Or perhaps she is thinking of very little after all—of love, a twilight romance, a wedding, a Mediterranean honeymoon. . . .

The woman is a genuine oddball; and going back through the years, one is tempted to suspect she always has been. I believe she was predestined. Her mother, Lola Rasmussen, was born in San Francisco in 1864—before the Civil War ended, mind you, as my grandmother would often point out. Now, Jews in San Francisco at that period of our history, and second-generation Jews at that—whatever they were, they were not common. Of course, there was the Gold Rush; that must have drawn at least a few. But I doubt that very many of our forefathers, fresh off the boat, would have been eager—or especially encouraged—to grab a tin pan and pistol and schlepp across the continent. Not when, right there at the docks, there were suits to be sewn, shoes to be soled, books to be bound, buildings to be built. No, somehow San Francisco was not the place, nor was a Gold Rush sufficient cause. And yet the Rasmussens had come West around that time.

Tanners, they were. They bought some redwood forests (for the tannin dye) and built a factory in Redwood City. The business went ahead for fifteen years, until around the time Lola was born. Perhaps the tannery was then beginning to founder, or perhaps there was simply nothing more left to do to it. But for one reason or another, which Grandmother will never divulge (she has probably forgotten by now), the family moved back East. Lola was then a small child, but old enough to remember a trip in a stagecoach. Were they ambushed by Indians? ("Highwaymen" —thus Grandma.) Escorted by a posse? Grandma would never say, but I take it the stagecoach was merely a shuttle between trains, as stagecoaches usually were.

Once again in New York, Martin Rasmussen (Lola's father) set himself up, or was set up, as a fruit wholesaler supplying the shipping lines. He had the good and infamous fortune to be associated with a fledgling outfit called the United Fruit Company. His job enabled him to travel wherever his clients sailed. He developed close contacts in Japan, and dealt increasingly with the Japanese. Grandma's house in New York as I recollect it was full of Japanese gewgaws—miniature monkeys, Buddhas and happy peasants—illustrative no doubt of the nature of Rasmussen's blithe connection with exotica. (At least such things were there the last I remember; though my uncle was driven, in times of financial hardship—which occurred increasingly through the years—to pawn anything that glittered.) Young Lola was taken around the world many times, finishing every trip in Japan. They eventually bought a house on Yokohama Bay, No. 6 Bluff, which they held for many years until after World War I. Grandma remembers it well; these long-term memories will be the last to go.

Lola was married at sixteen. Her marriage however did not stop the yearly peregrinations with or without her new husband Howard Frankel (he was caught up in business: for his father-in-law was easing him into a controlling position at United Fruit), but always accompanied by her sister Minnie and the English bulldog Bunk, who it appears often did for an escort—though this animal chaperonage did not in any case prevent Aunt Minnie (young, spirited, American Aunt Minnie) from getting tangled up in a sordid affair that ended in her arrest.

Minnie, it seems, was carrying on in Yokohama with a married man, a Dr. Davis, physician to the Marquis of Redding. Whether or not the lovers tried to make any secret of their conduct is not known; in any event they did not succeed, and the Japanese police—or private detectives, or the Adultery Guard, or whatever was used to surveil naughty alien couples in Japan in those days—entered the house and slapped handcuffs on Aunt Minnie. (The lapsed husband was already in prison, they told her.) Minnie, though, refused to budge, and they all politely sat around the house, waiting for someone to give in. I'm not sure how it was resolved. I believe both parties were simply booked and fined, and in time learned to live with their ignominy. (One is led to the inference that Aunt Minnie wasn't "a very nice person.")

Yet Grandma doesn't seem to have been too scandalized. It was before her time (I don't think any of her older brothers had even been born yet), and to her mind the whole affair no doubt adds a certain verve to the remembrance of a maturer Aunt Minnie, of whom she was really very fond. Minnie and Uncle Irwin (whom Minnie married years after the scandal, and who was never, to my knowledge, a cuckold) later kept a goat farm in the Berkshires, where Grandma often spent the summers. She told me she loved to play with the goats, and to drink the fresh goats' milk. ("It cleans the blood," she claimed.)

Uncle Irwin was a self-made man, and though he was not a blood relation, Grandma managed to respect him. A German shopkeeper's son, he had run away to America at a young age. Though slight of build, he worked for a while at the docks, and then became a longshoremen's labor organizer. He bragged of the many fights he had fought, and the many times he had been beaten within an inch of his life. Yet, I heard, he wore no scars and was actually handsome, in a diminutive way. He was also an amateur naturalist, knew his way about a farm, and even taught himself to play a good game of tennis. In fact he died on a tennis court.

Grandma has always admired athletic ability. She herself

loved to ice-skate and ride, and was always telling me what a good "table tennis" player my father had been. But all these encouragements must have fallen on prematurely deaf ears; at athletics I have always been a basket case. Yet somehow my body is trim enough, and seems to be fit—although I have never bothered to test this hypothesis by exertion. I do enjoy the beach, and can swim if I have to. But best if there are no waves, and I can placidly wade and float undisturbed. A friend of mine, who has set for himself comparably unambitious physical limits, has observed that the habit of exercise sets artificial standards that are annoying to maintain, and yet deviation from which results in eventual atrophy and death. We thus refrain together from establishing trends which might kill us.

(My grandmother does not approve. "You'll be a lump," she says.)

As the baby sister in a brood of brothers, she soon developed a taste for sports, and the accompanying nickname "Cissie," which has stuck with her for life. She told me that her mother often dressed her as a boy, less out of a wish to conceal her sex as such than to enhance a sense of virile continuity already established by her brothers. They were Norman, Norbert and Nelson. Cissie's given name was Nora—as seems reasonable. (Just what magic, if any, the initial N held for Lola or her husband is yet unclear.) "They were all nice names, except for mine," explains Grandma. No one has ever called her by it since I have known her.

The three N's all turned out to be business-minded, in varying degrees: Norman successfully, Norbert unsuccessfully, and Nelson psychotically. The story of Nelson, the eldest, has always interested me the most. It appears that he possessed, and was possessed by, an insistent, mysterious talent that no one, including himself, could quite figure out. Although he had received his education and degree in Organic Chemistry, he wanted to be an inventor. He denied even to his relatives that he was a Jew, yet to perfect strangers he would refer to himself as "the old Jew." He was often accused of anti-Semitism, yet

30

as a young man he had been much concerned on the side of the French Dreyfusards in that scandal. He even skipped Japan one year to go to Paris and march in the rallies. He returned with a pamphlet in which he claimed to have printed a pseudonymous Dreyfus-lionizing article under the byline "Un vieux Juif americain." (He would have been twenty, at the oldest.) He stayed in Paris for a while and enrolled in the Sorbonne; but his father, weighing the possibilities of a French pogrom, ordered him home. And, strange fellow that he was, he complied.

But the pogrom never occurred, and Nelson began once again to sneeze on the Jews; it was part of an allergy he had. (This recalls to me a medical anomaly in which the patient is actually allergic to himself, yet has no choice but to live with himself in varying degrees of organic and irremediable discomfort.) This complicated and sad man found that living with himself was a full-time job—indeed, it was the only one he had.

Not that he didn't hatch plans and schemes. He wanted to build a game reserve in Montana. He drew up plans for a flexible, transparent swimming pool. He thought of developing a herring slicer that would save the juice (and perhaps the world). It was this last idea that killed him; he slipped on a piece of fish while haggling in a market on Fisherman's Wharf in 1924, and died of a fractured skull.

This is really too bad, for if I had ever known this man I feel I might have loved him. However, much of him survived in my uncle Joseph, who, as you will see, tried to go him one better.

I have no particular interest in the stories of my other great-uncles. Norbert, the youngest, was, according to Grandma's accounts, an insufferable snob who worked for a bank in the insufferable city of Boston. When he died he was cremated; his ashes, I imagine, sank glumly into the Charles. Norman, the sole survivor, is a ne'er-do-well, that peculiar curse of middle children. He used to be a sports-equipment salesman, and is now, I believe, an alcoholic—or used to be. At eighty-eight, he is probably too old even for that. I don't know how he got to live so long; he certainly didn't do anything to deserve it. As Grandma put it, he didn't even marry a rich girl.

So these were the companions she grew up with, played with, fought with, traveled with, studied with, conspired with—felt inferior to. For she did feel inferior to them; she told me so recently.

"Why do you feel this way?" I asked. "You're so much better than any of them." She hates compliments, though; when she receives them she puffs air out through her dentures, disdainfully.

"I am not good, I am wicked."

"Wicked? Don't you think that's a little strong? You're not that bad."

"I should have done so many things differently. . . . Now, my mother . . ."

"Yes? Your mother what?"

"Now, I say, I don't mean to sound wicked—"

"Stop saying that!"

"I'm afraid she wanted to turn me into a man. You know my hair was quite short when I was a little girl."

This is true. One summer Grandma had caught typhoid fever while swimming in the Hudson. I somehow never associate such diseases with our continent—but then, as I understand it, it was a question of contaminated water. She was very sick, and they shaved her hair off, probably to make her more comfortable during the fever, or as a sanitary measure, I don't know. She soon took to wearing caps and bonnets, a custom she retains to this day—though her hair is now long, to the small of her back when it is down. Until you have seen Grandma walking along the Venice boardwalk in her light green summer-worsted suit, topped by a matching bonnet, strolling breezily by a group of shirtless conga players and other types—until you have seen her unexpectedly stop and, after peering up at one of these formidable-looking male bacchantes and deciding that, in spite of his "scraggy looks" he's not "a bad chap" and could "do with a sandwich," extract a

32

bill from her Scotch plaid change purse and tastefully, modestly, charitably slip the money into his powerful palm—I say that until you have seen this sight, as I once did, "eccentricity" must remain undefined.

How can such a person think herself wicked? I would have passed it off as merely another turn of her strange speech, but I am beginning to understand that the woman does not like herself at all. She blames herself for the misfortunes that have befallen her family: her first husband's philandering, which led to his dissipation, divorce, consumption and eventual death; her second husband's fatal heart condition; and my uncle's numerous unhealthy indulgences, bordering on the pathological. She would even have blamed herself for my parents' tragic accident, if she had not barely escaped annihilation (herself).

I would ascribe her self-flagellating tendencies to a selfish disposition to meddle, the impulse being more or less: "I am clearly the center, the sun of these people's lives, and it is therefore my duty to radiate outwards as much of myself as I can spare, so as not to deny them the warmth, light and gravitational stability that they crave. And I must also make sure that this radiation reaches them, and is not wasted on minor satellites." (That is, friends or even her late daughter-in-law, my mother.) So that—to continue my illuminating metaphor—when my grandmother's efforts did not always produce the desired effect, she, in her Copernican delusion, believed that this was due to an inherent fault in the radiating body (her "wickedness"), and not simply to the natural oscillation, predictable and normal, of orbiting planets.

So much for the scientific explanation of her self-denigration. But as she saw it, her "wickedness" was not the only thing wrong with her. Also at fault, she conceived, were her "homeliness," "lack of education" (and even "intelligence"), "inarticulateness" and "naïveté." How curious it is that we always discover and harp on those faults in ourselves that are least offensive, and often even endearing to others—not even faults, really, but just the idiosyncratic ruffles in the exterior we would so much like to present to the world as smooth. But our professed deficiencies are really nothing more than a concealed form of self-advertisement; or one might even interpret them, in the case of particularly vain people, as a perverse coyness, a sort of false clue, but leading nevertheless to the truth—that ultimate vanity inherent in each of us: the conviction that we are a unique and misunderstood creature and that, if others could only interpret correctly our misleading signals of communication, they would find deep inside all the contradictions to these little personal foibles and, lying even deeper, the secret virtues of an unsuspectedly profound character. Whereas in the real world we learn eventually, through disappointment, that there is probably no such thing as "profound" or "inner" character, at least as distinguished from superficial appearance—or if there is, that this unknown quantity is too complicated and ambiguous to be recognizable as part of the person we thought we knew; and that it really is much easier in the long run to learn to identify (if not to know) each other simply by the constant and often discouraging modification of our earlier impressions, which may be misleading but are seldom wrong.

Anyway, these were some of my grandmother's faults as she saw them. Yet she appeared sublimely unaware of the greater ones, such as the meddlesomeness I have described, and also some quirks that might be judged pretentious by those who did not know her: the English accent and anglophilic habits.

About the accent. It was acquired, oddly enough, in Japan, where Grandma was instructed by an English speech therapist enlisted by her mother to treat a supposed speech impediment. (I never learned just what this was, but in any case I am sure it helped to develop her fear of sounding inarticulate.) After the therapist, they packed her off to a convent school in the mountains, run by English missionaries. There she divided her time between English nuns and Japanese acolytes, and came away with the accent she now has.

Grandma's fears regarding her education are perhaps explained by the desultory nature of her instruction. A little New York grammar here, a little English missionary there, a sprinkling of wisdom from the kind lady on the crossing, etc. The Japanese convent school was the farthest she ever got in the way of formal education. But her father, I understand, when he was with her, was forever quizzing her on the local culture: "What did you see today? What does it mean? Do you know why the Japanese do so-and-so?" She tells me he had the answers to all these questions written out beforehand, and expected her to respond correctly. I am sure this did little to promote her self-confidence.

One of her favorite sayings has always been, "You can say anything if you say it politely." This little phrase reveals much about Grandma's peculiar perspective on the world. Politeness, "good manners," discretion, aplomb: these are the weapons with which we fight against the forces of darkness—bluntness, uncultured honesty, vulgarity, desperation, all the unsavory traits exhibited by those who are "not very nice." I have pointed out to her that if one goes by her definition of what is "nice" and "not nice"—a definition fairly loose and contingent—then there are not very many "nice" people left in the world.

"Well, that's their loss," she answers with a sigh. Perhaps this is so. If Grandmother only read, I would strongly suggest the works of Flannery O'Connor. But she insists she doesn't have the time or the eyes or the brain to read, and if she did, she would read the writings of the "great wise men of Israel."

"But there is so much, so much. . . ."

3

I mentioned before that my great-uncle Nelson reminded me of, or rather alerted me to, certain aspects I was to remark in my uncle Joseph—in the same way that in trying to explain certain obvious faults or disturbances in a problem child, we are tempted to ascribe them to their supposed antecedents in some legendary mad ancestor. Such specious causalities have the dangerous effect of satisfying us while the child rages on unchecked.

The analogy is not arbitrary. My uncle was a child; and he was my grandmother's child. She said it herself on that day early last fall when the telegram came announcing his arrival from the Far East.

"That child," she sighed. "Only he would think of coming to see me on such short notice. How does he expect me to prepare? We will have to buy beer—oh, how he loves beer! And ice cream. After such a hot journey I know he will be screaming for ice cream. And the sad thing is we will never have enough for him." The rest of the day was spent shopping for the things she remembered he liked; for as far as she was concerned, his tastes had never changed.

We went to meet him at the airport. I had never seen so many suitcases in my life; I counted thirteen, not including a flight bag marked Singapore Airlines, containing candy and colored paper flowers.

"Materials," he said when he noticed me eyeing all the luggage. "Materials and supplies—tricks of the trade. Sure I'm overweight, but what do I care, in the long run it's worth it to me. That's what you've got to figure in business, Peter— whether or not it's worth it in the long run. Because that's what makes a good businessman, separates the guy who knows from the guy who doesn't. I'm one who knows. Mom, have some flowers."

I had seen my uncle now and then over the years—though more seldom than I might have wanted while my parents were alive, for he and my father had gradually become estranged for reasons then unclear to me. But even encountering him as infrequently as I had, I was always fond of him. I remembered him as inordinately silly. Once he left a can of frozen orange juice on the kitchen table, and returned to find the can exploded and the walls covered in orange concentrate; he then attempted to sue the orange juice company, claiming their product was "a grenade" and could have killed him. Another time, in a restaurant, he opened mussels by throwing them on the floor and stepping on them. A story went that one day while he was driving in France, the engine fell out of his car— right out the bottom and onto the road. "Those French cars are just awful," he complained. What always amused me more than anything else I think was my intuition that these events were simply part of his everyday life, the mere thought of which delighted me, and to the implicit hilarity of which I sensed he needed to add no further effort than that required to live it. In other words, he was naturally funny; and I accepted this condition as a premise of his existence. He always seemed much funnier to me than did my father, who was a professional comedian—and well he might, for his brand of practical humor was, after all, more appealing to a child. And doubtless too, many of his antics were enacted solely for my benefit. Perhaps he felt in this a rivalry with my father, who could command an audience whenever he wanted, and for that very reason refrained from the more facile bids in front of his family. My uncle may well have been envious both of his brother's ability and his success—or more profoundly, of the secure audience my father had in wife and son, which my uncle must have guessed he himself would never have.

Be that as it may, I knew now that I would be obliged to see my uncle in a different light, colored not only by the intervening years of family history, but also by the diluting wash of my memories of him, which had no longer the brilliance of a child's, but the faded sobriety of a man's. An aging clown is a sad thing to behold, and I hoped that time, if it had not done him the favor of abolishing the necessity of his performance (which was part of his temperament), had at least gracefully modified and dignified his technique.

"The flight was just *terrible*," he now complained. "The air stunk—I think they put something in the ventilators. It was just awful. It smelled like a searchlight—ever been near a searchlight? Well, that's what it smelled like. Paul, how are you? *Wie geht's?* You think I need a trunk? Just like old Grandma, huh, Mom? Then we'd never get off the ground. Hah!" He embraced his mother in a clumsy bear hug. Her arm, emerging from within this affectionate mass and flailing, attempted to pat his shapeless shoulder. My uncle had a peculiar body. It was wide and solid; yet the impression of his torso was that it was ineffectual. His shoulders were rounded, their shape beginning to form the top of the pear of which his waist and hips outlined the overripe bottom—so that the legs were, as they would have been also on a pear, otiose appendages, which, neglected in the manner of sprouts, had now grown unmanageable. They were covered in dark flannel trousers, baggy and cuffless (this last a touch he had picked up in Europe). He wore a dark blue blazer, a pale yellow shirt, and a red tie with a pattern of green frogs, giving the overall impression of an oddball refugee from the Princeton Club—which in a way he was. He was in fact such an ardent and eternal Princetonian that he had encouraged me in my childhood to give him the nickname of Uncle Tiger, after the Princeton mascot. He then rewarded me with numerous stuffed tigers, all of which he had named beforehand. He wanted to leave nothing to my imagination—and he was right, for in regard to him I never needed to consult it.

Now he stood amid a jumble of luggage, trying to conjure up a porter. One skycap passed us and shook his head.

"Mr. Lorditch you better get yourself a moving van, a Bekins is what you need," said Paul, arraying the bags in two neat rows. "Otherwise I gonna get me a hernia sure. Let me find once a porter." He flagged down a skycap and discussed the situation with him.

"I can't handle that no way with one of these," said the skycap, a thin Negro, indicating his insufficient dolly. "What you got there, a circus show? Well, let me see, I'll bring a cart around, think we can do it in a cart." He bounced off and returned pushing a metal cart. He began to load the cart with spritely ardor. In spite of his thin build he was amazingly strong, and in no time he and Paul had stacked the massive bulk. My uncle cautioned them about the valuable content of the suitcases: "Now be careful, guys, that's precious research material, all the way from Singapore. It's fragile."

"We got it, boss," piped the skycap, and then to Paul: "What's he smugglin', anyway?"

We made our way out past the baggage-check station and into the sunshine, the slight Negro guiding his load as if it were a baby carriage. Paul went to bring the car around. My uncle, squinting, drew from his inside coat pocket a pair of pink sunglasses with heavy black rims. They made him look like a giant fly. We stared at each other for a few moments; then he said to me in a low voice, drawing me aside and into his confidence, "You. Listen. I didn't know Paul was a cripple." He uttered this last word with an emphasis of mixed shame, embarrassment, sympathy and disgust—as if Paul were not only a cripple (which he was not), but a distant relative of whose condition my uncle had until this moment been unaware, and the shocking public spectacle of whom, together with its consequent effect of repulsion on him, my uncle was now attempting to conceal by a sudden show of surprise and pity.

"Well, he has a bum leg," I answered, "but he's not exactly a cripple. He's always had a limp—didn't you know?"

"No, I didn't, no one ever told me, Mom never said anything." (As if Paul's injury were vital information concerning the general good of the family, which a mother, under normal circumstances, would never withhold from her son.) "That's a rough deal, the poor guy. What happened—he lose a leg, or what?"

"I don't know, I never asked. He seems to get along just fine."

But my uncle did not seem willing to accept this sanguine appraisal; and he made a point, before Paul had returned with the car, of emphasizing to the porter that this was a sick man who should not be allowed to lift any more baggage.

"You know what I mean," he said to the skycap, and added, on an impulse of both mystery and discretion, the purpose of which remained absolutely cryptic, "Keep it under your hat."

My uncle set up house in the room over the garage that had been my father's office. It was really more a study than an office, with overflowing bookshelves, a blue overstuffed easy chair, a long desk made from an uncut door, a round butcher's block weighing a good three hundred pounds and used as a lamp table, and a bed set into the wall, closed off by thick red drapes. There was even a stovepipe fireplace in one corner, though this was never used. A grandfather clock, with magnified insects painted on the face of the timepiece, stood near the window. To reach the study you had to climb a metal spiral staircase on the side of the garage. The room was deliberately isolated from the rest of the house. It had no phone, only a buzzer connected with the living room. Over the years this buzzer had developed its own language. One buzz meant you

40

were wanted for a telephone call; two meant dinner; three, come here, I need you. After the death of my parents, the room went unused for years, until I began to read (I was a late starter in literature, as in most things). Then I would spend all day in the deep blue chair, pulling out book after book from the shelves over my head. My father's library was stocked chiefly with the "light classics": Perelman, Bemelmans, Evelyn Waugh, Kingsley Amis, Beerbohm. For a stand-up comic, my father had peculiar literary tastes—in fact it is peculiar that he had any literary tastes at all. As far as I can remember, he never talked much about books, except to answer without hesitation when I asked him what was the best book ever written, *"Zuleika Dobson* by Max Beerbohm." I daresay he was wrong.

I was, and am, a desultory reader. I can rarely read more than twenty pages without skipping on ahead, often to another book entirely. In this way I would spend hours combing the bookshelves, mingled strains of different styles and voices swarming through my brain. In between books (temporally, I mean, not spatially) I would sometimes masturbate. This activity provided a welcome release from hours spent alone with musty Englishmen.

So I was somewhat put out when my uncle occupied this room. Of course, it was better than having him in my room. But I had looked on the study as a retreat. Now I must live again with only a door dividing me from Paul and Grandma.

I wasn't really sure why my uncle was here. Ostensibly he was "just passing through" after a trip to the Orient. But when he began to talk about having a phone installed "up there" (for we were forever having to summon him by single buzzes), I began to wonder. Something was up.

"Come to lunch with me today," he said one morning. "I want you to meet a friend of mine. He's from Java. Great guy—smallest guy I've ever seen." He put his hand to his waist. "Not much taller than that. But smart."

"Is he a midget?" I asked.

"He's pretty small, that's all I know. He's married, though—

41

got a wife and family. He likes to have a good time, too, just like anyone. Why don't you come along with us—I'm treating."

I admit I was curious. My uncle had not mentioned what his friend did, only that he had met him—Achekosa was his name, Thomas Achekosa—in Djakarta on his recent trip. "It's good for you to know someone there," he told me. "You never know what might happen, you might need him some day."

My uncle liked to live amid possibilities. I was learning that this was how he saw life—simply gushing contingencies as a cornucopia gushes fruit. Indeed, life was almost insufficient to hold all the glorious possibilities he envisioned; the choice between them was made all the more difficult because of the indiscriminateness of the selection offered; and, as in cornucopias, it was all a little disgusting.

We were meeting Achekosa at a restaurant in Westwood called the Velvet Horn.

"What sort of a name is that?" I asked my uncle. (Although I could imagine what it would be like: overstuffed red vinyl banquettes, hunting reproductions on the walls, chill air conditioning throughout, an immaculate salad bar with tongs to help yourself, no windows, a medicated dryness to the air, and cloying, Reddi-wip-covered desserts.)

"Well, what do you think?" he answered, leering suggestively. Then: "Never you mind. They've got terrific French food—and cute waitresses, too. They all know me in there—you'll see!"

And I did. The restaurant was much as I had imagined, except it had windows—of simulated leaded glass, which, however, had a genuine enough effect, for it was impossible to see out of them. The interior was requisitely dark. From somewhere came the computerized recreational bleep of a Pong game. Pictures, not of hunting scenes, but of dogs in old-fashioned men's clothing, hung on the walls over each booth, the overstuffed banquettes of which were not red vinyl, but black. The reception area smelled of carpet cleaner: an antiseptic tang, with marine overtones. There was Achekosa, sitting on a low bench; his feet did not quite touch the ground. He was indeed a little fellow.

"Tommy!" boomed my uncle. "Jesus, aren't you ever late?"

The Javanese rose to his feet with a neat, simple kick of his legs. "No, Joe, not like you," he replied, smiling. Then he blinked his eyes spasmodically twice, and issued a faint snorting sound through his nostrils. We were introduced.

"Yes, your uncle told me lots about you. You a writer. What kinds of stuff do you write." In his inflection there was no question mark.

"I write for a food magazine, articles for a food magazine," I answered him. "Not real writing."

"What magazine."

"Bon Vivant."

"Aha, so you like this restaurant," he somehow inferred. "You could tell us something about it. So what's cooking." A snort and violent blinking followed his little joke. (Either the man had a tic, or I was about to witness for the first time an attack of Javanese epilepsy.)

"Oh, I've never been here before," I said. "But my uncle tells me it's very good."

"Yeah, so what's cooking," he repeated. I had no idea what he meant by reiterating this foolishness, so I laughed and muttered—as one answers a nonsensical question with something equally nonsensical, because one hopes to conform somehow with the terms of the hidden alien logic—I muttered, "Well, you'll have to ask them." Now in cases like this, I have observed, the interlocutor (always a foreigner) can respond in either of two ways: he can demand another answer to his unanswerable question (thus proving what was always suspected, that he has an aggressively poor grasp both of the language and his place in it); or he can play along, accept your answer and pretend you have not only understood one another, but have an implicit agreement on things. Fortunately for me,

43

Achekosa took the latter course; he laughed uncomprehendingly but sympathetically, and we followed my uncle into the dining room.

My uncle and I slid into the booth, wedging Achekosa between us. Seated, he seemed less Lilliputian, although I was sure that under the table his legs dangled nowhere near the floor. The waitress recognized my uncle and said "Hel-lo," spacing the syllables. She had a deep, projecting voice.

"Hello, dear," said my uncle. "How are you today?"

"Oh, I'm fine, just all right, fine." She seemed to be giving a deliberately bored, singsong tone to her voice. But the eyes were not at all bored; they raked us over, seeming especially intrigued with Achekosa. Wide and round, they pierced and parried. Now they rested on me. My mouth opened. I wanted to say something but I could not speak, and I shut it stupidly. She looked back at Achekosa.

"Will you be having any cocktails, boys?" she asked. The way she said "boys" was, in my experience, unique. The voice itself was low, throaty, with a slight drawl, almost Southern. And the sassiness of it—that she should address us as boys! But after all, she was in a sense correct: Achekosa was no larger than a child, my uncle had a boyish mischievousness about him, and I . . . well, in some ways, which perhaps women can sense, I am not terribly mature. . . .

"You bet we will!" clucked my uncle. "Yes, we will—even before we look at the menus. Tommy, you'll have a—"

"Gin-tonic."

"A gin and tonic, a Heineken, and for my nephew—this is my nephew Peter; Peter, this is Shirley—"

"Mary."

"Mary, this is my nephew Peter."

"Hello." She did not look at me now, not even when she asked me what I was drinking.

"I'll have a tea, please."

"Tea," sneered my uncle. "Look what a nephew I've got, Shirley. Why don't you have a beer?"

44

"No thanks, I'd like tea." (I never can drink during the day; it puts me right to sleep.)

Eyes still averted, she said into her pad, "Real swinger, huh?"

I pretended not to hear; this was the least I could do, for I felt myself blushing hotly.

"Huh?" she repeated, knowing I must have heard her question. I was too confused now to come up with a snappy reply. I answered, "I will."

"You will? You will what?"

"I will have tea," I bumbled.

"You will have tea. So you will," she mocked. She gave a low, throaty chortle, and was off.

"She's got a lot of spunk, that one," said my uncle. "Independent. Good for her." He looked at me. "She seems to have an eye for you. Watch out." Again I was made aware of my uncle's fecund world of potentialities. He and Achekosa began to talk business. Achekosa was telling him about herbicides in central Java. It seemed the farmers didn't know how to apply the chemicals to the land; often they mistook herbicides for fertilizer.

Our waitress brought over the drinks and menus. As she set my tea before me I noticed she was smiling faintly, with pursed lips.

I made little effort to follow the conversation of my companions; I could hardly read the menu. The idea of food, when we are not interested in it, bears little resemblance to the same when we are hungry. Such concepts as "chicken pot pie," "salmon quiche," "spareribs à la Français" (whatever in God's name that is), "health salad," even a prosaic fried chicken, tantalizing and familiar enough when we have an appetite, appear when we lack it as strange and doomed experiments in the field of malignant cookery, the mere tasting of which we are convinced might very well mean the end of us. In this anorectic state, our vision of the forthcoming meal, if we have the courage to order it, becomes drearily vague; all descriptions in menus lie—none can seem even remotely appetizing. Thus a "chicken pot pie" assumes qualities of a Ubangi cannibalistic banquet; a "health salad" is an insidious euphemism for indigestible promiscuous roughage; and "spareribs à la Français"—well, this dish is simply catered from another planet. And of course, whoever is with us at these times is, with a vindictive foresight, always eager that we order the most impossible item on the menu. Thus my uncle: "Have the 'velvet deep-sea casserole.' It's delicious!"

Such a menu was a hopeless task. I finally ordered clam chowder. My uncle was not pleased with the choice. "Clam chowder, hell, I'm having 'spareribs à la Français.' "

"But uncle, I thought you were recommending the 'velvet deep-sea casserole.' "

"No," he said, adding assuredly, "that stinks. Tommy, what are you having?"

I had overlooked for a moment our diminutive guest—an easy oversight, since he was nearly concealed by the long menu, which appeared to dwarf him as an encyclopedia dwarfs a child. His eyes convulsed as they ranged over the list of alien, forbidden foods—but then he surprised me by saying, with polite tractability, "I'll go with your choice, Joe." I wondered if he knew he was ordering pork; but it was clearly not his first trip to America, so he must have known. Or perhaps he did not adhere to Moslem dietary laws; perhaps he was not even a Moslem. I thought I could detect an anticipatory sinning twinkle in his eye, the betrayal of a closet pig-eater.

The waitress returned to take our orders. My uncle ordered another round of drinks.

"Another tea, too?" asked the waitress, still in that teasing tone, and now staring at me impudently. In my confusion I grew inspired. "No thanks, I'm still nursing this one." This drew from her a laugh—a single honk of amusement. For a moment her buck teeth were revealed, then instantly withdrew behind her lips.

The food was brought, and my uncle's mouth was soon

covered with a sticky brown sauce. He attacked the ribs as if they were corn on the cob. Achekosa was daintier, nibbling along the edge of a rib with a punctilio born of suspicion. Yet he seemed to be enjoying his food; and his eyes, now with something better to do, had stopped their convulsive blinking.

"Eat your chowder," my uncle slobbered at me. "What are you, sick or something? You have diarrhea?" His solution to the supposed problem was to hand me a pleated paper cup of gelatinous sparerib sauce. "Put some of this in your soup—it'll taste better," he assured me.

He and Achekosa were now discussing the industrial triangle of Africa—copper, yogurt and matches—which my uncle had just discovered and wanted somehow to exploit. To this end he had formed a corporation, Sheba Enterprises. He wanted to know if Achekosa was interested in the deal. But Achekosa was skeptical; he wanted to know more about it.

"All right, look," explained my uncle. "There's copper in Ethiopia, right? We know that. As for yogurt, that's what a lot of Africans live on. We know that, too. Look at these wandering nomads in the desert—what do you think they live on? That's right, yogurt—and sometimes blood, which they get from their animals and mix with the yogurt. But I'm not talking about that. I'm talking about just plain yogurt. In Ethiopia you already got a market. What you don't have yet is mass production. A lot of these guys, they still get their yogurt from the sheep farmers. Now that's peanuts—how much can these guys produce in a year? A hundred gallons? A thousand? Ten thousand? I don't care, it's still not enough. Demand exceeds supply, we know that—"

"How you know that?" Achekosa questioned mildly.

"We *know* that," my uncle repeated. "Don't you ever read *Forbes* magazine? Don't you read the *National Geographic*? It's all there. Besides, I've been to Addis Ababa. I've seen how these people live, and let me tell you, they're not exactly having a picnic over there. Even in the city, you got people sleeping out everywhere, some in tents, but mostly right out there under the stars. It's a sad sight, Tommy. I bet you've never seen anything like it, even in Java."

Ignoring this presumption, Achekosa asked, "So how they going to buy yogurt?"

"All right, look," explained my uncle once again, "they eat a lot of yogurt. We *know* that. You might say yogurt is the bread of Africa—well, no, it wouldn't be like bread, it'd be like—ice cream. That's right. I like that, it's a good slogan: 'Yogurt is the ice cream of Africa.' " (He repeated this several times.) "All right. Now it's so hot over there, you can imagine how much ice cream they eat, just 'cause of the weather—"

"Yogurt, you mean yogurt, they eat yogurt," reestablished the fact-minded Achekosa, eyes blinking confoundedly.

"Right. Yogurt. Now everybody's eating yogurt all day, but where are they getting it from? Small farmers, like I said. Now the small farmers, they're milking their cows or goats or sheep or whatever they have over there, maybe it's a water buffalo or a camel, I don't care, that's not the point. The point is, they can work all day long, they're still not going to be able to meet the demand, 'cause it's just too great. And the sad thing, Tommy, is they don't even know it."

He paused. "That's where we come in. We can mass-produce yogurt like it's going out of style. Hell, all you need is milk, and a little bacteria, which you could probably pick up off the ground over there. Actually, it's hygienic bacteria we're using for yogurt—acidopoulos bacteria" (apparently a Greek strain of the germ) "which you can grow in a laboratory, so you know it's safe to eat."

But Achekosa was a dogged skeptic. "How you going keep it? Yogurt spoils if you don't refrigerate."

"You think they refrigerate it now? I bet you a million bucks they don't."

"So maybe they don't eat so much yogurt," he offered.

My uncle was outraged. "I tell you I *know* they do. I've done research on the subject. I went to school with the ambassador to Ethiopia—Paul Malcolm Sargent. He should know."

"So?"

"So," concluded my uncle, impeccably casuistic, "the third point of our little triangle is matches. Maybe the most important. You realize how important matches are, Tommy—I know they have them in Java." (My uncle's conception of Java must have been that of a country known to be technically more sophisticated than Ethiopia—an opinion he perhaps thought would flatter his friend.)

"You mean they don't have matches in Ethiopia?" inferred Achekosa, at this point expecting the worst in regard to that pathetic nation so desperately in need of exploitation by Sheba Enterprises.

"They do," said my uncle, "but they're not very good. In fact I have some right here."

He produced from his coat pocket a small matchbox, on the cover of which was a drawing of a snarling red lion. He struck a match. "Sometimes they splinter." He blew it out. "Or they don't always go right out when you blow them out. They smolder—see!—could be dangerous. All you have to do is drop a match before it's out, and you could start a forest fire—I mean a jungle fire—that could cost millions of dollars. It's the wood they're using—must be some kind of dry root that burns forever. Anyway, it's obviously not suited for matches. But nobody so far has come up with anything better. That's where we come in. We get rid of this root and replace it with good, dry, quick-burning firewood. It'll be a lot safer for everyone concerned."

"Wait a minute. How you going get that wood?" demanded the thoughtful Oriental. "How you know they have it in Africa?"

"I'm not talking about *that*," my uncle shot back. "You're not listening. They *have* this wood. It's just a question of transporting it to the factories—"

"What factories?"

"The match factories we're going to build. Jesus, Tommy, you think I haven't thought of all this before?" My uncle was now very excited, inebriated as much by the possibility of Ethiopian industry on a grand scale as by the liquor he had drunk. He was sweating. His lower lip was curled downward in an expression I had never seen before—a look of almost nauseated disdain for the insane language that poured from his mouth— the words reduced to the state of an effluence that was the useless, overflowing and mildly putrescent by-product of his weird creative process. This expression, which was later to become characteristic of him at such moments of inspiration, caused his face to appear forlorn—an effect raised to pathetic heights by the exaggerated and impossible magnitude of his ambitions.

"And I know what your next question is going to be," he went on. "How does it all go together? Copper, yogurt and matches—what do they have in common? How do they fit? What do they mean? Is that what you're thinking, Tommy?"

"That's right, Joe," said our patient guest, blinking mystifiedly. To judge from his expression, the forthcoming news that these three materials might be combined to produce a beauty soap, a meat tenderizer, or shoes, would have been a possibility that would not have surprised him in the least—and even one toward the realization of which he seemed to believe he might be able to offer some practical suggestions, if only he could get a word in edgewise.

"Well, don't you worry," reassured my uncle, "it all fits together just like a jigsaw puzzle. Listen. You build a match factory in Ethiopia—could be anywhere, I don't care, it just so happens it's in Ethiopia. Now what do you need to build a factory? Raw materials. Right. And one of those raw materials is copper, which Ethiopia has in abundance. I know that; I've done research. Okay. You can use copper for lots of things— pipes, electrical wiring, circuits and such, tools, money even— bronze too, they make bronze out of copper and tin. Thousands of uses—a very useful metal, copper.

"Okay. Now here's the simplest part of all. Tommy, what's the first thing you need in a factory?"

50

"Copper," answered the alert Oriental.

"That's right—but even before copper, what do you need? Even before anything else, before a single match is made, before a single copper circuit is switched, before a single copper tool is raised, before—"

"People. Workers."

"Right. Workers. People," my uncle repeated in a more humanitarian inversion. "And people—what do they do? They eat. They do it often—sometimes less in Africa, but they still do it. Everybody who can, does. Thousands of people working in a factory, they eat too." He paused, sweating, climactic, allowing his observation to sink in before hitting us with its inevitable conclusion: "And they eat—yogurt."

At this point my grandmother would have said, "So there you are." But I said nothing; nobody said anything. What could you say—no? I suppose you could have, and someone should have. My uncle's industrial triangle was nothing but an absurd tautology founded on an unnecessary premise—which is not to say it was not fascinating. It held for me the fascination of the demented—a shuddering glimpse of an incomprehensible yet vaguely familiar terrain, at the sight of which one recoils in terrified relief, and in the (often mistaken) belief that it is not one's own territory.

The waitress came over with the check. Achekosa quickly snatched it up; my uncle of course objected, and they began to wrangle. The waitress stood by, amused. Her dimples appeared again; I was in love. My uncle finally succeeded in wrestling the check from the little man, and slapped a hundred-dollar bill down on the table. "I hope you have change," he said.

I came back to the restaurant the next day. It was a busy lunch hour. I had come at that time to be sure of catching Mary at work. I sat at a small table in what I hoped was her section, and waited for her to appear. But another waitress came up and handed me a menu, and my heart began to sink. I said, as politely as I could, "May I be served by Mary?"

"Mary's not here today," the waitress replied. "I can take your order when you're ready." She spoke without inflection; it was thereby to be understood that she disliked her fellow worker. I felt gratified to be able to say, returning the menu, "That's all right, I'll just have clam chowder, thank you."

"Large or small."

"Small, please."

Spite glittered bright in her eyes. It was surprising, refreshing even, to feel at once how much we disliked each other. I experienced an anticipatory tingle of adrenaline as I rehearsed various appropriate offensive remarks—those imagined noble, incontrovertible blows, which, as they promise to exalt us in victory and debase our enemies, somehow never seem cheap or vulgar or even unfair, until the moment we utter them—if we ever do utter them—for rarely can we approach through the spoken word the universal, compassionate, just yet inapplicable wisdom or our ideal fantasies of revenge—which emerge, if at all, only as a paltry "Oh yeah?" or "Who are *you*?" or a sarcastic apology or, the most cowardly of all, a "Let me speak to the manager."

I have often succeeded in convincing myself, even when a woman shows an interest in me, as Mary had done yesterday, that she is making fun of me. You see, the whole thing seems so much a game that I find it hard to believe anyone can take it seriously. Which is not to say I don't take it seriously myself. For me, it is a miserably serious affair; and if it is a game, it is a grim and vital game of survival, whose rules I have never quite learned, or at least have failed to follow. Yet I attempt to play along; and sometimes my ignorance in the matter is not immediately noticeable. But such halfhearted participation is painful for me; I fear I am losing something irreplaceable; I feel I am bestowing something irrevocable: myself.

Now I realize it is a sad and perhaps misguided conceit, this

idea of "bestowing" oneself. (Please excuse the digression—
though you must be used to it by now—but I feel you know
much more about my family than about me. Which is perhaps
as it should be, in the better interests of narrative, of drama, of
life—and I want at least to offer you a brief glimpse at the
shuttered windows of my musty soul, after which you will no
doubt want to proceed on to airier rooms.) Maybe it comes
from being an only child and an orphan; or perhaps it is the
legacy of a nearly forgotten sense of early childhood stability,
which I experienced in the shelter of my parents, as contrasted
with later intimations of chaos under the guardianship of the
German goose-fat-eater and Grandma: that is, an overgrown
sense of self, or rather of the inapproachable uniqueness of
self, taught me by my parents, and challenged by all others. I
do not mean to say that no one else but my parents believed in
me, but only that they believed unquestioningly, wholeheart-
edly, eternally. I like to think that they believe still; and I am
afraid they might be disappointed at what they see. . . .

Paul claimed that he had always believed in my intelligence.
But what this really meant was that he abidingly cherished the
memory of my father's "wisdom"; he was dedicated to the
continuance of my father's will. And its living example was
me. So it was almost inevitable that I should receive from
Paul, regularly and religiously, his own idiomatic professions
of faith.

"You got there some head on your shoulders," he would say.
"You gonna work from your head, like your pa. He always told
me to 'Watch that boy, Paul, he gonna grow up to be a smarty-
pants.' I always said to him you was one already, and you was
gonna get a lickin' if you was too smart."

With Grandma it was different. I was made aware of unknown ancestors; I was steeped in the lore of atavistic eccentricity; I learned the crotchets of the dead. (Perhaps this has
encouraged in me my inordinate sense of the past.)

"Now your Aunt Minnie," she would begin, "she was a very
lively girl." (Although she was speaking of her as an adult,

53

to Grandma her mother's sister was forever a girl.) "She was a girl who loved life, and lived it to the full. And it showed. Strangers on the street would compliment her; they knew at once she was a lady. People don't do that nowadays, of course. Unless you're rich or famous, they won't look twice at you. Money, money, money—yes, money makes the world go round," she said contemptuously—a contempt apparently directed both at the undeniability of this substance in its universal reality, and the supposed indifference, to her, of its unfair circulation. And yet this attitude of hers was really disingenuous, since the force she so contemned had helped to propel her own progress through the world.

"But it was different then," she continued. "They liked her not for her money, but because she was a real lady. And she certainly lived up to the name. So vivacious, so entertaining, so worldly, so considerate always. To the help, too. A pity she was arrested. . . ."

"What?"

"Yes, she was arrested," Grandma repeated placidly. "You knew that, didn't you?"

"No I didn't," I lied; I wanted to hear the story again. "That's incredible. What for?"

"Oh, I don't think I should go into it."

"Oh, you have to. Come on, Grandma."

"No no, it would be wicked, she wouldn't want . . . not that it was her fault, mind you . . . and then they were so silly really, the Japanese, they made such a scandal, we all could have been ruined . . . of course it really *was* her fault, I suppose . . . but she wasn't the only one . . . he was really disgraceful, that man, wicked. . . ."

"Please, Grandma. Don't tease my curiosity like this."

"Well, now, you must promise not to tell. . . ."

Surely Grandma was aware she had told this story before; her very placidity betrayed a loving familiarity with the story and characters. And after all, to her mind, what was really so surprising about the affair? It needed no explanation; it was

54

simply Aunt Minnie, her aunt, part of her family, her world, and thus possessed an implicit justification.

What an extraordinary vestigial creature, this grandmother of mine. In many ways, of course, she was not so extraordinary: a little old lady, mild-mannered, with a slight stoop, more active and agile than most her age, but certainly as hard of hearing and as nearsighted and as forgetful and as doting as the next. Yet these inevitable marks of aging were not, for her— as they are for most elderly people—the chief concern or interest in life; they never claimed much of her attention. For my grandmother had something better to do. She was in the process of rejuvenation.

It wasn't that she couldn't admit to her eighty-one years. Yes, she allowed that she had been for some time identified with the septua- and octogenarian named Cissie Samuels, and this, we assume, had suited her well enough. But now she was moving on to something different; one might say entering an altered state of being—though such an idea would scarcely have been comprehensible to her. Recent developments in her life suggested a historical process in reverse. She was moving backwards, back to a younger century, in search of purity, innocence, ignorance perhaps: the solace of an age in all ways more congenial to her, and of course more ignorant, which nevertheless—perhaps consequently—with the zeal of a trusting, dumb midwife, had been all too eager to help bring our own age into existence. (The metaphor was one Grandma might have used herself.) That the offspring, this hideous century, had proved to be a monstrous child, only brought out to greater effect the midwife's frustrated good intentions. My grandmother sympathized with the woman; for so, in the face of horror and deformity, could she imagine she might have felt. But what to do? She could not live in the same house as an ugly child, so she sought out the company of the antique midwife. Unfortunately she did not know that her old friend had died last century. And no one was about to tell her. Besides, even if someone had, she wouldn't have believed it.

55

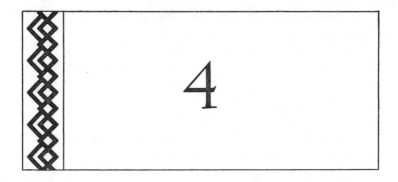

4

It wasn't long before my uncle found what he was looking for—more than even he had bargained for, and according to his ravings the buy of the century. It was a colony of condominia in the Marina called Mariner's Village. The word "village" applies only in a thematic sense, for Mariner's Village was so very much more than a village that its name cannot even approximate the raging metastasis that had engendered this cancer-by-the-sea. It was like nothing I had ever seen, which is to say—in the words of a quizzical earthling who had just caught a glimpse of an extraterrestrial entity bigger and stranger than his dreams—it was like something from another planet.

But I should say something first about our Marina—for without the Marina, Mariner's Village would not exist. Or, to carry through our metaphor, the Marina is the other planet from which Mariner's Village came.

The Marina is the product of a vast real estate development project begun by various speculative interests in the early sixties. The full name of the project is Marina del Rey—the King's Marina. Reasonable enough, for it is a veritable Versailles of landfill. They must have filled in at least five square miles of coastal swamp, backwaters and idle canals that previously had comprised the waterworks of the city of Venice, bordering on the Marina. Atop this landfill they sank pilings and built piers, docks and quays—or esplanades, really, since the boats don't use them, and they serve mainly as public sundecks and atmospheric locations for several small "neighborhood cafes," Riviera-style, catering to the local swimsuit generation. It has always struck me as someone's (someone ignorant of the Riviera) idea of a concrete St. Tropez. Set back from the esplanades are the more opulent condominia, whose second- and third-story balconies give out a view over the glittering walkway edging the placid waters of the bay.

And there are the boats, bobbing in the sunshine—thousands and thousands of boats. The Marina was built as much for boat-owners as for singles. Before development was begun, there was a small-craft harbor—five hundred boats at most— and no residential community to speak of. It was all very Spartan back then; you simply rented space on a pier in the bay and kept your boat there. You didn't want to stick around, since there was nothing to do but drive back and forth across the swamps, which had an unpleasant sulfurous smell.

But speculative interests soon changed all this; they expanded the bay, built a breakwater, dredged the swamps dry and built a little city, easy as pie. It took, all of it, under ten years. They promoted it as very swinging: a "casual, sun 'n' sea environment" with a "carefree lifestyle." It was the place to be young, a Shangri-La-by-the-sea, a drive-in Disneyland with residential accommodations. The Disneyland parallel here is really quite apt; with a little imagination the Marina complex can be seen as a toned-down Fantasyland, very hip, without rides. The number of Porsches and Mercedes-Benzes in underground Marina parking lots must surely rival the population of West Germany; and all the gold taken from around people's necks would have embarrassed even Cortez.

How did my uncle end up here? And not just anywhere in the Marina, mind you, but in a condo in Mariner's Village, the jewel in the throne. He didn't own a boat (although I imagine he was "working on one"; what else could he have told his realtor?), and his car was a Stingray—sporty, as he called it, but after all a Chevrolet. And then, my uncle was fifty-four—a senile fifty-four. If everyone else was out there swinging, he must have been barely dangling. Still, there were more than a few older boys his age cruising the Marina, red as beets and cultivating melanomas through their sunroofs. Some wore on their heads the sun visors so prevalent among surfers. Driving through the Marina any weekend, one could spot these creatures waddling in and out of their souped-up specials, adjusting on their foreheads the emblematic visor, which is murder on a toupee.

And so into this Eden, out of the East, came Joseph Lorditch, banished man. His mother, you see, had expelled him from her realm. Perhaps "expelled" is a bit harsh—it was more a state of prolonged exile in which she hoped he might come to his own recognizance, cease from his erring ways, which he had lately been trodding with abandon, and once again enter the family fold cleansed and purified, worthy to serve. This of course was madness on her part, and probably the worst thing she could have done. In her righteous search for the proper mode of maternal chastisement, she unwittingly secured for him infernal damnation and burning in a hell of saunas and Jacuzzis.

She asked him to leave the house. They had for some time— really, since his arrival in the fall—been at loggerheads. She objected to the hours and much of the company he kept. The "shady business types" lurking about late into the night made her uneasy; she feared he was setting us up for future trouble— these people could only bring unnecessary expenditures, and dark unpleasantness of mind and body. He argued with her, of course, saying that she was being unfair, that these men were his "associates," important to his "business," and furthermore, if she cared to know, brilliant (top of their classes at USC and Pepperdine), influential, and unquestionably honest: his friends. He accused her of being old-fashioned and narrow-minded. She gladly accepted these labels on behalf of her family, if it would help to protect them. They don't need your protection, he told her. If you don't feel you do, she replied, then you must leave. Taking your telephone with you. The incessant ringing is like the bells of hell to my ears.

This arrangement, though painful, was in the long run, I think, better for both of them. I had been worried that she might suffer a stroke during one of their arguments; her face would become pale and rigid, her eyes hooded with worry. Her love, I feared, clutching desperately, in vain, at the inaccessible, would kill her. And I think that my uncle, stubborn and selfish as he was, was finally frightened also. He began talking about a condominium in a place called Mariner's Village, where his friend Ed Richardson lived. Richardson knew of a deal he could get, Uncle explained, whereby through a mysterious "transferral of stocks" he need pay no cash for a year, and could also avoid a protracted mortgage.

"That will not be necessary, I can lend you the amount," offered Grandma, who, now that the prospect of his independence was suddenly upon her, did not feel so eager to let him go. But he was impatient to make the move; he wanted to deal through his new friends, and besides, he did not want to let her off so easily by accepting her offer of help.

So, during Christmas of that year, shortly after he was moved in (he had not allowed us to assist, but had hired a moving company Ed Richardson had suggested), he invited me to come over and see his "digs" in "the Village," as he called it. He asked me to say nothing to Grandma; he felt she still needed time to get used to the idea. He was right.

I found him lounging in a djellaba. "I bought this in Morocco," he said proudly.

"I should think so," I said. "Isn't it a bit warm for here?"

"Yeah, well, I've got a sunburn—I fell asleep on the sun porch and I got all sunburned—even under my arms. Can you beat that?"

It was true, he was quite burned; when he smiled, his usually yellow teeth looked like white buttons stuck into a tender red pincushion. My uncle was a stoutish man of medium height, but slouched now in his favorite overstuffed green chair, with the djellaba on, and with such a red face, he looked like a fat pasha. His bare feet, also burned, were crossed and resting on an ottoman. I noticed again a peculiarity of his right foot that I had remarked before: the arch of the sole was abnormally high, making the foot appear curled, like a Persian slipper. He had suffered a mild case of polio as a child.

"You should be careful in the sun," I said. "You might get sunstroke."

"I think I've already got it." He put his hand to his brow.

"Do you feel hot?"

"Christ, don't I look it? I just fell asleep, that's all. I'm lucky I woke up before I caught fire." He took his hand away from his brow, looked at it and shook it as if it were a questionable foreign object. I wondered if he had been drinking. I didn't see any bottles or glasses around.

"Have you been home all day?"

"Of course not," he said. "I had lunch with Richardson. Hell of a guy. And a damn good lawyer in the bargain. An important person to know." I wondered if he was so soon in need of Richardson's services. "I want you to meet him. We could have dinner tonight. Sure, why not?" He picked up the phone by the easy chair.

"But I thought you just had lunch with him," I said.

"So what? This is important. Most things are accomplished over food, anyway."

I was willing to grant this, and questioned no further just then. I stepped out onto the sun porch. Scattered about it were a deck chair, a picnic basket, several towels, and yellowed sheets of *The New York Times*; the bare boards were blotched with tanning oil. Walking up to the rope railing, I squinted before the shimmering esplanade below, and the bright happy launches in their slips. Farther out in the bay, past the breakwater, sailboats were scudding silently. It was the prettiest time of day in this land, the late afternoon. The sky was an infinite blue; against it the windows of tall glass buildings in the Marina Center reflected in mosaic a magnified and disintegrating sun. On a slip nearby, a young couple were loading a crate onto a boat. The woman was wearing snug white shorts and a jersey. As she bent over, her jersey hiked up on her back, and two dimples were revealed. (I have always wondered about these fascinating parts of the female anatomy. What are they?) For a while I watched her dainty, decisive movements; she seemed to know so well who she was. Who was she? Presently I turned from the balcony. Stepping into the darker room, I was temporarily blinded; I could barely see the outline of my uncle, draped in loose folds, standing at the bar. Had he just been sneaking a drink?

"So did you get in touch with Richardson?" I asked.

"He's going to come around for a drink at six—he lives just over here on Tahiti Way. Then I was thinking of taking us to Davy Jones' Locker. Great steaks. It's a swanky place, too. I call it the Locker Room. Lots of young things running around. You should see it. Richardson goes there all the time."

This wasn't, to my mind, a sterling recommendation. I said, "Why don't we go someplace else, then? I mean, if you've both already been—"

"Why should I?" he snapped. "I know the place, they know me, it's convenient. Plus it's fun. You'll see."

It sounded like just another Marina clip joint—but then they all are nowadays. I'm afraid that in our constantly growing city the number of honest restaurants is actually decreasing—restaurants, I mean, whose modest purpose it should be to graciously encourage one to eat enjoyably; not to flirt, guzzle cocktails or leer at the floor show, but to relax in one's own company and be gratefully spared that of others whose only regular or extended thoughts are directed principally at the problem of what to have imprinted on their personalized license plates.

61

(Please understand that if I am a snob, I am not an insensitive one; and my uncle seemed so proud now of his discovery that I could question it no further.)

"You better get dressed if he's coming at six—it's a quarter to, now," I told him.

"Well, he might be late. I think he was going to pick up his babe."

"Not cracking cases, eh? And I'll bet you he's even married—he is, isn't he?"

My uncle said, "Shh." This expression, emanating from a bright red figure in a hooded djellaba, struck me as insane. I broke out laughing.

"What's funny?" he asked.

"Nothing. Go get dressed."

"Okay, okay, we've got time, you know. It's not a formal place."

"So are you going to go dressed like that?"

"Don't be ridiculous," he said, as if this were out of the question. He got up carefully and wandered into the bedroom, testing his tender armpits as he went.

A half-hour later he came out, groomed, scrubbed and sparkling, ruddier than before. He was wearing a pink blazer. It glowed like a blister on his skin. "Richardson's not here yet?" he asked.

"You've got to be kidding," I said, staring at his blazer.

"Snappy coat, huh? I got it in Southampton, with your father. Twenty years ago, must have been."

"Will they let us in?"

"Are you kidding? This is a formal coat. Haven't you ever been in Southampton?"

"No." I had never even been to Long Island.

"Well, that's how they dress there—they know all about it. This coat's got a history."

"I bet it does—I'll bet it's got a record."

He unbuttoned the coat, then buttoned it again and moved to the bar.

"You're not going to drink now?" I said, but he paid no attention, and poured the contents of a little ounce bottle into a whiskey glass.

"Richardson's late," he remarked. Then he put his hand to his brow. "Jeez, I still feel hot."

"Well, you should—you're just about the color of your coat. And alcohol will make you hotter." But of course my remonstrances were lost on him. He had a way of ignoring a voice that he didn't want to hear; he talked right through it. Or he negated, irritatedly, "I'm not talking about *that*," and cut you off.

"Did you make a reservation?" I asked.

"They know me. There's always a table saved for the Tiger."

It was this confidence that kept us waiting for the tardy Richardson. Uncle spouted on and on about this singular man's achievements in the fields of law and women. It was a good hour before the slightest tone of doubt entered his monologue—and by that time he was well on his way, and didn't care.

"Richardson's not coming, Uncle. Let's eat. Come on, I'm getting hungry."

"Now wait a minute, let's just see if—"

"No, I'm sure he's already eaten by this time. And he was supposed to come for cocktails. Forget it. Let's go."

But Uncle gave one last rally. "You don't know if . . . maybe something happened, he could be clinching an important deal, maybe he's moving on some of the ideas we were talking about. . . . Did I tell you about Vox-Tone, where it amplifies the voice of a dying man on the street so that anyone can hear—"

"No! He was supposed to be here an hour ago, and he's not, so let's go!"

Uncle paused. "Maybe he had a heart attack," he said suddenly, and his face drooped at the thought. He stepped up to the screen door of the sun porch, now in shadow. A last band of light glowed a luminous pink at the tips of the tall masts bobbing in their slips.

63

"Fuck him," he decided.

A twilight world was creeping out and taking hold of Mariner's Village as we finally walked down to the restaurant. Obscure, darkling shapes seemed to twist out of the buildings, forming themselves into eels, whales and crabs; but they were only lengths of rope draped along the sides of the buildings. Rope was everywhere: coiled on the top of worm-eaten pillars (the worm holes were simulated with drills), bordering the walkways, ready to spring from every lamppost as if from a gibbet. The marine motif was stretched to its limit. Gold-tile fish lurked gloomily at the bottom of the children's shallow swimming pool. In the adults' pool, black numbers shivered beneath the ripples in the water. A woman's laughter, hollow, merciless, splashed over us from one of the balconies above; the sound was profoundly frightening. We walked along in silence. Under the vapor lamps the pink jacket shone an unnatural lavender, like the advanced stage of a burn.

The restaurant entrance was below ground level; the whole building seemed sunk into a pit. Steps led down to a wood-and-rope bridge crossing a shallow pond. The pond was lit up from underwater, and large fish—and their shadows—hung motionless. At one end of the pond was a small-scale replica of a sunken ship, bathed in blue light projected from lamps in the shrubs. The bridge led to a landing paved with smooth stones, and then we reached the door—whose handles, of course, were rope. One side of the door opened and a couple came out laughing; their hair was the color of margarine. Even when he had stopped laughing, the man's upper lip did not quite close over his teeth.

As soon as we had stepped inside, the hostess, a trim, pert young woman, greeted my uncle. "Good evening, Mr. Lorditch, I love your coat."

"Joan, this is my nephew Peter. Peter Lorditch. This is Joan. Did you save a table for the Tiger?"

Joan showed us immediately to a table in the far corner of the room, by a picture window looking out onto the pond and shipwreck. The restaurant, I recognized, was simply a condensation of the rest of Mariner's Village. Rope and nets hung from every inch of the low ceiling—as well as cork buoys and colored glass balls, fishing rods, rusted lanterns with red and green bulbs, lifesavers, oars, and huge, varnished fishes mounted on plaques. All this together produced the cluttered effect so prevalent in pretentious maritime bars.

The restaurant was well-filled with customers—all couples. I didn't see one pairing of the same sex, except for me and my uncle.

"This looks like a swinging place," I remarked. I was already depressed.

"I told you so," said my uncle. "Joan will take care of everything. Won't you, Joan?" But Joan had turned for a moment to another table and did not hear him. "Sure she will," he said. Eventually he caught Joan's attention and ordered a drink while we looked at the menu. It was a standard "surf 'n' turf" selection of food—that dreary, promiscuous mix of seafood and steaks that marks a third-rate restaurant's idea of adventurous dining. This is food one can only eat when drunk (one could hardly conceive of it sober)—which, of course, is why it is served in places like this. I was reminded of a teacher I once had for high school biology, who found it amusing to throw together, in the same jar of formaldehyde, creatures with no possible affinity for each other when alive: birds with frogs; a small sand shark with rats; long, segmented worms with a pig embryo. This obscene, defiant violation of nature's laws of ecology seems also to be the operating principle of surf 'n' turf restaurants, which thrive on our secret delight in forbidden combinations. (For this perverse thrill see also the ancient Romans, who would punish parricides by enclosing the live criminal in a sack along with a monkey, a rooster, and a snake, also alive, then throwing the whole mess into the Tiber.)

But Uncle was tantalized by the wide selection, and also by the salad bar in back of us that was being plundered from all sides. "I think I'll wait and have my salad afterwards, like the

French," he said. "Unless they have anchovies," he added. "I don't want anchovies. I hate them. Look, they've got medallion of beef. I'm telling you, they must have a French chef here. I bet they've even got chocolate mousse for dessert . . . yep, here it is, what did I tell you."

Joan came around twice to take our orders, but Uncle said we weren't ready yet. He kept reading out dishes as soon as he saw them; he read through the whole menu in this way.

"Uncle Tiger," I said, "you've got to pick out one dish and order it, otherwise we're never going to eat. I'm having the sand dabs."

"OK, OK, I just want you to see what they've got here—see all this? It's some place."

"I know, I can see that. Please order. Have the sand dabs."

"I haven't had that here, but their fish is terrific. . . ."

"Have it."

"Not so fast. I want to be aware of all my options, as Richardson says. Jeez, it's too bad he didn't come. That's a hell of a thing to do. I'd never do that to a guy."

"Here's Joan again; can we please order?"

"OK, OK. Joan, dear, for my nephew, for my nephew Peter, he would like the sand dabs Capitain."

"Sounds great," said Joan. "Soup or salad? Soup is German cream of leek. Salad? All righty. You can get it right up there at the salad bar. And for yourself, Mr. Lorditch?"

"Call me Tiger, Joan. That's my name, the Tiger."

"All righty, Tiger."

"That's right." Uncle leaned his elbow heavily on the table. His face seemed to slant to one side—not his head, just his face, which gave him a look of distress. He seemed to have forgotten about his order.

"Yes?" said Joan.

"That's right," Uncle repeated. "Tiger Joe Lorditch and his nephew Peter."

Joan looked at me, then poked her pen at the pad in her hands. "And what will you be having, Tiger Joe?"

66

"You'll have the sand dabs, won't you, Uncle?" I prompted him.

"I certainly will *not*!" he thundered, as if defending himself against an unfair accusation—he was no fish-eater, nor was he ever to be mistaken for one. Then, more quietly, he said, "Joan, dear, I'll have a sirloin steak. Rare, with lots of cooked onions. And another drink please, dear." He pushed his empty glass away, with a deliberate gesture of disgust.

"And do you have the gestapo tonight?" he asked.

"Gazpacho? No, we have cream of leek. Would you like some?"

"Hell no, that stinks. Forget it." Joan gathered up the menus. My uncle repeated, "Cooked onions."

"Got you," said Joan. "Have a nice meal." Serving Tiger Joe Lorditch was clearly no picnic; lucky she was a pro, and could handle it.

"Have you talked to Grandma lately?" I asked him. With his drooping face he indicated no, or something negative. I felt he should at least attempt a show of concern; after all, he had left her when she really hadn't expected him to. She cherished the hope that he was going on to greater things—or to something, at least. She was convinced he possessed that vague gift, "a business sense"; but I'm afraid he had little sense of any kind, and I had tried to disburden her of this misconception. I did not realize at the time that certain of our misconceptions—the most personal, the ones that keep us going day after day, the true ones, as it were (true for us as the misconceivers)—in time become organic to ourselves, and cease any longer to relate to the original pressing concerns for which we fabricated them, or if they still do relate, they do so independently of our faculty of reason; so that what others, and even we ourselves, might once have recognized as our misconceptions become, finally, simply conceptions like any others: the unfounded opinions, vague ideas and delusions that help us to express, day in and day out, the dream of our own identity, to build that prison of illusion in which the soul is kept.

Yet I would like to think that my uncle's soul was freer. It was certainly more expressive. I told myself that this was not strictly his fault. I had felt it might have something to do with his blood chemistry. A doctor of mine whom I had consulted about my uncle had explained a condition having to do with insufficient oxygen transferral to the tissues, including parts of the brain, causing a person to feel light-headed when even the smallest amount of alcohol was introduced into the system. I told myself that perhaps this was what my uncle suffered from. But the idea was most disturbing and I could never bring myself to tell him about it. Besides, like his mother, he abhorred doctors. So I told him instead to watch his drinking; and sometimes he did. Around me he usually limited himself to one beer—which was enough for him.

"Go to the salad bar," he said now. "Get yourself some salad."

"I don't want any," I said. "I don't like salad bars."

"Go on. What do you mean you don't like? Look at that selection. It's healthy, too. They say it stops cancer."

"Oh, really. I would say it causes cancer."

"No no," my uncle drawled with a tired wave of his hand. "It's roughage, and doctors say roughage prevents cancer. That and Vitamin B-12."

"B-15, you mean Vitamin B-15," I corrected.

"No no, what are you talking about, it's B-12, that's the health drug, Vitamin B-12," Uncle said impatiently, his sad face drooping. "I should know, I've done research on that drug. It's Vitamin B-12 that's the health drug. And that is a fact."

"Well, whatever you say. I suppose you're something of a health bug, eh?" A health bug pissed to the gills. I do not doubt that Uncle knew something about these "health drugs"; it was just his way to lecture all evening on them while drinking himself unconscious. But then I suppose he would argue that alcohol is good for hypertension. I can hear him ranting, "That's what my doctor said—it dilates the vessels."

"They're discovering all about it now," he went on. "These doctors are miracle workers, any day now they'll have the whole human race cured. They're full of shit, is what they are. Just a bunch of crooks banding together to scare us all and get us to buy their drugs. They're in cahoots with the drug companies. Remember what I said. I knew Johnny Upjohn. Went to college with him. He told me all about it. He wasn't in the business, though—wouldn't have any part of it. Knew all about what goes on, and he wouldn't have any part of it. You see, that's because he knew too much—too much for his own good. That film, *The Man Who Knew Too Much*, well, that was him." He paused, nearly breathless.

"That's what happens, Peter, when you know too much. You think you're smart, you studied the Classics. Well, you can know just so much, you can just know too much. Johnny Upjohn—a case in point. Dead at fifty-four." Here he paused again, as if to listen for the echo of his own voice. Then he made a violent gesture to his forehead with the back of his hand.

"Jesus, that poor bastard," he sputtered. "He just dropped like a dog on the street in Holland, just like Adlai Stevenson when he died. You don't remember that. Because that's what he was—Dutch."

"Adlai Stevenson?"

"No no no, Johnny Upjohn. You're not paying attention. Johnny Upjohn. With all his drugs and his millions he just dropped like a dog on the street. You can't believe it. Well, it's true. He was a good friend of mine, and now he's dead." He said this last word with angry contempt, as if he were speaking a filthy word. I don't know what was going through his head just then, but I can guess it was something—many things—not very pleasant. He was trying to get at it, whatever it was, but every time he tried to describe it, it would elude him. I wanted to help him, but I could not get a word in edgewise.

"The world is not pretty, Peter," he went on. Couples at other tables were staring now. "Because with all their drugs they can't keep you alive. You're going to go someday. Walking across the street and you're hit by a car transport and that's it, baby! You never had a chance. They can't keep you alive. And what do they care? They don't care. They make their millions and they keep you taking all the drugs in the world, and then something comes along and kills you that they never heard of the cure. That's the way the world operates, Peter. Somebody takes your place and then the poor slob, he dies from the same thing, and what do they know? It takes them years to figure out what you got, and by that time how many people have kicked off, and how many more were born? Can you count them? Can you? It's a mess, it's a terrible mess, you should see India, and who can figure it out? Those drug companies can't, I can tell you right now. They don't know the first lousy thing about what they're doing. And that's a fact. Did you know that the drugs used to cure cancer—treat cancer I mean, you can't cure it, there's no cure—no cure!—the drugs they give you for cancer can cause cancer!" Here he gave an ungodly drunken laugh, mixed with a hiccough. A tendril of snot flew out of his nose and landed across his cheek. Now he was laughing.

"Uncle, your nose," I gasped, bringing a napkin to his face. I was afraid he would soon do something really uncontrolled—he was talking himself up to it.

"Uncle, calm down, just take it easy. Wipe your face." He wiped his cheek absentmindedly. I looked for Joan, but she was busy at another table, probably trying to avoid an embarrassing scene. I wondered what it was like when he came here alone. Did he rant to himself?

He seemed to have settled down then, and soon a waitress brought over the food. He poured a lot of sauce on his steak, cut it up into small pieces, mixed it around with the potato into a brown sludge, but did not eat a bite. I asked him whether it was too rare—it looked raw—but he said it was done just right. Then he said, "Leave me alone, I'll eat it the way I want to," staring gloomily into his plate. His mood had turned sour.

I ate my sand dabs. They were tender—so tender, in fact, that they had a gelatinous quality. Joan came by to ask if everything was all right. She didn't seem to notice that he wasn't eating, or if she did, she made nothing of it. Fortunately, he did not order another drink. He was forever picking at his plate, and ate one or two bites, but that was all. I had finished my fish.

"What's wrong, Uncle?" I asked him. "You ordered a whole big steak and you're not even eating it."

"Yes I am. You just wait. I'm taking my time," he said haltingly. Flecks of brown sauce speckled his lapel.

"You got something on your lapel. Some sauce."

He looked down and brushed carelessly with his napkin, spreading the spot.

"Get some club soda," I said, "dab some club soda on it."

"Forget it. It's gone." He looked away toward the salad bar. "Lots of babes around here," he remarked with a frown.

"They're all with men. Everyone's in couples," I observed. Indeed, it seemed a general law that at night in Mariner's Village no one went out without a protective escort of the opposite sex. These couples radiated health. The women seemed tantalizing trinkets ornamenting the vanity of their men. Gold glistened around bare necks and earlobes, setting off the tanned skin that looked so impossibly smooth and pliant. Wet white teeth sparkled in the flash of a smile, and when they chewed I could see the delicate muscles of their cheeks working silently. That one of them should work on me . . . I found I was cultivating an erection. It remained for several minutes, useless but insistent.

I was observing couples observing each other. A woman with dark feather-cut hair, sitting with a stoutish man wearing a trim beard, glanced every so often at a mustachioed man sitting diagonally opposite her. Her look was challenging and contemptuous, and referred somehow to both men—as if a doubt, the same doubt, were constantly recurring to her. But the man in the mustache did not notice her glances. Another woman was sitting with two men, and when she talked she

71

looked at neither of them, but at some incalculable object in the distance. Once one of the men turned around to see what it was.

A group at a table behind us was laughing. "Peterson, you turkey," a man's voice said. "I don't believe you just did that, Mike," said a woman's voice. "It's fu-u-ucked," a different man's laughing voice said, drawing the word out in a squeak and breaking into a lower register at the end. I cannot say why, but this sounded like the rudest remark I had ever heard, and without even seeing him, I hated the man called Peterson.

Through all of this my uncle sat still, sunken into a gloom, just staring at his plate. During the lull I was conscious of music coming out of a life jacket in the netting above. The words said, "Before I make love to your body, I want to make love to your mind."

Abruptly my uncle roused himself and said, "Let's go to the salad bar, want to go to the salad bar." Then he was pushing at the table, trying to rise from his chair, and having difficulty.

"Uncle, maybe you should sit down and finish your meal, you've hardly touched anything," I tried to reason with him. I knew that once he started to make a scene he would make a nice big one. "Please, or let Joan help you."

"I don't want that shit," he snapped. "I want salad. There's the salad bar." He pointed with a twisted arm, as if the salad bar were an oasis far in the distance, and he a desert straggler. He stumbled towards it. There was no stopping him. Joan was nowhere in sight. I placed a hand on his arm. "Leggo. Gimme some salad." He walked with his legs stiff and his arms swinging out at the sides.

"Look at the guy in the coat," said the Peterson voice. Everybody was watching. Now he had arrived at the bar, and stood gazing fascinatedly at the banal cornucopia of iceberg, romaine, spinach, red cabbage, mushrooms, cucumbers, radishes, sprouts, cauliflower, celery, celery root, garbanzos, beets, Bac-Os, and the tubs of dressing sunk in ice. For a moment he just stood there; then he began to rave in a loud, slurred voice,

"This is the stuff, Peter, this is the stuff. Don't let anybody serve you. Stay away from all that meat, that's pure cancer. And the goddamn butchers, the restaurants, know it. Sure they know. Just like those drug companies, they're all working together to screw us on this cancer thing, just as long as they can keep on feeding you the cancer and keep on going, keep on going, what do they care, they don't have a cure, there's no cure, what do they know, the whole thing's money, Peter, money and cancer, money and cancer, money and cancer. . . ." He was lurching towards the garbanzos, his sleeve caught on a ladle and pulled a tub of dressing to the floor; he jumped backwards with a hideous laugh, a mixture of anguish and hilarity; the tables were laughing also; and as I jumped forward to salvage him I felt a block of lead in my back, together with the very palpable thought, "This is the worst moment of our lives"; and staggering as I fell forward, I turned to see the face and gold medallions of my assailant above me, growling in the Peterson voice, "Leave the pink coat alone!"

Then I was sprawling underneath the salad bar. I could hear my uncle whining like a child, "Where's Peter? What'd you do with Peter?"

"Who's Peter, man?" said the voice with medallions—you could actually hear the medallions in it. It was a dumb-sounding voice, with a certain crushed quality, as if it had had to struggle through layers of sinew and stupidity to make known its shabby will.

"Peter is my nephew. You hit him. I saw you," said my uncle's voice.

"I didn't hit anyone, man. I thought he was hassling you. Fuck you if you don't want any help."

"That was my nephew just coming to get some salad," said my uncle's voice again. "You had no right to hit him. And you have a filthy mouth, young man. Peter, are you all right? This is disgraceful. Where's the management? Joan!"

But the management was already amassing. Mike Peterson grumbled and went back to his table, as if he had merely been

73

disturbed for a silly reason. From under the salad bar where I still lay, I saw his feet plod back to their chair. He was wearing a pair of those thick, multi-layered, indestructible, supposedly everlasting synthetic sandals.

"You come back," my uncle called after him. "You can't knock a man down and leave the scene of the crime. You can't do that. Besides, you have a filthy mouth."

Slowly I crept to my feet. Several people, including Joan, had gathered now around my uncle. I overheard Joan explaining to them: ". . . gentleman . . . customer . . . Mr. Lorditch's nephew . . ."

"That's not true!" raged my uncle. "He hit him, knocked him to the ground. I saw. There's Peter now. Are you all right? I think he was knocked out cold."

"I'm all right," I said. "Let's get out of here."

A man in a red blazer stepped forward. "You're the nephew?"

"Yes. He's drunk. I'm going to take him home. Come on, Uncle Tiger."

"Did someone hit you?"

"Yes they did. Knocked me under the salad bar."

"Who?"

"Mike Peterson." I pointed to his table. "Guy with the Hawaiian shirt and medallions."

The red blazer simply stared and winced. "This is terrible. I hate to make more of a scene than we already have. Are you hurt?"

"I don't think so. Shaken up a little."

The man sucked his lips inward. "I'll tell you what. What's your name?"

"Peter Lorditch."

"I'll tell you what, Peter. You point whomever it was out to me and I'll handle it myself."

"What will you do? He assaulted me. The man is a barbarian. I should press charges."

"I know," said the red blazer. "And he's gonna get his. The

thing is, Peter, I don't like to make a scene, what with the other customers. It's generally a bad policy. You can understand that, Peter." The man was appealing to my name as if it were that of a famous person he wanted to show me he knew intimately.

"I suppose so," I said. "I really don't care. I want to leave now. Uncle Tiger, let's go." But my uncle, peculiarly invulnerable, impermeable, was talking at Joan. A busboy was sweeping up the mess.

"The man's vicious," I said to the red blazer. "He's a really scummy type and he shouldn't be allowed in here. He's dangerous."

The red blazer nodded. "I know, Peter, I know. Let us handle it, champ."

"I hope you do," I said. "Uncle, come on." I caught Joan's eyes, and together we escorted him to the door.

"What a lousy break. There's always guys like that," Joan remarked, as if this sort of thing were regrettable but normal. "I'm never serving him again, for sure. They should never let him in again."

"Well, I hope they do something stronger than that."

"Lock him up, Joan, lock that bastard up," my uncle intoned.

"We're going to lock you up tonight, Mr. Lorditch," said Joan, and winked at me.

"Yeah. Lock me up and throw away the key. Hah."

"Might not be such a bad idea," I muttered. At the door I turned and saw, at Mike Peterson's table, the red blazer leaning over and talking to my assailant, his arm around Peterson's shoulder.

The world, I am forever rediscovering, is disgustingly vulgar.

75

5

He was one of those specimens of whom it is said, by those who bother to examine them, "They don't fit in anywhere." Yet in Mr. di Barnaba's case this judgment was not invidious—people did not resent him for it, nor were they reacting against a superior attitude on his part. It was not from any physical peculiarity, or inadequacy of character, either, that he set himself apart. Indeed, it was part of his special gift that he never appeared to have contrived his exclusivity; it was inherent.

Although he was a foreigner, he was never really an outsider to our ways. If anything, he was the consummate insider, gazing placidly on the world outside from within the privacy of his courtyard—a structure airy, open, yet impregnable. He did not bother to segregate himself, never shut himself off or locked himself in; he did not have to. No need for him to become a recluse; the world was already very far away.

His differences, if profound, were not obvious. His manners were impeccable, because he really did not care at all. His charm was always ready and attentive, because he himself was often somewhere else. Yet the only outward sign of detachment he showed from matters terrestrial was in the way he made excuses for himself. I would have thought that anyone self-conscious enough, considerate enough, to admit the need to explain his actions in this way would not, in that case, be as detached (at least socially speaking) as someone who felt no such obligation—who saw himself bound by no conventional rules of conduct, whose selfishness or inconsiderateness or injuries to others were absolved in his own mind, or simply ceased to exist by virtue of some mysterious authority known and wielded by him alone. This in fact is how most selfish or deluded people can manage to live with themselves.

But Mr. di Barnaba was not selfish or deluded, and his excuses were not merely an attempt to explain or absolve his conduct. They were rather the least possible concession he could make from his world to ours, in order to retain our sympathy and respect, and at the same time ensure our indulgence for future infractions, which, when the time came, would no doubt be as charmingly nullified as those before.

Yet he was not a manipulator. He sought (or so I believed) nothing other than to be allowed to live apart. Among us, but apart. He loved company, loved to tell and receive stories and confessions; but he was never at a loss when he found he had the afternoon or evening to himself. At such times, opera was his pleasure. Los Angeles has no company of its own, though, and unless a very good one was visiting, he preferred his records and his sun porch to actual attendance. "As acoustically sound as any box at the opera," he told me, "and much better for a suntan."

I have mentioned that he was a foreigner, but this is partially incorrect. For although by birth he was an Italian—a Southern Italian—he had long since become a naturalized American citizen. He spoke and wrote a beautiful if idiosyncratic English. He had even lifted a self-sworn, lifelong ban on politics in order to memorize the list of American presidents. And he confessed to me a preference that was decidedly un-Italian: "The best meal of all is a chiliburger." Although perhaps it was precisely as an Italian that he allowed himself this one blasphemy.

All things considered, he was really more foreign to his century than his country.

Mr. di Barnaba was not exactly pleased with the twentieth century. This was probably because he had to live in it. That is, his body, subject to the immutable laws of biology and physics, was temporally constrained to inhabit this century, this moment. But his mind, in compensation for this regrettable necessity, functioned retroactively, seeking its natural source and element in the past. This curious physiology was nourished by his personal history.

He was born near Taranto, in the village of Godega, on the bay outlining the instep of the boot. Imagine any Southern Italian town, washed by the eternal action of sun and sea into a sleep of centuries, broken only by the periodic cycle of festival days; a town of mixed history, bearing still the worn but persistent marks of its stubborn atavism: the stolid Norman steeple of its church; the curling, Moorish arches of the porticoes leading off the town square, whose massive flagstones suggest the paving of greater Northern cities, especially Venice; and the Spanish Baroque façade of the Palazzo di Giustizia—the town hall—whose sandstone contours receive and reflect a guardian benevolent warmth from the sun, and whose coloring enriches itself by imperceptibly deepening gradations as the day wears on, and finishes in a blaze of saffron.

Mr. di Barnaba would go into long rhapsodies on his home-town—its colors, smells and sounds at all times of the day and night. He analyzed in detail the machinations—the eternal stasis—of its provincial society, its gossip, its deaths. In short, he gave me such an expressive account of his childhood in this town that he rendered it both unnecessary for me ever to visit it and pointless, I thought, for him to return. It had already ceased to exist for him in its "real" geographical location; perhaps it had always been a dream. And it was only now, when he had expressed no intention of ever visiting it again—when he had virtually demolished it forever—it was only now that he could bring himself to begin the awesome job of reconstruction. Stone by stone, building by building, street by street, he was reassembling the structure of his birthplace.

I listened to his stories for hours. I really had nothing better to do. I worked for the magazine as seldom as possible now, and if I was ever bothered about this, I could always ask him for an "authentic Italian recipe," spiced with his own anecdotes by way of an introduction, which I could then submit to *Bon Vivant*. They were curious about how I obtained my occasional material; but I never revealed my anonymous source. I wanted to keep them away from him, ostensibly for reasons of professional self-interest, and also so that he would seek no other audience; but really I liked to feel I was the only witness to his secret, an intermediary between the Old World and the New in this act of historical conjuring. Or I was his adjutant, his "familiar" in the magical arts, the most supernatural revelation of which this week was the discovery of the trick by which Signora Graziagigante finally succeeded in eluding her husband and sleeping with the baker. This intelligence could be arrived at only after numerous installments explaining the principals, subordinates, and the legendary but prevailing Meridional Code of Honor, which propounds, as a major premise, the division of all women into two camps, whores and virgins. (But makes no corresponding distinction among men, as I remarked one day to Mr. di Barnaba.)

"That is not necessary, my lad," he answered. (He always called me "my lad.") "You see, in the South, in the Mezzogiorno, all men are scoundrels. It is *a priori*, it is inescapable, it is something to be proud of. The man who is not a scoundrel is a woman."

"So, then," I pursued with arch casuistic reasoning, "by that token, the man who is not a scoundrel is either a virgin or a whore."

"Aha, you are too clever for me, my lad."

Of course, Grandma never heard us talking like this. I liked to think this was because I was at that time the only one who shared his other world with Mr. di Barnaba, the only one who was even then growing, if not to understand this mythic land, at least to be able to grant its existence. But perhaps it was simply that he thought himself too delicate in her presence, and her in his, to mention such things. From what she had indicated, Grandma imagined the South of Italy as a land of quaint pageantry, inexplicable festivals and bloody vendettas—all of which it was. But she would have been hard put to imagine it was anything more, and for her it did not have to be. She had heard tales of bandits in the hills, and fifty-layer wedding cakes (perhaps she wanted one herself). To disabuse her of these notions would have been cruel and misguided, for as Mr. di Barnaba could assure me, there were still—in the Godega he had left, the Godega of his mind, the only Godega now—wedding feasts and mountain outlaws. But these institutions were growing old and exhausted, while the youth of the South were fleeing to the industrial cities of the North.

"The Mezzogiorno is now an economically stagnant region," explained Mr. di Barnaba. "Like Ireland and Greenland. Can you imagine anything like Ireland and Greenland? Ours is a tired people, this is the problem. Greeks, Arabs, Normans—all have visited our land, all have fled. All have left their mark. It is a real melting pot—much more than America. But now the pot is old, there are many cracks and the broth is leaking out. All that remains are the lumps and dry bones."

This was how he spoke. Sometimes the metaphors were labored, sometimes rhapsodic. He often appeared entertained by his own turns of speech, impressed by his tropes, the fluid cadence of his peculiar ictus. But his language did not sound studied or pretentious; he simply needed it to express his world—as a scientist, often to the perplexity of the layman, uses a specialized language to precisely describe phenomena.

Mr. di Barnaba's language was descriptive as well as persuasive—as my grandmother's marriage to him would attest. Although I wouldn't say that she was persuaded so much as overcome. Anyway, it amounts to the same. The charm was the main thing. It was one of those relics Grandma was always searching for, hoping to rediscover, as one might hope to stumble upon an unknown artisan still practicing a traditional but neglected craft—a search undergone not so much for the sake of the craft itself as for the assurance its continuing practice gives to the elderly that some things, albeit some very little things, are "still the same"—and that they, the elderly, have not lost touch with these testimonial remains, that the world is not utterly alien, and still holds a small place reserved especially for them. This is why old people set such store by appointments and schedules, even when they are often incapable of keeping them. And to their eyes, a superficial charm lends to troubling depths of character the same specious intelligibility as the application of a schedule to the abysmal vastness of time.

There was an Italian delicatessen in Santa Monica where my grandmother liked to buy cheeses for her afternoon tea. She had been famous there for years, probably from the moment she first set foot inside. She knew the staff, could identify all its Latinate generations and bifurcations. Like a genealogist, she kept scrupulous track of who was getting married, never failing to supply toys to the frequent issue, as well as congratulations to the parents, grandparents and even great-grandparents, whom she held in special esteem. They in turn called her "*la signora inglese*." (Paul, who drove her there and sometimes did the shopping for her, was "*il signor tedesco*," and supposedly her husband. When Grandma heard of this rumor she was very upset, and corrected it immediately: "Mr. Kirschner is my kind, good friend, my handyman, and my chauffeur." But in her absence he referred to himself as "housemaster for the boss lady.")

She knew not only the staff of the deli, but also most of its regular customers, many of whom were members of Santa Monica's elderly community. She maintained relations politely and unambitiously, according to her way—which, she sometimes complained, led people to consider her aloof and a snob. "I suppose they expect me to gossip with them," she sighed,

81

adding sarcastically, "but I'm not clever enough for that—I can never remember all their stories."

I was surprised one day last winter when she mentioned a "pleasant gentleman" whom she had seen before at the delicatessen, and who had surrendered to her the last slice of a fontina already designated for himself. This act of supererogatory graciousness, although it greatly impressed her, was resisted, then finally accepted only with the obligatory show of reluctance and displeasure with which the "undeserving" receive the respect and recognition, the homage they so secretly and so ardently crave.

She described her benefactor in bland terms that belied her interest—although they turned out to be accurate enough. "He seemed like a kind, well-educated man. I believe he said he was Italian, but he spoke a beautiful English." Even Paul, forever unimpressed with the Mediterranean races, had no criticism on this score, and could corroborate, "Ya, a nice fella, and dressed nice like a fancy gentleman"—the most generous compliment he could bestow.

I met the "pleasant gentleman" one evening in Big Steve Scroflone's restaurant. Since my uncle's "business connection" with this man, we had begun to patronize his restaurant—chiefly because my uncle would go nowhere else without considerable protest, claiming that Big Steve was a kindhearted, hardworking man who deserved our business. And let me tell you, he deserved no better. He certainly did not *need* our business; the restaurant was always filled.

But Uncle Tiger did not mention another reason for our patronage—the chief one, I am sure, but one that went undiscussed except by Grandma, when she confessed "I feel ashamed" or "It's really not right," yet which somehow never resulted in her refusing an invitation, for she loved the desserts. The reason was this: that more times than not, whenever Big Steve was at the restaurant, the check either never arrived ("The boss he lost it, sir . . . is all right.") or, if it somehow did, was aggressively destroyed by the massive owner himself, with a specific violence reserved, I would hope, only for that purpose—and documents from the IRS.

But to us Big Steve was always too kind. No matter how crowded it was, and even if we had no reservations—which my uncle had usually neglected to make, deliberately, to show his "influence" with the management—there was always a table waiting for us. Big Steve had taken a special shine to my grandmother. He renamed her favorite dessert—a wedge of tortoni ice cream on a bed of sponge cake soaked in liqueur—"tortoni Cissie," and always made sure her meat was well done. "Cissie, you do to veal what I wouldn't do to my worst enemy—but I love you. Plinio! One piccata, cook it to death!" Then he would plop his massive bulk down in the aisle seat of our table and talk horses with my uncle, in a bullying whisper that stood for a roar—and would have been a roar, had we not been sitting in his restaurant:

"Whistlin' Dixie's heart's gonna explode in the fourth, so fuck—pardon my French, Cissie—forget her, Tiger. Now that I think of it, forget horses, it's a dead end. I got something you wouldn't believe. Cereal that bleeds—real gory, huh? Well, it's just food coloring, you see. . . ." And so on and so forth until the meal came. Then Big Steve would rise up out of his seat, like a whale breaching. *"Ciao, bambini,"* he blew, "later. You got a sweet tooth tonight, Cissie? I certainly hope so. Plinio! One you-know-what when the little lady's ready." And, flashing the flukes of his leviathan hindquarters, he swam on to other tables.

One evening he informed my grandmother, "You've got an admirer here tonight. He says to say hello from the Bay Cities Deli."

"Who could that be?" said Grandma. "I wonder if it's Kenny, is Kenny here tonight?"

"No, it's not Kenny," said Big Steve, visibly amused at the thought of the counterman eating at his restaurant. "This is one of my regular customers, a charming gentleman." Big Steve used the word "gentleman" in the way parking lot attendants or movie theater ushers will use it—indiscriminately, wearily, euphemistically—since prolonged contact with the public has proved to them that the male half of humanity is in fact a hateful and ungentle thing. Whereas the word in this case, as grandmother's growing interest would indicate, and despite Big Steve's usage, was really quite apt. However, she did not relent in her innocence.

"Bay Cities . . . why, perhaps it's Pat, or Andy, it's not Andy, now, is it? Andy and his family? Do ask them over, I'm so glad . . ."

"No, Cissie," said Big Steve, "it's a gentleman dining alone. A good personal friend of mine." (I later learned that this was nowhere near the truth.) "A wonderful gentleman. An Italian gentleman, as a matter of fact."

Big Steve gestured three tables away, to what looked like a small man, wearing eyeglasses, sitting alone. The man appeared to have a dark but warm complexion. His forehead broke below a receding reef of black hair, strikingly black; his mustache, however, thin and well balanced, showed traces of gray. His cheeks seemed to shine, illuminating a skin that looked youthful, although the man could be no younger than sixty. It was his glowing cheeks and forehead that gave his complexion its warm quality.

He was eating daintily but eagerly. He broke off a crust from the small loaf of Italian bread he had removed from the basket and set on the bare tablecloth. As he glanced up from his plate he noticed us looking at him—noticed, rather, Big Steve quite obviously pointing him out to us. He raised his glass of wine in acknowledgment, as if it were we who had first remarked his presence, and not the other way around. Grandma, who was seated facing him, lowered her eyeglasses and set them halfway down her nose, so that the frames were pointing downward, and instead of adjusting the angle of her glasses in order to see, she was obliged to adjust the angle of her head. Perhaps she thought this pose was one of haughty indifference, but it was so affected that it achieved quite the opposite effect, and revealed an excited curiosity all the more obvious in its mummery.

"Is that the gentleman over there?" she asked. "Yes, I see now, I do recognize him, if he's the same one . . . oh yes, that's the nice man who saved me the cheese that day. . . ."

The gallant saver of the cheese! Grandma could not soon forget such an act of chivalrous courtesy, or the knight who had bestowed it. Although from where I sat, her silent benefactor looked more like a Sancho Panza than a Don Quixote.

"Well, let's get him over here, bring him over, Steve," blurted my uncle, ever the champion of good deeds. "Bring an extra chair, or what the hell, he can sit here next to me, I don't care"—as if my uncle, in turn, were rewarding chivalry by this sacrifice of his comfort, this gracious subjecting of himself to the proximity of an unknown Italian.

But already the stranger was politely smiling his refusal. He still had not spoken a word to anyone. However, an unspoken refusal was to my uncle no refusal at all. He was the most verbal of communicators—or of non-communicators, since people rarely had any idea what he was talking about once he had begun to explain it, and their mystification increased directly in proportion to the verbosity of his explanation.

"Bring him over, Steve," he continued. "What's he say there? Bring him over. What's his name?"

Here compassion—compassion for a man so desperately in need of an explanation, or at least an introduction, as my uncle was—must have won out over his natural shyness, for the stranger set aside his glass of wine and rose to approach our table.

I saw at once that he was not at all short or paunchy, as I had thought at first, but tall and robust. Although his jacket was buttoned, the width and depth of his chest were striking. His hands were large, and though not a worker's hands—they were not worn or calloused—they looked powerful. The nails were shiny, lending an additional oddness to their spatulate finger-

85

tips, which they appeared to ornament with a not strictly masculine effect. His clothes, like the outlines of the body they covered, looked more British than Italian, modest, insular rather than declarative or revealing. His jacket was a darkish gray with a fine herringbone nap. His trousers were darker still, but not black, and of a cheaper-looking fabric, perhaps a synthetic. He had cuffs on his shirt, and silverish cuff links. His tie was a bright saffron yellow. He must have felt terribly hot in these clothes, for besides being heavy, they were not at all loose, and fit his large frame almost too well.

He strode up the aisle and stopped just short of our table. He laid a broad hand across his chest in a strange gesture suggesting an effort at deference, but without yielding to its fuller expression. It was a gesture that was in itself a disquisition on the fine and perhaps imaginary line between necessary politeness and inevitable imposition, as if the arm and hand were there to restrain the natural instincts of the torso to incline itself out of a natural friendliness. The tension between the two parts of the body thus opposed resulted in a version—infinitely, effortlessly, unnecessarily urbane—of a bow.

"Well, well," began our knight in tweed, "what a pleasant surprise." (I had been hoping for a more unusual introduction, for something, perhaps, in another language; and yet his natural inflection of the expected in our own was gratifying, almost relaxing.)

But if it was a surprise for Grandma, it did not seem an altogether pleasant one; at least she showed no recognizable signs either of pleasure or surprise. And she made no indication that he might sit down.

Uncle Tiger, who only moments before had been so eager that Steve should bring the stranger over to our table, now made no special effort to accommodate him—doubtless because, now that the latter had proven he was real by walking and talking, my uncle was confronted with a situation that involved not merely the idea or verbal support of someone's reception, but its literal enactment, and he preferred to leave such offices to the wisdom and experience of his mother. He made a movement in his seat as he craned around to look at the stranger: one of those diplomatic and noncommittal motions of the body which are meant to suggest the idea of welcoming, but without actually summoning the effort of rising and greeting someone.

Grandma said briskly, "I'm sure that I know you, but I can't seem to remember your name. You're a friend of Mr. Scroflone's, aren't you?"

The stranger, still keeping his hand across his chest, allowed himself a gently contemptuous laugh, in which he was able to express toward the big man—but discreetly, fondly even, since the other was nearby and looking on—both the affection of familiarity and, to modify this slightly, his sense of the distance required by inherent social differences.

"Yes I am," he said. "But I am also a friend of Bay Cities. That is how I recognize you. You are very fond of fontina, if I remember correctly."

Grandma dropped her guard just a little. "Oh yes, you are the gentleman . . . I wasn't sure from a distance . . . what a coincidence. . . ." She paused. "Well, I suppose we both know good food when we see it—when we taste it, that is."

"Yes," said the stranger, smiling, "this is one of my favorite restaurants in Los Angeles. You can always trust a place where the owner so obviously appreciates his own food."

Big Steve, eavesdropping nearby, roared his appreciation:

"Go on, you character! Are you gonna introduce yourself, or do I have to do the honors?"

The stranger brought down his arm from his chest and came one step nearer. Now he was almost up to the table. "That's all right, thank you, Steve," he said. "I can do my own honors. My name is di Barnaba. I presume you are all—but I'm sorry, I don't even know your name."

My uncle was unusually silent; I think he was impressed to the point of speechlessness. (Absence of the speech that in his case was a natural and constant oral effluence was a sure sign of recognition or respect.) His mouth drooped slightly as he looked on; the only motion in his face was the blinking of his eyes.

My grandmother hesitated here for the briefest moment—only just long enough to consult perhaps the deeper vestigial reaches of her social instinct, to determine whether this was an appropriate question for him to be asking, and for her to be answering. The process took less than a second—"Oh yes, I'm sorry, you don't"—and offering each of us up for introduction with a generous gesture of her arm—for she was bestowing the knowledge on him—she graciously explained us in turn: "This is Joseph Lorditch, my son, and Peter Lorditch, my grandson, and my name is Mrs. Samuels."

"I hope I can keep track of all that," laughed the stranger. Good humor was not incompatible with his formality—which, for that matter, was not all that formal. "I am very pleased to meet you all—and to re-meet you, so to speak, Mrs. Samuels." His arm now came again across his chest.

My uncle abruptly broke his silence. "Well, sit down, Mr. Barnaba—Steve, bring Mr. Barnaba a chair."

"You've already got one there, Joe," said Big Steve. "I don't think he needs two—unless he's like me!"

"Oh, but you haven't finished your dinner yet, I don't want to intrude," demurred Mr. di Barnaba.

"That's all right, all right," my uncle went on, "we're all going to have 'tortoni Cissie'—that's named after my mother, 'tortoni Cissie,' what do you think of that, isn't that something? Isn't that right, Steve? And you can have one too, Mr. Barnaba. Sit down, or one of the waiters is going to walk into you."

Mr. di Barnaba hesitated a moment, then said, "Well, then, just to prevent an accident," and slipped into the aisle seat. He moved his tall frame gracefully, as a man of smaller proportions might. Perhaps it was this facility of movement that had given me my mistaken first impression of his size. He linked his large hands together on the table, and I saw that he was wearing a gold band on his left middle finger. This ring drew attention to itself not only because of its unusual placement, but also because, as I would soon discover, it was Mr. di Barnaba's habit to twist it around below the knuckle while he was listening to someone else talking.

He sent for his wine from the other table, mentioning how well Big Steve's cellar was stocked. Even, he whispered, if Big Steve himself didn't know the first thing about good wine, fortunately he was assisted in his ignorance by the excellence of the cheaper Italian export wines.

"So you're a wine expert," my uncle concluded. "I thought so."

"No, I would not call myself an *expert,* but I have grown up with wine. In fact, I think that is even understating it."

"Sure, so you know all about it—you might as well be an expert," continued my uncle inexorably. For he had already decided that his new acquaintance was an accomplished enologist, especially in the field of Italian wines, and he did not want to be contradicted in his judgment. Any challenge to this premature appraisal would be taken as an insult to his ability to detect and promote talent. That was the way he was.

"How are you on French wines? Do you know French wines too?"

"I really don't know much about wines at all," answered Mr. di Barnaba patiently, becoming slightly embarrassed. "Although I have spent some time in France."

"Really? Whereabouts?"

"In the South, near Cannes."

"Not in the wine country, eh? Never been to Bordeaux?"

"No, I haven't—though as you probably know, they make wine almost everywhere in France—anywhere they can grow grapes, actually."

"Sure, sure," said my uncle. "I know all about that. But Bordeaux is the best, everybody knows *that.*"

My uncle's abruptness did not come from any wish to humiliate Mr. di Barnaba. He was not mean or insensitive. In fact, quite different impulses moved him to speak the way he did. He wanted to establish for his new acquaintance a ground of preeminence; for it was inconceivable to him that he could associate with anyone who was not preeminent, was not "tops in their field," as he called it. Thus he had decided that I was a Classical scholar, when I had no more than a B.A. in Classics and no further interest in those things. And thus he had decided that his friend Richardson was the Clarence Darrow of the Marina. Not only were such delusions self-serving, elevating him to the level of his accomplished fellows, but they also made the world more interesting. So it was important that Mr. di Barnaba, now on the threshold of my uncle's world and about to enter it brilliantly on the strength of all the latent talent promised by his appearance and manners, should prove himself, should make his own outstanding contribution—even if it was totally imaginary.

Mr. di Barnaba now addressed my grandmother. "I don't believe I've seen you here before, Mrs. Samuels—although it is certainly a welcome addition. Did I hear you say that there was a dessert named after you? Is that so?"

Before my grandmother could answer, Uncle Tiger broke in, "That certainly is so—the 'tortoni Cissie'—just like fettucine Alfredo or a brandy alexander. It's a famous dessert now—everybody knows about it. Just go into any good restaurant, even in Europe, and you can see them order it."

"Oh, Joseph, I don't believe I'm all that famous. If I were, I would be rich. My son is a terrible exaggerator," she explained to Mr. di Barnaba. "You mustn't pay attention. Mr. Scroflone was just being kind."

But my uncle continued to rave. "It's a hit—it's internationally famous! They even have it in Maxim's!"

"Well, then, this is a historic occasion," remarked Mr. di Barnaba. "I am witness to the creation of a new dessert. I consider myself most fortunate."

"Sorry, Mr. Barnaba, but the dish was already named before

you knew about it. Big Steve invented it months ago—right, Mom?"

Grandma frowned and muttered in my direction, "I wish he'd *stop* it."

Ever so gently, ever so pleasantly, Mr. di Barnaba placed a hand—the ringed one—flat on the table and leaned forward slightly in my uncle's direction. "It's *di* Barnaba, there is a *di*."

Since it had not been my uncle's intention to be sarcastic or derogatory (he was simply carried away by the grandeur of knowing that a dessert had been named after his mother), he took the correction in stride. This was one of the most disarming features of my uncle's character, and of its effect on those who did not know him well, or had just met him: namely, that once they had discovered (and this discovery often took a while) that he was not assailing their ignorance, invalidating their contributions, or utterly ignoring their half of the conversation, but was merely indicating to them, by means of the confused semiotic jumble that was his natural mode of verbal communication, that he was managing, or attempting to manage, the discussion from the dizzying and precarious vantage point of a separate reality—once they had understood, or thought they had understood, that he was a little bit mad, then their defensive responses to him disappeared, and they treated him with the humoring condescension deemed appropriate in dealing with the sociably insane. This "dropping of the guard" on their part actually enabled some of his acquaintances to eventually trust my uncle—as one might feel secure in the presence of a benign madman. And this was where they made their mistake; for my uncle was neither mad nor particularly benign—and his associates were not nearly as sane as they would have liked to think.

My uncle immediately appreciated the significance of this correction. "You must be a noble, then," he deduced. "You must be a count."

Mr. di Barnaba laughed heartily at this idea. "Not unless I am Count Dracula," he said. "No, it is a simple name, quite common, Tullio di Barnaba, it means only that I am the son of Barnaba. But I don't care much for that sort of thing. I am an American."

"American?" my grandmother repeated.

"Yes, a naturalized citizen."

"Oh? And how long have you been in this country?"

We learned he had been here since the thirties. He had left in 1935, after having been drafted into Mussolini's army to fight in Ethiopia. "I was a fencer. They wanted me to lead the cavalry charge in Africa, with sabre flying. But you see, I did not like to fight for real—I preferred to fence at the Academy." He was referring to the Military Academy in Venice, where he had been enrolled at the time of the invasion.

How had he gotten out of it, then? Had he deserted?

"I do not like to think I was a deserter. Instead, I drank castor oil and feigned illness. Actually, I ended up making myself quite sick; I gave myself an ulcer."

"That's a helluva way to get out of the army!" laughed my uncle. "I should have tried that myself."

"No, no, believe me, it catches up on you," said Mr. di Barnaba. "There are easier ways—such as eating the food of the military."

Big Steve's voice nearby boomed agreement. "Believe you me, this gentleman's right. I don't know about the Italian army, but the American, it's like they dredged their biscuits up from the bottom of the barrel. That's what made me get into the restaurant business. There's got to be a better way, I said to myself. If it wasn't for that hope, I wouldn't have made it through the war—I wouldn't be what I am today."

"That's for sure," said a customer near us. "What'd you do, Steve—rent a whole mess hall for yourself?"

"You better believe it," barreled Big Steve. "Now if I'd've been in the Italian army, things would've been different. Yessir. After a week they would've had no more pasta left. Then they would've been forced to surrender. I could've won the war singlehanded. Now there's a thought!"

Mr. di Barnaba stayed on at our table through dessert, radiating tidbits of information and anecdote as a nugget of plutonium radiates particles. After such exposure, one could not avoid being contaminated. I sensed I had met at last a great conversationalist; and even after we had left him, snatches of his conversation, archaic phrases, rhapsodic evocations continued to bombard with their lasting radiation the reactor of my brain.

I had to have more. I sought him out in the Italian delicatessen. We sat outside at stone tables next to the sidewalk, and he declaimed amid the traffic on Lincoln Boulevard, apparently undisturbed by vulgar noises and the unremitting sunshine. I was amazed that he did not seem to mind; he did not seem even to be aware, as I so readily was, that life here was inferior, nature inadequate, and people barbarously uninformed. Did he not miss the golden pink light of Venice, strained and diffused to an ineffable delicacy through the gauzy air of the Adriatic? Was our light in contrast not too harsh, too young, too bold, too shallow, and did not everything under it pale accordingly? Evidently not. I had a store of such questions designed to elicit his response; it is a wonder how he put up with them all. Surely I must have had less fatuous things to ask him, but somehow the fatuous ones drew the best replies. And my curiosity was not totally ingenuous; I had guessed that although Mr. di Barnaba's sense and manners might be cringing at my questions, his vanity stood proud and eager to answer.

"It is not so bad here as you imagine," he replied, eating a mortadella sandwich. "It is one of the nicest places in the world to live. As far as comfort goes, it is really quite superior. I know—you in your youth disdain comfort, you disdain the life of ease in which you were raised. My lad, how could you know differently? But it is a knowledge of books, not life. Travel, you must travel.

"Venice? Venice is a dying princess—you know Ravel's little

piece? It is just like that, slow, resigned, yet in the case of Venice it is not a very pretty death. Or rather, it is pretty, it is beautiful—but excruciating. The doctors of restoration are doing their best. They are very good at what they do, the best in the world. But how much can doctors do? They cannot prevent the inevitable. Venice is on her deathbed, a deathbed of centuries, and the whole world is her next of kin, watching her every breath, terribly concerned and utterly helpless. Some of the kin are merely greedy legacy hunters—the German tourists, the Japanese—who want to squeeze as much as they can out of the old lady before she dies. Others are more considerate, satisfied with less. Some are there only out of a sense of obligation, so that they can later tell their friends that they did not desert her in her final hours. The old lady is taking a long time to die; some are frightened, but they continue to come around, for her death is a glorious spectacle."

A van, bright metallic blue with mirrored windows, revved its engine and roared past, disgustingly vulgar. Mr. di Barnaba did not seem at all disturbed. He sipped his Pellegrino water and looked into the distance, past the Safeway parking lot, past Big Fella, past Love's Pork Pit.

"I think that most Europeans, given the chance, would want to come to America, to live for a while at least. Culture? European culture is a saddle, an uncomfortable saddle on old nags. Yes, we are old nags, all of us, driven too long and too hard by History. In our old age we want to run free; that is, we want to die. I am afraid that is the only way most Europeans know how to be free. What fools they are. But it is not their fault, or it has only gradually become their fault through History.

"History is a very slow poison. It takes longer to act on some than on others, but eventually it destroys everyone, no one can resist it. Now if medicine could come up with a remedy for History . . . but I am afraid that would be terribly expensive. And besides, then Europe, cured of its malady, would soon be empty, they would all move to Australia. That would be a tragic fate.

"How is your grandmother?" he asked abruptly. I thought perhaps I had missed a subtle connection; or perhaps he thought she was Australian. "It is a pity you did not bring her with you today," he said. "I enjoy hearing her talk, she has a lovely accent."

"She's not Australian," I said.

Mr. di Barnaba laughed at the thought. "God forbid! How could you think that—she is so obviously British!"

"No she isn't."

"What?"

"She was born in New York City," I explained, and told him the story of her accent as far as I knew it—including the speech therapist and the Japanese convent.

"Well, then, she must have traveled a good deal," inferred Mr. di Barnaba.

"Yes, when she was younger—almost every year when she was a girl, to Japan and Europe."

"Aha," said Mr. di Barnaba with a satisfied smile, "I had the feeling she was a woman of cultivation." One had the impression that his feeling stood for some greater sense of vindication—perhaps of snobbish expectations, more likely of hopes he had cherished for sympathy with a "cultured lady," for identification and communion with the dying old nag he made out to be European culture—which, even having known Mr. di Barnaba as briefly as I had, I was sure he craved more than he would admit. Besides, his endorsement of the life here—just as my indictment—was overzealous, smacking of an opinion not so much held as attempted, not so much felt as contrived, and the ringing of its praise was actually criticism by default, through which, as if by sympathetic vibration, he succeeded in sounding also, clear, mellow, nostalgic, the church bells of his homeland.

"Yes, she has an air of sophistication," announced Mr. di Barnaba. "And yet she seems so youthful. I know she is your grandmother, but it is really quite extraordinary, you must know that. She seems to be a very active woman, and not at all self-pitying." (Though from what he had just said, there was really no reason why she should be self-pitying.) "I can feel great dignity there," he continued, "a self-esteem which is not incompatible with her natural modesty."

"Can you really tell all that?" I asked.

"Yes, of course, it is clearly written on her face. She has an innocent face, she does not know how to wear a mask."

I suspect that what Mr. di Barnaba first saw in her was his idea, now realized and tangible, of an "English Lady." Not that he could pretend she was really a member of the landed aristocracy, a peer of the English nobility. But the knowledge that she had traveled widely, had received a desultory but exotic education in faraway places, had consorted, through her mother's connections (and unquestionably, chastely enough), with a marquis or two—had had, in short, that tasteful yet adventurous upbringing of a young woman of the upper middle class in the early part of this century, a class that existed tangential to but forever removed from the life of the European nobility, and yet could never admit to its own impossible aspirations to join that higher order—it was this knowledge, I believe, that attracted Mr. di Barnaba's interest at the start.

"Tell me more about your grandmother," he would ask, and when I had finished (for example) the story about the banquet served by Cossacks on horseback on the shore of the Black Sea in 1911, he would murmur, full of wonder, "And to think that that same woman still consents to live our comparatively tame life. She must have a rare courage. Tell me more about the horsemen."

Around this time she began to ask him to tea, first with others, then by himself. She had met in Santa Monica two genuinely (if not genuine) English ladies: Mrs. Marsh and Mrs. Podspur, relics of the English colony that has existed in Santa Monica for some time. These ladies were her most reliable tea mates. Not that my grandmother particularly enjoyed their company.

They were prone to the gossip she so detested, yet out of politeness (or some secret, less definable inclination) felt she ought not to prevent. Grandma set such store by the ceremony itself that she believed it would be worse to neglect it than merely to sacrifice herself in entertaining the company of these two muffin-warmers. And perhaps also, simply because they were English, she believed that their gossip, with its English inflection, was less an expression of personal vindictiveness than of cultural charm. Whether she ever led them on to assume that she was a compatriot, I do not know. This is not an impossibility. I am sure they would have enjoyed the brief illusion. And I am just as sure that when Mr. di Barnaba was introduced into the trio, they did not appreciate the addition of the new Mediterranean element. Other offenses were in turn added to this, such as the gradual replacement of relevant gossip with travel anecdote, in which my grandmother, if only because of her inexhaustible stock of material, displayed over the others an unexpected superiority. Perhaps also at fault was the growing list of compliments Mr. di Barnaba was letting slip her way, to the general neglect of those two fine and deserving tea-cozies. The visits of Marsh and Podspur dwindled to umbrageous monthly visitations, and the sun of the South shone more frequently in our home.

Paul, as I have mentioned, had at first been favorably impressed by Mr. di Barnaba, if only because of the way he dressed. But he soon began to give signs that the other's presence was "drivin' the ladies away." I don't believe Paul had any great attachment to these two; nevertheless he could not forget that he had once been the only male at these functions, and an arbiter of sorts. That is, he made the sandwiches and served the tea. Yet Paul conceived of his place as much more purposeful and beneficial than the newcomer's—however well he might be dressed. Mr. di Barnaba to his mind was an idler, "makin' sweet talk and romance with the ladies," a "storyteller," a "play-actor." "Where's the makeup? That's all he's missing, that one," Paul would remark as soon as our guest had

97

left. For he felt he knew a good deal about actors and their ways, having been formerly employed by two great practitioners of that stellar art, Jack Holt and James Arness, who—he lived in the secret and perpetual hope—might someday again require his services, although Jack Holt was dead, and James Arness, from what I had heard, was in retirement, at the very least.

"What I say," opined Paul, "is a man who's gonna be an actor, he should be an actor, not a society baby." Paul had an unsure and unique conception of the word "baby," which he appended to certain other words with novel results. Thus he imagined the term "war baby" to describe not someone born during the war, but rather someone who liked to argue, criticize, provoke or otherwise disturb the order of his life. A "society baby" meant not a person born into the upper stratum of society, but a person who aspired to be a socialite, someone who showed a taste for socializing and social functions (which Mr. di Barnaba, incidentally, abhorred). And so Paul could blithely dismiss Jackie Onassis as a "society baby" in the belief, since he was totally ignorant of her origins, that she was a social climber—without ever realizing that, even if this were the case, she had already reached the summit.

What did they talk about, my grandmother and Mr. di Barnaba? Travel, as I have said, formed a good part of their conversation, allowing them to explore also the topics of food and music. Grandma was able to hold her own quite well in these fields—which was especially commendable considering the gradual blunting in recent years of both her hearing and palate. Still she refused to wear a hearing aid, and continued to eat indifferently, when I happened to cook them, what she was told were spicy foods. But there was one food above all others she retained a taste for: potatoes. Whether fried with onions, boiled, baked or mashed, she pursued this bland vegetable, in all its conceivable modes, with the Hibernian implacability of a survivor of the Potato Famine. Usually one to avoid extreme expressions of devotion or dependence, she nevertheless made an exception to this rule in the case of the potato; and if you had pressed her for a confession of her love in the most drastic terms ("Grandma, admit it, you'd kill for a potato.") she would not have contradicted you, but would have allowed, quite simply—almost as one obsessed will finally give vent, under pressure, to a great personal truth that has been so obvious, for so long, to so many: "Yes, I *do* like potatoes."

But somewhere amid the menus, travelogues and musical programs must have risen between them the skeletons—now fond, benign, stylized perhaps, Halloweenish—of defunct marriages.

My grandmother, as we know, had already survived two. The first was to Nathaniel Lorditch, the father of my father and uncle. He was a retailer not lacking a rakish flair, a gadabout, a player of horses, but a keen businessman nevertheless, whose commercial foresight served him well until the one big mistake that killed him. He was the founder and owner of Lorditch and Company, a ladies' clothing store on Fifth Avenue, as fashionable as any of its time. The store was successful from the start, but Nathaniel Lorditch, always thinking ahead, predicted that while Fifth Avenue would always be Fifth Avenue, 57th Street was the dark horse of fashion—and he didn't want to miss out on that race. He believed he could always move back to Fifth Avenue in any case, so he closed shop and moved uptown twenty blocks to 57th near Fifth, to the very location where Henri Bendel now stands. (Grandma swears you can still discern on the front of this building the washed-out traces of the old Lorditch plaque.)

About one thing Lorditch was right: 57th Street was beginning to boom—to such an extent that the city saw fit to widen the sidewalk, and plant trees. During construction the existing sidewalk was torn up, and many retail businesses were temporarily wiped out. Lorditch, who had made the move only months before, was now threatened with bankruptcy, and was consequently unable to obtain the loan that would have enabled him to reinstall the business at its former location. In his desperation he gadded more and more about, with the result that during a prolonged absence of his wife and mother-in-law in Japan (the children were at school in England), women were seen and believed to be living in the house. (By whom this was discovered it is not known; my grandmother has never really discussed it. I learned the story from my uncle one night when he was drunk—for which reason I do not doubt its truth for a moment.) Learning of this news upon her return, Lola demanded that her daughter divorce Lorditch immediately, which she did—rather more quickly than perhaps was wise, considering the children, who later returned from England to find their mother no longer married to their father, who had disappeared in the bargain. This does seem rather harsh punishment for infidelity, even from as tyrannical a matriarch as Lola. She must have had something else against the man. But then again, those days were not our own, and to both ladies' minds, I imagine, he had defiled everything he had touched—including themselves, their family and their home. It is testimony to the power of Lola over everyone that she was able, apparently without hindrance, to deprive her daughter and son-in-law not only of each other, but even of the company of their children, which by any rights they should have shared together, for better or worse, in a home of their own—which Lola also had never allowed. When she learned then of Nathaniel's infidelities, it must have been with a certain recognition of irony amid the horror, since by imprisoning him in her home and refusing him his own, she had also provided him with the inevitable location of his adulteries.

So the wretched Lorditch, bankrupt, evicted and ostracized, could think of no better place of exile than California, Pasadena in fact, whither he fled—bringing with him nothing but a virulent and neglected case of tuberculosis, from which he died four years later.

For fifteen years thereafter, Grandma led the life of an only daughter in the house of her mother, amply provided for by her father, although she was herself the mother of two young men, whose lives were now managed by Lola. It was college for both, their grandmother decided—Princeton for Joseph and Brown for Alfred. Joseph went on to law school, then six months' practice in a New York firm, after which he quit the profession with an explanation illustrative of his unique frame of mind: "Too much paperwork!" But his precocious aversion was not for paperwork alone. For the rest of his career he spared himself work of any sort; and labored, when he had to, only under delusions.

Already war had broken out. The Lorditch brothers entered the service in the winter of 1942. My father became something of a hero after his plane, the leader in a group, was shot down over Italy, and forced to make a belly-landing without wheels in the mountains, where he and his fellows hid out for months until they were captured. He spent two years in a prison camp in northern Germany.

My uncle was stationed in Miami.

At this time, back in New York, my grandmother was wrapping Red Cross packages for the prisoners overseas, taking the El in the morning and often not returning until late at night. Her hands, she tells me, were sometimes cut and bleeding from the rough cord she had to handle. A woman who never before in her life had had to wrap a package (or most likely even lift one), who had traveled only in carriages, chauffeured autos and ocean liners—now my grandmother, day in, day out, cut and calloused, hopeful and despairing, went trundling back and forth on the El. Yet she speaks of this period simply as "the War"—as if it had been, for her, only that period of our history following the Depression, when, wherever one was, whoever one was, one got along as best one could. I have to remind myself that she lived for almost a year with no news of her missing son, who was last recorded shot down behind enemy lines. It is hard for us "postwar babies" (and I use this in the more accepted sense, not Paul's) to imagine a country—our own, and recently—in which so many millions of people were living this way, under so much (yet with so little) hope. Life in these circumstances must take on qualities with which we are unfamiliar, perhaps one of the most important being that it ceases to exist as merely the setting for one's own drama, one's own mind and actions. It is no longer lived for oneself alone, and cannot be justified, if for a moment we were to stand back to look at ourselves and our lives, by those hollow contemporary standards: the personal, the self-regarding, the "I-for-myself." Yet this is very difficult for some Americans of my generation to appreciate. The suggestion that "life is hard" means usually to us, "my ambitions are as yet unfulfilled," "my expectations are constantly being disappointed," "my relationships are not profound," and not infrequently, here in Southern California, "my Mercedes eats gas and is a hassle to get fixed." But I hear that it was once different, and that one was sometimes called upon to imagine the sufferings of others.

One evening, coming home on the El, my grandmother met an army major. He helped her with her packages, and noticed that her hands were bleeding. He showed concern, and wondered what she had been doing to receive such ugly cuts. He must have been very impressed with her and what she told him, for after the war they were married.

The major was a chemist for the government, and was at the time researching the development of new non-ferrous metal alloys. His name was Albert Samuels. He was a Jew, born in 1898 in St. Thomas, Virgin Islands, and schooled in New York. On his mother's side he was Sephardic; the family had been in St. Thomas for generations, having fled originally from Portugal. Albert's father had been an exporter of bay rum, a stern, busy man with little time for his son. After sending Albert off to school in the States, his father made only one trip there, on business, stopping by the school for a brief chat. Both parents were absent from high school and college graduations, and when Albert returned afterwards to St. Thomas for a visit, his father's first question was, "Why are you here?"

It is hardly surprising that Albert developed a heart condition early in life—how many times had it been broken already?

102

I remember, on the visits back East I made with my parents, that his angina was beginning to limit him to the life of a semi-invalid. He continued to work—like his predecessor in the House of Lola, he was the founder and president of a company, CP Chemicals—but rarely left the house in the evenings. Of course there were no children by this marriage; it was all Albert could do to get along with his stepson Joseph, who had never pretended to welcome him into the family.

He was a kind and honest man—traits uncommon enough in a corporate chief—and I do not doubt that it was these qualities, and his misplaced trust in his subordinates, that contributed to the eventual foundering of his company in 1958. He believed the collapse was engineered by anti-Semitic competition in collusion with his associates; he had long complained of the Jew-haters from DuPont. Now he saw, with the futile satisfaction of bitterness, that his lonely life had come full circle. He had never been part of any family, neither his father's nor his wife's. (Lola, growing senile, was increasingly suspicious of this outsider—was he even a Jew?—who spent so much time in her house.) Abandoned by his business, as he had been by his parents, he reverted once again to what he had always really conceived himself to be: the insular Jew surrounded by enemies. With his anguish rose his angina, and bound his heart forever in perpetual pain, which withheld from him even at this late date the favor of killing him straightaway. He died on the toilet after his third massive coronary, and was buried in the army cemetery, not the family plot. Of him Grandma has said, "He was a good, good man; but I am afraid he never had much fun." And how could he? I myself had a certain feeling for him. I have still his autograph collection, compiled throughout his life, bequeathed to me after his second heart attack.

Mr. di Barnaba had made only one previous marriage, which left him a widower—thus the wedding band in altered position on his left middle finger. He had met her in Venice, where he was fencing at the Military Academy, and she studying at the Art Academy. She was an American named Ellen Anderman, from Colorado—as he described her, "a real Venetian blonde, from Denver." His drinking of the castor oil after induction had to do with her. ("Bad enough to be sent to fight in Africa. And when one is in love! I would rather live with a hole in the stomach than die of a hole in the heart!") They were married first in Venice, at the Chiesa Santa Maria dei Miracoli—"Yes, a miracle that I was still a civilian, and now married to the woman I loved"—and once again in Denver. Ellen's father encouraged them in vain to settle there. He owned copper mines, which, with the outbreak of war six years later, were to double his already considerable fortune. Generously but unperceptively, he offered to include his son-in-law in the reaping of this Depression windfall. But young Tullio had his eye set on architecture. Perhaps Ellen had had something to do with this—and Venice too had contributed her share. At any rate, to a Renaissance eye such as his, the open spaces of the West were crying out for buildings to fill the emptiness.

They came to Los Angeles. With the endless Anderman dowry—property prices, too, were the lowest then that they will ever be, certainly in this part of the world—they bought a house in the Pacific Palisades. Jobs were scarce, though; somehow Mr. di Barnaba was not immediately asked to become senior partner of an architectural firm, although he made it known that he was ready, for he had taken a course in drafting at the Academy. He finally found a job as second assistant draftsman for a miniature-golf contractor, and soon quit. He began to acquire a record collection. Ellen continued to paint and sculpt at home. She did several portraits of him, which he says bear striking likeness to him at the time when he was a "dangling man." Yet he must have known even then that he had attained, at an early age, the only life he ever wanted for himself—the only one he could reasonably be expected to lead—one which some might criticize as idle and unproductive, but which provided him a dignified alternative to the always complicated and disillusioning necessity of having to make a living: that of having one already made.

But if money was secure, life was not. In the fifties, Ellen was stricken with cancer; she fought it, and was rewarded with a seven-year remission; but in 1960 (only shortly after Albert Samuels, as it happened), she was dead.

There had never been anyone else for him, said Mr. di Barnaba, looking significantly at his ring.

"Yes, I know," commiserated my grandmother, "that is how I felt—twice."

"So you should be wearing two rings here," he said.

"No, I don't wear jewelry," she informed him stoically.

"Not even your wedding ring?"

"No. They are safer in the strongbox than on my fingers— who knows what could happen?" Yet the mysterious possibility did not seem to her unwelcome. Elderly people often refer to their forthcoming extinction with a complacent suggestion of vindication—as if, when the time comes, they imagine they will be pleased to be able to say, "You see? I told you so. And after all, what can you expect?" But this attitude in my grandmother surprised me, because she seldom appeared bitter or world-weary. Perhaps, though, I was mistaken about the nature of her expectation; perhaps she was merely curious about her end, and the business it would leave unfinished—like Herr Settembrini in Mann's novel, who complained of his doomed condition only because he knew it would ultimately prevent him from finding out how the turbulent situation in Europe would resolve.

I could not really judge how Grandma took these discussions, which may have been quite different when I was not there. I think Mr. di Barnaba was more voluble in front of me; perhaps he was even a bit pompous. He felt I had much to learn—and here was a golden opportunity for me to drink of knowledge from its clearest font, himself. Not that he took himself altogether seriously. His manner was to pass off much of what he said as diversionary trivia, which could be valuable only as light entertainment. But the tilt of his head and the strength of his back, the dignity of his wide chest when he spoke, gave him away. The posture was not one appropriate to comic relief or merely anecdotal delivery; these were important words, pronouncements, expressive of his deepest beliefs, elements of his world, part of himself. His head and body were proud to give issue to them, and his pride was twofold, deriving both from the assurance that he was educating us in something dear to him, something that perhaps would have been otherwise lost to the world—and also from the attitude he was submitting to my grandmother: that of an outmoded gentleman who was finally appreciated by one of his own, for what he was, and without need of explanation. The satisfaction of this dual achievement coursed up his spine and shone on his features.

Grandma, for her part, seemed comfortable enough. Over the topic of marriage—or rather, of its effect on her—she glossed with laconic authority, which in her case one was apt to attribute to "tastefulness" rather than evasiveness. She had felt great sorrow, every passing had left its mark; yet each had prepared her better for the next, and after all there was a bright side to everything: you were never dragged down but you were built back up again, and you learned from all experience, good and bad—and so on and so forth, concluding with her favorite tag, "so there you are."

Grandma's maxims would have sounded drearily platitudinous had she herself succumbed to them; but she jumped from one to the next so desultorily, so unsatisfiedly, with so unfulfilled a desire remaining always at the bottom of her search, that they seemed to annoy her more than anything, and she quoted them only as if to show how empty was their wisdom, how inadequate their relief—as if to say, "Now this is what they tell me works, but I don't believe it is doing any good. Can you suggest anything better?" Her attitude relied on an obligatory show of discomfort that I don't believe she really felt—much as we take vitamins to supply a deficiency we think we might have, but have never actually experienced, and would probably not notice if we had. Grandma could not complain of a hard lot in life. She could not regret many lost opportunities. She could not have lived in any time that would have more enabled her to do what she had done, see what she had seen, believe what she still believed. She had been tremendously fortunate, and she knew it. But then she had to talk about something.

Mr. di Barnaba was a great conversationalist because he offered to his listeners ready—and often misplaced—belief in their own intelligence. He made us feel privy to revelations of special significance in his company—whether it was because of the lofty tone in which they were delivered, or the conspiratorial nature of the listener's interest, which assumed the qualities of participation in an act of sacred ritual, the unfolding of a strange preserved antiquity that was reenacted each time Mr. di Barnaba opened his necromantic mouth and the mummified words miraculously issued forth, exhumed, brought to life, to speak again—their meaning quaint, but still vital. Hearing him talk, one felt the same gratification as after having successfully translated a difficult idiomatic passage of Latin and finding that it describes phenomena one had experienced directly the day before. For my grandmother, who was always apologizing for her inadequate education, this must have been a welcome new sensation—assuming that she could make out everything Mr. di Barnaba was saying. But even if she couldn't quite catch all the words, the tone, the cadence of those rising and falling periods, the tinkle and drone of his voice like a supporting Indian musical instrument in the background—monotonous, soothing, basic—these sounds alone, even without the accompanying sense, were welcome and reassuring to her ear. Woven together in her mind with the idea of afternoon tea in the cool, sunny garden, attended by her Teutonic servant, her grandson, and the caressing tones of this disarming European, his voice must have assumed the textural quality of gold thread in an

107

ornamental tapestry depicting her final kingdom, where she reigned supreme, uncontested, if at times unacknowledged. For her power had become so comfortable to her, so benevolent, so assenting now in her old age, as to pass almost unfelt by her subjects.

But I don't believe that even the divine power of kings could have barricaded her against Mr. di Barnaba's proposal of marriage. Whether he stormed right in, or besieged her for weeks, I do not know. He never gave me any indication of his intention, aside from showing a great interest in her, and drawing me out about her whenever we were alone. I never imagined he would actually pop the question—much less that she would say yes.

So there you are.

6

The ambitions of Mr. di Barnaba were not immediately apparent to me; I was still very much under the spell of his charm. Yet perhaps I should have taken a clue from my uncle, who was not—whose very pixilation rendered him immune to the enchantment of anyone else.

"I don't trust that Mr. Barnaba," he said one day. "What's he hanging around for? What's he want?"

"He's not hanging around," I said. "He enjoys our company, and we enjoy his."

At this my uncle sneered, then opened his eyes wide in warning. "He's a shark," he proclaimed, finger upraised. "Watch out."

Not that my uncle wasn't hatching his own schemes. Tommy Achekosa, as I have mentioned, had introduced him to a man named Richardson—a man we never saw, but who nevertheless was to assume an unremitting and almost vatic presence in our lives. Richardson this, Richardson that; Richardson says buy lots of Mattel; Richardson says don't pay your property taxes if you own a condominium, if your maintenance expenses exceed more than one percent of the total cost of the building; Richardson says Merv Griffin is a homosexual; Richardson says don't eat meat, it'll kill you. However, my uncle ate a lot of meat.

My uncle invoked the aura of Richardson as if it were a spirit from the world beyond—all-seeing, all-knowing, and especially adept at tax and property law. It may be remembered that my uncle himself was nominally a lawyer; he had attended law school at Virginia and somehow passed the New York State bar exam. I suppose he considered himself thereby knowledgeable enough to appreciate the genius of Richardson, whose extraordinary gifts went unappreciated, and even unsuspected by the laity. For us, Richardson must remain at best an unknown quantity, attested but not proven, a mystery witness who was somehow never available for comment.

My uncle had begun to lunch regularly with his new mentor. For one reason or another he never invited me to come along, as he had with Achekosa. I doubt that it was because he feared I would not find his friend interesting, even invaluable; his concerns went deeper than that. He would drop occasional hints that at these luncheons monumental deals were being made, pioneering breakthroughs in the history of business that required for their delicate negotiation the utmost secrecy and discretion. No matter that my uncle was the most indiscreet and public of negotiators, whose first impulse upon conceiving an invention was always to publicize its ingenuity. No, he saw his meetings with Richardson as laying the groundwork for a new entrepreneurial infrastructure, whose intricacy it was probably even a waste of time to try to explain. In time we would know; in time we would fully understand the importance of it all. Until then, "not a word" (as if this were possible in our ignorance), "keep it under your hat."

But for his idea ever to be fact, he realized he needed money. He advised his mother of this need. It was not the first time he had done so, nor would it be the first time she had acted on his advice. Her alleged destitution and, more truthfully, the actual disappearance over the years of a large proportion of her capital, could testify to this repeated and utterly fruitless process—which as far as she was concerned was nothing more than an act of faith: faith in her son, misplaced faith in his ability, contradicted faith in his word—the faith of a mother, implicit, incorruptible, and lacking a memory.

She wanted so much for him to be a success in business that she overlooked not only the potential danger posed by such an eventuality (danger both to the business community at large and her own immediate family—what was left of it), but even its fundamental impossibility. Hadn't the road to riches for her family proved already rocky enough, without the massive boulders of her son's blunders to bar the way and forever seal the escape? Hadn't she seen too much risked and lost on more defensible ventures? Hadn't she finally had enough? Or more to the case in point, couldn't she recognize sickness when she saw it? Why didn't she help to spare him this final death-agony, if only for his own good? If her devotion to the mere fact of his existence (which was what it all boiled down to at this point; his doomed ventures were becoming for him a matter of life and death—much more, I am afraid, of the latter) was really as unquestionable and unquestioning as it had always appeared, I asked myself, would it not, must it not win out over even his most strident protestations of insolvency and lost opportunity?

No. Remember, this is a woman passing strange. Her ways are not our ways, her mind is not like ours, her world is not the one we live in. . . .

She gave him the money. (I will tell you shortly how—the method in this case is important, for it was not exclusively to him that she gave it.) It had to do with her vanity, I think. She was pleased that he still needed her in that way, that she still figured as an important and indeed crucial factor in his plans, in his life. This was a privilege she reckoned she deserved, and must live up to. Not to live up to it would be to shirk her duty, not merely as a mother, but as the operating principal of the drama, the guiding light, the sun of reason and of beneficence. Her contribution, as she saw it, was necessary to furnish not only the substance of the investment, but the meaning. And conversely, a failure to contribute, at whatever cost, would be a failure of meaning, a triumph of disorder and chaos. This alternative was dreadful enough to keep her paying interest.

Meanwhile, Mr. di Barnaba was not idle either. The engagement had been announced, the marriage was set for May 11. As far as the ceremony was concerned, Mr. di Barnaba was deferring to my grandmother, who was set on a religious Jewish one. The matter had been decided as soon as the question arose. As I have said, I had the impression that to her betrothed it was all the same; one ceremony (or religion, for that matter) was as good as the next. Mr. di Barnaba had an ornate mind, but not necessarily a ceremonial one. His love of delicacy and distinction was more internal. I have suggested the image of a nobleman reclused within his courtyard; to this I might add the observation that the courtyard held also a well-kept garden and many fine sculptures, which, however, the proprietor was at no pains to advertise. It was enough for him that he knew the details were there. Those who were particularly interested—if there were any—might hope for a special invitation to visit the grounds, which would be kept up regardless of whether anybody was looking. But the visitors (which we were) didn't see everything that was growing there, and the landlord himself wasn't aware of all his holdings, even as he was working to increase them.

Just how he was working I did not know. I had only an intuition, deriving from my uncle's vague hunch, that he was cultivating something he did not want us to see just yet. It was so improbable: here was a sophisticated, worldly European—to all appearances a conscientious widower, cautious, tasteful, unaggressive—suspected, invidiously no doubt, of mercenary motives by a mad inventor who, in addition, would have little to gain by his mother's third marriage. . . .

Or would he? It was not impossible that my uncle, like many people unfamiliar with the inconsistent correlation of money and social position in modern Europe, had assumed that Mr. di

Barnaba, because he was a "cultivated European," was therefore rich; nor was it impossible that he (Mr. di Barnaba) would have relied on this assumption for purposes of his own. However, Mr. di Barnaba, for his part, and this also for purposes of his own, had been something less than completely ingenuous in the way he had handled references by my uncle to the future groom's financial situation, and had given indulgent and by no means disabusing rein to my relative's fantasies on that subject. It must have been clear to him that my uncle had somewhere been grossly misled in the matter, yet he was not at pains to put him just yet on the right track; he would let him wander a little. . . .

But whether or not my uncle had anything to gain by the marriage—what did he have to lose? Not discounting other valuable if abused possessions—a mother's unstinting attention, encouraged by his position as confirmed bachelor (although she had never admitted this to herself); freedom, hitherto, from any challenge to that attention, and from the likely prospect of such—not discounting these things, the threatened loss would be, first and foremost, one of money. His mother's money, and by extension his own—the squandering of which had up until now been exclusively their own affair (I was out of the question; I had always been out of the question), but which might very well soon cease to be so.

Not that my uncle was so unregenerately greedy and selfish as to see the entrance of Mr. di Barnaba only in terms of a threat or a blessing to his available funds. He wanted to give the newcomer a fair shot, wanted to see him succeed—if only on his (my uncle's) preconceived terms. He had already given Mr. di Barnaba one chance to prove himself as a wine expert; he imagined it was through no fault of his own that Mr. di Barnaba had failed the test (because, in fact, he had failed to lie about the extent of his knowledge, and had even been overly modest in describing it). My uncle was after all a generous man, up to a point, and he would not withhold from the charming Italian another chance to cut the commercial mustard. (The most fascinating thing about my uncle's judgments in this regard was, as I have already mentioned, that they had their basis not in observation or even reasonable expectation, but rather on his own unique set of criteria, the foremost of which was that all of his "fellows" should be as successful as he, and vice versa. And the only proof of success was my uncle's deeming it so.)

I doubt that Mr. di Barnaba was wasting time worrying whether he would pass the next test. If he had any impression to make, it was primarily on my grandmother that he wished to make it; and he could rest assured that she would not make things so hard for him, that it was most likely his efforts would prove not in vain. He was also perhaps not unaware that his relationship with me, as well as being an agreeable pastime for himself, was a serviceable medium for his signals to her. We went places together, often unaccompanied by Grandma.

One day, when my grandmother was detained by essential and interminable meetings with lawyers and insurance agents (the "not very nice" people), Mr. di Barnaba took me to the Self-Realization Shrine in Pacific Palisades. When at first I balked at the name (it did not sound exactly like his cup of tea) he seemed surprised—not only that I hadn't heard of it, but that I seemed to impute to him a spiritual motive in wanting to visit it. After all, he explained, it was only a question of a placid lake with noble swans.

"You have never been? Oh, it's the most peaceful place in Los Angeles, an oasis among freeways. The spirits of all the sages must inhabit that place, I am sure. It is a landscape of serenity. I have spent hours strolling among the paths and shrines, admiring the tropical plants in the botanical gardens. And today is such a fine day! We must go."

When we pulled into the parking lot off Sunset, he had already begun his horticultural lecture. Did I not appreciate the way the flower beds bordered the herringbone pattern of parking spaces? The trellised arbor leading from the parking lot, overhung with bougainvillea and Spanish moss? The pontoon pavilions floating at the end of the lake? We began to walk alongside this lake, Mr. di Barnaba continuing to lecture on the vegetation. He recognized several plants we had also in our garden, which caused me to wonder to myself if my mother had ever been to this park. She must certainly have known of it, and in that case might have visited it to gather information and suggestions for her own garden. I asked Mr. di Barnaba when the Shrine had been built. He answered that it must have been completed sometime shortly after the war, when he had first visited it. I realized then that it was very possible my mother had been here. And as I was making various chronological reckonings, with a curious but detached consciousness of the past and my possible place in it, I became aware of a little fold of time that my memory had preserved unrecalled and intact; and my thoughts reared suddenly backwards from projected imaginings into the country of forgotten history. This history was immediately quite tangible to me; it was, in fact, my own. Certainly I had been here before, with my mother! I had stood looking at this lake—remembered now more as an immemorial sea, alive with giant floating creatures, which were, if perhaps not the same birds of my mother's time, then certainly descendants of those, and so claiming a prehistoric, anachronistic link with the extinct era of my mother. She had been with me when we watched them so long ago. And the monument across the lake, appearing as a small gateway with two golden onion-topped minarets at either end, my mother and I had stood there too on some forgotten unforgettable day; we had paused at its base as I ate an egg salad sandwich she had bought for me, and which ended up soiling my pants. There had even been a Wil Wright's macaroon for dessert. My mother was suddenly so present for me at this moment that the objects around me—perceived now as relics, testimonials of that day: the lake, the lily pads, the swans, the eastern gateway, the general plangent thrum of life preserved—all of these things, so suddenly recalled into their proper original relationship, became at the same time not quite bearable; they held much more for me now than they could reasonably be expected to contain in and of themselves, and in one abrupt merciless rush, they disburdened themselves of my unwelcome (to them) nostalgia by turning suddenly and irrevocably transparent. And this was, after all, only natural for them; they were only things, always would be things. This park would not, could not allow me to preserve it as it had once momentarily been; and it now mocked me further by denying, in its impatient rush back into the oblivious present, that it had ever been otherwise for me. Yet I knew, with the organic persistence of memory, what the objects before me sought vainly to conceal: a vestigial part of me, elements of my dead mother and that day of a mythical sunny childhood. More painful for me than mere imaginings, these impressions were nevertheless now scarcely more than a dream—a dream of innocence in a subtropical pleasure garden, a dream grown neither into experience nor disappointment with time, I felt, but diverted, gradually forgotten, all but disintegrated—and suddenly invoked now, when it was too late. My mother was dead. The overhanging trees of the park proclaimed my sadness; the sun upon the leaves, the birds upon the water, even the shrines, all of these now stoically declared the blunt impassive fact: my mother was dead.

I was not particularly talkative as Mr. di Barnaba and I walked on the path around the lake. He kept up an affable chatter, although he must have been able to see that for some reason I had for the moment turned sour on things.

"It is really a pity your grandmother could not be here," he said. "It is a place she would truly appreciate. Has she never been before?"

"I don't think so. At least she never told me about it."

"Ah," he answered, "she would know it if she saw it. If I had the money I would build her a garden like this."

"A pleasure-dome?" I suggested.

"Yes yes, good for you: 'A stately pleasure-dome decree: / Where Alph, the sacred river, ran / Through caverns measure-

116

less to man / Down to a sunless sea. . . .' It's too bad I am not Kubla Khan, or I might be able to do it."

"Like that palace on Sunset Boulevard?" I asked roguishly, referring to the mansion in Beverly Hills that a sheikh had recently bought and remodeled, and on the front lawn of which he had erected nude statues with painted faces and pubic hair.

"Well, perhaps I would not need to be quite as rich as that— but with decidedly better taste," qualified Mr. di Barnaba. "That all comes under the heading of Patron of the Arts. As you say in your Hollywood here, 'We make them and break them.' Or we used to, we art patrons, up until modern times. Ah, where have they gone, in what modern sea have they drowned, those great noble *padroni* of the *rinascimento*—the Renaissance—*'di quella nobil patria natio,'* the immortalizers of talent, the 'soft touch'—no—of the art world?" He turned to me. "How would you like to have been established in the Doge's Palace, in the special 'artist's wing'? Not a bad deal, eh? And called upon to produce the whole year long only a couple of processional masterpieces perhaps, a bust of your patron and patroness, or their child, or possibly even simply to design the palatial float for the Regatta? All expenses paid, of course, plus a handsome commission (if they liked it). Those were the days for artists, were they not, before government grants and special fellowships? All one needed to succeed was a little nod from the Duke—and the same, for that matter, to end up floating facedown in a canal," he laughed. "Life then was simpler, cheaper and richer—no?

"But now, to be even Art Patron of the Pacific Palisades, say—that is another matter entirely." His eyes glittered with amusement at the idea. "One would need to establish relations with that detestable travesty of a museum up the Coast" (he spoke, I presume, of the Getty Museum) "if only to make oneself known. And then whom, after all, does one patronize? There is always that problem of material, and the closet in which to store it. Whose closet would it be? And we would

117

need a padlock, at least. Not to speak of the money involved—
these artists are very demanding, you know. One would have
to be a very good businessman. . . ."

"Is that what you want to be, 'Art Patron of Pacific Palisades'?"

"But of course, my dear Peter. There is certainly a hole to fill
there, wouldn't you agree? I would be performing a much
needed service."

His manner was for some reason irritating. Of course it was a
joke, and more self-deprecating than anything else. But it was
precisely this sense of himself and his facetious ambition that
made me wonder. I asked myself whether that ambition were
connected in any way with the impossible position to which he
always aspired, for which he had been born centuries too late
and millions too poor—and in his failure to attain to which he
saw, perversely, his one victory, perhaps even his one proudest
achievement. For it was this failure, or rather his choice to
adopt this anachronistic role of courtly esthetic emcee—it was
the consciousness of his contemptuous persistence in the face
of modernity that gave one a sense of his charm, his symbolic
quality of "gentleman," his irrelevance, his lasting value. And
it was upon this consciousness that he so irresistibly and necessarily drew; it was his talent to do so.

Yet it was not really enough for him to get by in this way,
merely on the strength of his peculiar talent. He needed, I
think, something more, something different—something more
vulgar, more modest, more honest. He needed money.

Money not to be an "art patron," but to be able to tell himself convincingly that he wanted and might expect to be an "art
patron." Money not to be rich, but to appear suitably as a
gentleman. Money not to be merely comfortable, but to be
young again. Mr. di Barnaba was not insensitive to the re-
generative properties of wealth: it kept you well-fed on good
food, well-stocked in antacids; it insulated you more or less
from menial occupational hazards, stress, and carcinogens; and

in the worst event, it promptly paid or otherwise handled your medical bills. Not to mention all the merely cosmetic amenities money was able to provide. Besides, he was accustomed to it. It had been, during his happiest years, his adopted way of life. It was, if not for him a natural element, at least a congenial one. How fortunate he must have felt to have found in Grandma a kindred partner who understood and could satisfy these acquired tastes!

But I am not sure either that it was only the satisfaction of his tastes that he anticipated as an outcome of his marriage. For even with this goal now in sight, he seemed restless. He was too scrupulous, or at least too polite a man to allow his perhaps less altruistic motivations to show through, much less dictate, his impatience; and yet, if such motivations had been at all present, however deep, however hidden, a sign in him would have eventually betrayed them. But it didn't. So I sensed that this restlessness, or whatever it was, wasn't immediately self-serving. It was not on the date of May 11 that he had his eye fixed, but rather on some more distant appointment, vague but impending—an event as yet unknown but in a sense already predetermined, whose momentousness for him would be felt not by any arrangements or expenditures he made beforehand, whose advent could not be better prepared for than simply by his remaining, inevitably, what he was, the figure that he cut.

My uncle was rooting for him—to the extent that he truly believed Mr. di Barnaba cut a splendid figure—and was now trying to find out more about him, find out just precisely to what use he could be put. Mr. di Barnaba had, in my uncle's eyes, lost much of his potential as a "wine expert"; nor was he much of an architect (as he himself admitted). We knew he had been a splendid fencer, but he had not kept up this skill, and had given away his fine sabres and epées. No, as my uncle saw it, our friend's field of expertise was fast contracting until it soon circumscribed itself around that one last hope: the restaurant business.

"Mr. Barnaba, I finally found the thing for you," said my uncle one day when he had come over for tea (beer). "I've been talking to some people. We're going to set you up in the restaurant business. How'd you like that?"

"Delightful," responded our friend. "What a pleasure that we have finally hit upon my one incontestable ability. But you must make sure that the restaurant has no wine cellar—I wouldn't want to give myself away." His eyes played ironically as he gauged the measure of the distance of his progressive fall from Art Patron to Wine Expert to Restaurateur.

"I'm not talking about wine, now, I'm talking about food—good food, something we all know about," my uncle plowed on. "And this isn't just another idea—I know you could do it." By this he meant he hoped that he, through the agency of a charming continental and the financial backing of his mother, might be able to swing "something like." The inclusion of Mr. di Barnaba in his scheme was apparently important for several reasons: primarily because it promised to add the element of what he would call "class" to his venture, and himself; because it would offer a congenial and appropriate way for the Italian to finally "prove" himself, if only to my uncle's satisfaction, and in terms of his particular ambitions of the moment; because it seemed—considering my uncle's degree of self-importance, and his conception of himself as the bellwether of genius—the "considerate" thing to do; and finally because of my grandmother herself, because the gentleman in question was, after all, her strange choice. My uncle was a loyal son.

"Ah," sighed Mr. di Barnaba, "I wish it were enough, Joseph, that you know I could do it. . . ."

"Why not? That's enough."

"But there must be others concerned?"

"I'm not talking about *others*." My uncle dismissed the

thought of these "others" with an impatient wave of his arm. "I'm talking about *you*. You and me. You, me and Mom."

This appeared to put it aptly for our friend: he gently smiled, as if in appreciation of the recognition dawning upon him that my uncle was forever condemned to the fate of being unable to separate himself and his from anything he touched. It was a perverted Midas touch, substituting for gold some deadly radioactive isotope.

"You and me, and Big Steve Scroflone's gonna help us. I already talked to him about it." This last emission registered high on the Geiger counter of Mr. di Barnaba's sensibilities: he raised his eyebrows.

"You're going into business with Scroflone?"

"I say, is that *our* Mr. Scroflone?" inquired my grandmother.

"Big Steve has it all set up," Uncle went proudly on. "He's got contacts. I mentioned your name."

"You mentioned *my* name?"

"Sure. He knows all about you. Don't you remember, that's where we met you? He agreed we could use somebody with a lot of class."

Hearing himself so described in a nutshell, Mr. di Barnaba didn't quite know what to say; and so he didn't say anything for some time, while my uncle went into detail concerning the project. He was going to buy property in Culver City—the location of a beer-tapping-and-accessories outlet on Sepulveda, just gone out of business and abandoned—and thereupon open an Italian-style ice cream parlor. "Real Italian—you know, the gooey stuff, the best in the world. We'll have people salivating all over the place. We'll have marble tops, zinc counters, palms, opera music, the whole thing. It'll be a smash. Just what people are waiting for."

"In Culver City?"

"Sure, in Culver City. Why not? Once it gets a reputation, they'll come from all over, even Europe. And it'll get a reputation, I guarantee you, because it'll be the best. The best ice

121

cream, the best music, the best *ambiance*. The best! I think I'll get a string quartet to play on weekends—just like in St. Mark's."

"I say," queried my grandmother, just hanging onto the conversation now by a thread, "are you talking of Mr. Scroflone's restaurant?"

"No, no, Mom, the one *I'm* going to open. An Italian ice cream parlor. The works. I'm just telling Mr. Barnaba that maybe he'd be interested."

"Oh, well, then, why don't you ask him?" she sensibly replied, with a tone of detached consideration in her voice. as if it were a remembered old acquaintance to whom she was referring, or someone hard of hearing.

"I did," laughed my uncle, "but he doesn't seem interested."

The man in question then spoke on his own behalf. "Oh, I am interested. I'm just a bit surprised, that's all. I hadn't heard anything about this. You move swiftly in the business world."

"You have to," explained my uncle. "I was telling Peter, it's all in the timing—timing and foresight. You prepare for an opportunity, and then grab it when it comes. Right, Mom?" (He seemed to envision the liquidation of a beer-accessories store in Culver City as a special dispensation, an act of Divine Providence operating in and for the business career of Joseph Lorditch.)

"Yes, that is correct," concurred my grandmother. "Many great men have fallen because they missed their opportunity: Napoleon, Caesar, Thomas Edison, Mr. Lindbergh. My mother always said, 'There are three things in life you can never call back: the spent arrow, the spoken word, and the lost opportunity.' And she was one to know; she spent enough! Yes indeed, she spoke them and spent them and lost them, and they cost her a pretty penny into the bargain. . . ."

Hearing my grandmother utter these sayings always gave me a feeling of security I would have found difficult to explain. Perhaps it had to do with a consciousness, an instinctual inner respect of peculiarly American speech patterns—a sense of the past, moreover of the basic commercial soundness and validity of our industrial heritage, a plain-dealing, honest-talking, straight-shooting mentality, which, if it had not been voiced (though unconsciously, implicitly) by my grandmother herself, might have seemed provincial or excessively pragmatic. Yet through her utterance it was infused with a special courage usually alien to proverbial wisdom—conveying a suggestion of continuance, prevalence, a proof of the ultimate victory, in our plodding country, of the dedicated and the patient. The effect of such phrases on me was all the more pronounced in that she used them so cavalierly, so familiarly, so evocatively that one identified them, in her, as the result of a process of organic linguistic habituation—real physical evidence of the growth of the language.

Her practical meaning, at any rate, was clear enough: Mr. di Barnaba should go along with her son's idea. After all, to her understanding of the matter, they stood a chance of making some money. How much she might herself be asked to contribute was evidently not yet a consideration, although she knew her son well enough to expect that this would be the inevitable next step. After all, she may have reasoned, her generous friend Mr. Scroflone was a consultant in this affair. So much the better; his advice was therefore to be followed, he being one of the "nice people," especially to her. She allowed that he was tremendously fat, yet this was in itself no strike against him. Her mother had never trusted thin people, especially with money; she would never have thought of dealing with a thin banker or lawyer. And Grandma understood this reasoning implicitly. For her it was a sign of the times that people were growing thinner. There were simply not as many good, honest, enterprising fat people as before.

"Is that what you're offering me, Joseph—an 'opportunity'?" questioned Mr. di Barnaba.

"Sure it's an opportunity. I'm telling you, there's never been

another like it—it's one of a kind. You bet it's an opportunity."
For a moment my uncle looked contemptuous, as if the self-
evident profitability of his proposition could escape the grasp
of none but an entrepreneurial moron. Then he leaned forward, looked over his shoulder, and finally spoke in a hushed
voice—as if there were secret agents from the Better Business
Bureau listening from the trees:

"Mr. Barnaba, look. This thing is gonna change the face of
ice cream in America. I'm not talking about Häagen-Dazs or
Clancy Muldoon's—people are already tired of that. It stinks.
They want something even softer and creamier, something
maybe they remember from the time they were in Italy and
they stopped at that little ice cream stand in Florence, and
they've never had anything like it since. Sure, you're Italian,
you're spoiled, but most Americans—"

"But I never ate ice cream," protested Mr. di Barnaba. "I
don't like it."

"I'm not talking about *that*," stormed my uncle. "I'm talking
about Americans—"

"But I'm American."

"*Most* Americans. Most Americans, they remember, or
they've been told, that Italian ice cream's the best in the world.
They're just waiting for the right place to open up. How do I
know? I've done research on the subject. Don't you read *Forbes*
magazine? Don't you read *Consumer Reports*? It's all there.
People are dying for it. Especially with inflation—people are
drowning their sorrows in ice cream. It's cool, soothing. Maybe
it reminds them of their childhood—I don't care. What I care
about is the consistency. It's got to be smooth and gooey, like
warm peanut butter, for instance. And why not have peanut
butter ice cream, with real peanut butter? Or hazelnut ice
cream—that's big in Italy, hazelnut. I don't care, it's up to you."

"Up to *me*?"

"You *know* what flavors are big over there. You can remember. Pistachio, that's big, isn't it?"

124

"Joseph, I have not been back to Italy in eighteen years. I have no idea what kind of ice cream they are eating over there. And what do you mean, it's up to me?"

"I mean you can choose the flavors with a certain latitude. It's up to you—I'm not asking for really weird flavors, just some unusual ones that people will try. But I want to have American flavors too. The big three—chocolate, vanilla and strawberry. And then alternates—licorice, say, or banana-pecan. Flavor of the Day, we could have. Baskin-Robbins has Flavor of the Month. Well, we could do better. A fresh one every day—make it up the night before. 'Fig-o-Rama,' something like that, or 'Peach-a-Thon.' You know. Once we get the machine it's no problem."

"The machine?"

My uncle raised his finger to his lips and forcefully sputtered, "Ssssh!" The saliva of excitement sprayed from his lips. "The secret machine," he explained. "The machine that'll make just the right consistency. I found out all about it. No more."

"Who sells such a machine? Is it from Italy?"

"I say no more. I've already said too much. Don't you think I've got it all doped out? Just leave it to me."

But our friend was understandably worried that perhaps too much already had been left to him—including the question of Mr. di Barnaba's function in the scheme. He could not conceal his interest in this particular.

"But you mentioned that I was to have some part in the selection of ice cream?"

"Of course, if you can decide. I figure there's no one who could know better than you what goes on over there."

"But Joseph, I told you, I don't eat ice cream, I haven't been to Italy in almost two decades, and I doubt whether I've been inside an ice cream shop—any ice cream shop—more than five times in my entire life."

"This is *different*," my uncle shot back. "This isn't an ice cream shop. It's an—ice cream caffè. That's what it is—'The Ice Cream Caffè.' That's what we'll call it: 'The Ice Cream Caffè.' " He repeated this several times.

"I'm afraid I don't really know what you're talking about, Joseph. You see, I've never—"

"I told you I'm not *talking* about that," thundered my uncle now, with a demagogic, preclusive sweep of his arm. "I'm not even *worried* about that. You're Italian, aren't you? What matters—Mom, tell him please—is that you're there when I need you."

"But what do you need me for?"

This question seemed really quite too much for my uncle. He looked around at my grandmother and me. "Isn't he modest! Well, good for him. That's exactly what I want—the low profile. That's class. That's Old Europe."

Old Europe sat mystified and defenseless-looking. At this point Old Europe could have done with a drink. Yet Old Europe maintained his ancestral bemused composure in spite of it all, as he appeared to contemplate, with the persevering good humor so convenient for his kind in the face of absurdity, the vague but nevertheless pressing idea of his future. He would put up a good if vain fight against the forces of irrationality; we had not yet heard the last of Old Europe.

My uncle's next move was to invite Big Steve Scroflone to the house. Upon first sighting this enormous creature in the doorway, Paul summed up the situation in his way: "What we got here, a circus-show?" he whispered. "Where's the clowns? So where's the lion hunter? Mr. Barnum he'll be coming in a minute, we better get us ready." However, when he had discovered that the object of his amusement was the owner of a restaurant, his attitude changed. He quickly donned the white "serving coat" that to his mind ratified occasions of importance, and represented his elevated though disused position as "personal manager to the boss lady"—all of this once again conveying the mysterious impression, which I had often remarked before, that he was "ready." Paul would not have felt he was doing his job were he not "ready" at a moment's notice; fortunately for him, his perpetual vigil kept from him the reasonable next question: for what?

My grandmother, having assumed this was a merely social visit, had planned tea in the garden as usual, but had overlooked the matter of whether or not Big Steve would be able to fit into the lawn furniture. He took one glance at the little white chair designated for him and laughed. "Sorry, Cissie, no way. You better get a couch for me. Didn't you see me coming?"

But Paul was on hand with one of the wider reclining patio chairs. "Here you go there Mr. Scallopini, you try this one, she ought to fit nice."

"Thanks, champ, where would I be without you?"

But before sitting down, Big Steve wanted to take a tour of the garden. "My mama used to grow plants and vegetables," he explained. "Mostly what you could eat—know what I mean?" he roared, slapping his front midsection. "Look at those orchids. Cissie, you're a genius."

"Well, now, I haven't really had much to do with the garden, I must confess, though I do love the flowers," admitted my grandmother modestly.

"Oh, go on, it's beautiful, and I know you do your share. Jeeze, I'd love to raise honeys like that—no matter what funny things my friends would say about me—right, Joe?" He winked at my uncle. "I'll tell you about me, Cissie. I'm a man who likes life—all forms of life. Except some people who work for the federal government. No, seriously, I love growing things. Love to see 'em push up from the ground and turn into something. Makes me feel that God's got a finger in the pie, know what I mean?"

"Oh, certainly," empathized Grandma. "I love the beauty of a garden. It's so comforting. Do you have a garden of your own, Mr. Scroflone?"

"Sure do, ma'am. Five and a half acres out in Thousand Oaks."

"Five and a half acres? Why, that's practically an estate—it must be beautiful."

"Yes indeed, ma'am. Avocado trees, orange trees, lemon—got my own vegetable-and-herb garden. You know, sometimes we'll feature my produce at the restaurant, if it's a good batch. I even got my own skunk cabbage. Don't serve it unless we're desperate, though."

"I say, 'skunk cabbage'? I don't believe I know that. . . ."

"Oh, you wouldn't want to."

"He's kidding, Mom."

"No I'm not—we got it," said Big Steve.

"Well, I'm certainly never ordering it. That sounds *terrible*," cried my uncle delightedly.

We walked back to the lemon tree and Big Steve spread himself thick over the reclining chair. "Only thing I don't like about gardens is the walking," he remarked. "Think I'm going to invent a drive-through garden. What about it, Joe—think it'd go?"

"Sure, if you had a speed limit. Otherwise you'd have people running over each other to get to the rosebeds."

"Ha! Your son's got a headful of ideas, Cissie. A real character. But I love 'im. You must love him too."

"Yes, when I'm not cursing him," she laughed.

"Well, did he tell you about his newest idea?"

"Which one is that?"

Big Steve looked briefly at his co-conspirator. "Why, the Italian ice cream parlor—"

"The Ice Cream Caffè," my uncle corrected. "Caffè Ice Cream. That's very important. It's the image."

"Whatever you say, Joe. Anyway, I think it's a very good idea, don't you, Cissie? But what am I saying? You've probably been to quite a few during your travels abroad—"

"No she hasn't," my uncle broke in. "This is utterly unique.

She's never seen anything like it—nobody has. That's how come it'll be so big."

Big Steve glanced knowingly at my grandmother, as if to say, "We've heard that one before, haven't we?" And yet I could sense already that it was upon this grandiosity of ambition that his vulturine intention preyed.

"Well, Joe, we *hope* it'll turn out big," Big Steve qualified. "That is, if we ever get our heads together on this thing."

"We are, don't worry, we are," answered my uncle. "I already talked to Mr. Barnaba about it."

"Oh, you did. And what was his feeling?"

"He went for it. Didn't he, Mom?"

But the Old Girl was not to be had so easily, even where her son was concerned. "Excuse me, Joseph, but I don't recall so. I don't recall he was very familiar with the idea."

"What do you mean he wasn't familiar? I explained the whole thing to him, don't you remember? Sure, it took some explaining—" He turned to Big Steve. "You have to kind of go over things with him sometimes, he's not so practical-minded, but once he got it, he went for it—really went for it! I think he was secretly happy to find something he finally knew about. He got very excited, didn't he, Mom? Sure he did."

I winced under the arrant distortion. I could not figure out why di Barnaba's approval should be so important to them. They referred to him as if to someone with whom they would have to deal, whose opinion was crucial, and whose authority would supersede even the responsibilities of flavor consultant and Italian reference that my uncle had recently conferred upon him. I already knew why they wanted my grandmother's backing. She too must have been aware of their motivations. But her resistance, if it came to that, would after all be fairly easy to conquer; Joseph alone could do it. Whereas Mr. di Barnaba presented another problem, an unknown quantity with which they would have to reckon, and which might very well influence her decision.

"I don't remember his being excited," corrected my grandmother. "Mr. di Barnaba is so rarely excited. It's not his way," she added rather fondly, evidently pleased to recognize that now she could be said to know his way.

"Oh, he's all for it, thinks it's a great idea—you know him!" blustered my uncle, anxious to thwart the possibility of an ambivalent reaction before it was too late. "I've never seen him bat an eyelash over anything—have you, Steve? As cool as ice, he is—Italian ice! Well, that's all right, that makes him perfect for the job!"

But Big Steve was not so sure. "I'd like to talk to Mr. di Barnaba myself," he said; and to my grandmother: "He's not coming today, is he?"

"I don't think so. I would have invited him, if I'd known you wanted to speak to him. Perhaps I could reach him on the phone—"

"No no, Cissie, please don't bother. I'll probably see him at the restaurant. Though he hasn't been coming around so much lately. You've been giving him too much of that home cooking, Cissie, you devil—you'll run me out of business! Who's your cook—out with your secret!"

Paul, approaching with the tea, beer and sandwiches, had overheard this, and he was beaming with happiness as he gave Big Steve a self-acknowledging smile.

"You name your price, Mr. Scallopini. My boss she's now working me too hard."

"Is that so, Paul? Not treating you right, eh? Well, we can't have that."

"Oh yes," sniffed Cissie, "I'm an absolute slave driver. You see, I even make them wear uniforms, just like the army."

"Mrs. Samuels come on, this here ain't no army fatigue, I got it special from Mr. James Arness when he made me Top Manager of his home." (Precisely what this position was, or in any case why an officer of such exalted station should be awarded a white busboy's jacket, was information Paul apparently did not care to divulge.)

"And so I should make you 'Top Manager' also?" answered my grandmother. "I can tell you that if I did, my dear, I'd give you a different outfit than *that*."

These skirmishes delighted Paul, and he adopted for them a contrived gruffness which was meant to convey his reaction to "abuse." He was fiercely proud of his job, though; and if he was no longer "Top Manager," he knew on the other hand that his value to the household was not to be sufficiently expressed in a title—which, if it were even attempted, would have had to describe a worker with more responsibility than "manager," more devotion than "nurse," more regularity than "housekeeper," more culinary pretensions, if not talent, than "cook," and more eclectic household knowledge than "handyman." He knew this, and knew that we knew it; and yet he persistently took pleasure, felt perhaps even an additional sense of worth, in pointing out to others our misappreciation of his value.

"Well, Cissie, you'd better start treating your cook better, or he's gonna see the light and come over to me," warned Big Steve. "Isn't that right, Paul?"

"Oh, I don't want to say nothing, Mr. Scallopini, or I might sure get a beatin' afterwards." He winked conspiratorily at the fat man to indicate that he was getting away with much.

"Well, go," muttered my grandmother. "See if I care. I'll have a vacation at last." (The prospect of respite might have been mildly tempting to her; and yet if Paul were not there merely to serve tea and sandwiches, overbuttered though they were, what would she do?)

"You two love each other, I can tell," said Big Steve. "No, I wouldn't think of separating you—you make a great couple."

Grandma did not find this at all amusing. "Yes—like oil and vinegar."

"Great, she's terrific," whispered Big Steve to my uncle, as if my grandmother were after all just an old worn-out pet he had not expected to amuse him anymore, but who had just accomplished, for his pleasure, cleverly and unbidden, a triple somersault in midair. Turning to my uncle, he whispered, "Did you really tell her?"

My uncle shut his eyes tight and nodded.

"Because she doesn't seem to have registered it."

Again my uncle nodded in the same peculiar, pained way. Big Steve grunted. Then he inclined himself in his chair and patted his hands on the armrest. "So, Cissie, what do you think of your son going into business?"

"What business is that?"

"Well, what we were discussing, the ice cream parlor. . . ."

"Oh, and what else is new?" laughed my grandmother. "If I had to count the businesses my son has started and stopped . . . yes . . . if wishes were horses . . ."

"We're kind of working on this one together," Big Steve informed her.

"Oh, so it's your idea?"

"No—both of ours. I'm just . . . giving Joe here a push in the right direction, you might say."

My uncle's eyes were still tightly shut, in the attitude of a malcontent, spoiled, ashamed child.

"Are you sure it's the right direction?" asked my grandmother bluntly. She was by now quite familiar with the words and the situation.

"We know it's the right direction. We're just not sure how far we'll have to go to get there, you might say."

"That's right," agreed my uncle, eyes still closed.

"And you need money to get there, is what you mean," laughed my grandmother. "You should have just said so. Don't you think I've heard it before?"

Big Steve was embarrassed. "Oh, we have *money*," he asserted, as if mere money were not the issue here. "We have *money*—we're in partnership." I think that Big Steve's claim of partnership here was intended to exempt him from the dependent role of shyster; and indeed, in that capacity he might have been said to be merely a co-shyster.

"I say, you're partners? Well, then, congratulations. I think

132

it's very good for Joseph to have someone he can talk to—about business matters, I mean. I'm afraid I don't know much about the subject."

"But from what I hear, you come from a business family," said Big Steve. "A very successful business family."

"Oh, those were my father and former husbands," Grandma confessed modestly (and rather inaccurately). "And they never told me much. I don't have much of a mind for figures. I don't have much of a mind, period, I'm afraid."

"Now that's not what Joseph told me," continued the flatterer. "Joseph told me you were a shrewd businesswoman."

"Oh really," she pooh-poohed, "I don't know what he tells you. My son is a great teller of tall tales."

The son in question lifted a beer glass to his unusually silent lips. He was enjoying the oblique attention.

"Well, thank you for telling me," said Big Steve. "Now I'll never believe anything he says again. I'm glad at least one of us knows what they're doing. But I still think he was right."

"Pardon me?"

"About your business sense. You look like the sort of person who wouldn't let a good opportunity pass—who knows a deal when she sees one."

My grandmother laughed. "Tell that to my lawyers. They don't seem to think so. They think I'm a 'patsy.'"

"A patsy? Oh no, I can't see that." (Not compared with some of the patsies he must have dealt with.) "Whatever would make them think that?"

"It must be the way I talk," my grandmother laughed again. "I believe it makes people think I'm old-fashioned."

"Oh, I wouldn't let that worry you," consoled our guest. "After all, what do people know? They're probably just jealous."

"Jealous? Jealous of what?"

The question stopped him for a moment. "Oh, jealous of your *style*. They probably think you got a lot of *class*"—she winced at the word—"and maybe they don't know how to react to it. I know the type. We get people like that in the restaurant sometimes. Show-offs. They might be big spenders, but they have no idea what they're ordering. We got one guy in there with this fancy babe and a couple of cronies, and he motions the wine steward over, like he's going to order something fancy, and he says, real cool, 'You got any "Ziffadel" wine?' 'Ziffadel,' right? 'Course, Bello—that's our wine steward—didn't want to embarrass him, so he went in the closet and brought out the 'Ziffadel'! Sure, I know those sorts of people," Big Steve concluded, with no question but that his example described accurately the substance of my grandmother's detractors. "You just can't let it bother you—just got to keep on doing what you do, the way you see it. . . . You got no one to live up to but yourself."

"Yes, that is certainly true," agreed my grandmother. "And it is often hardest to live up to your own expectations." She then sat back in her chair, with an emphasis suggestive of some conclusive discovery. Her son sat motionless with his eyes closed, still with the foolish, pained expression on his face, waiting. Big Steve said "Yes indeed," and then he too appeared to be waiting, almost reluctant to pronounce the next words that came creeping out of his venal mouth.

"Cissie, we need your help."

Disregarding the euphemism of this last word, his plea, I suppose, was frank enough. Even the euphemism could be forgiven him, granted that to Big Steve's mind money *was* help—to the degree that if he ever hoped for salvation (and in his position, such hopes must have recurred often) it would unquestionably have to come in the form of more money. But he had only a slim basis, if any at all, to hope that to him the Lord might prove so generous. His chief supports, I concluded, were mortals of perhaps finite but by no means inconsiderable resources—of whom my grandmother I suppose was one. Besides, he must have reckoned, if she had any idea of business, or even of her son's position in it, she would have to understand. She could be counted on to understand. She *must* understand.

134

"I say, Mr. Scroflone," she said, "a big boy like *you*, need *my* help?"

Big Boy Steve glanced at his partner, whose eyes had now opened; but my uncle did not offer to speak. As usual, he would leave it to his mother.

"Well, I can't see what I could tell you," she went on. "You seem to know very well yourself what you're about. There are so many clever ideas today, and so many clever people to think of them; I confess I can't keep track of it all. Of course, then, who needs an old lady, everyone's in such a big hurry, so ambitious, so many plans—I must say it all escapes me. There used to be so many *nice* people, I wonder what happened to them. Now Kenny, the counter boy at the delicatessen, he's very nice, always so good to me, but I suppose he's not very important, at least in terms of his 'position,' so no one pays any attention to him. . . . Before, it was different; before, my mother always had nice things to say to the help, always had time to be gracious— the gardener always had iced tea to drink when it was hot. Of course, that's all different now. I try to offer something to them, something cool to drink or some chops, but they don't have time. No time anymore. I suppose they'd prefer liquor instead." She sighed.

Big Steve listened to all this with dreadful attention. Things were getting complicated, he could see. All he had done was ask for money; now he had to listen to a historical survey of the decline of civilization.

"That's very kind of you, Cissie," he offered submissively.

"Yes, you'd think it was, wouldn't you, but nobody seems to care, they're just there to pick up the check—and I can't say I blame them. It's as much as anyone can do to keep head above water these days. Inflation is wicked. I know that someone is making a sinful pile of money—whether it's the Arabs or the government, you never know. And the pears I bought yesterday, so bruised, as if someone had taken a whip to them. Simply wicked . . . but no one seems to care . . . yes indeed . . . another day, another dollar." She laughed quietly to herself.

135

"Another million dollars . . . I say, and the lawyers' fees are disgraceful, highway robbery—or perhaps it's just my lawyer, he always tells me I underestimate working expenses. He's right, of course; no one could ever underestimate his work— you simply couldn't get any less. Nothing from nothing is nothing, as they say. I wouldn't dare suggest that to him though, he has such a high opinion of services rendered, you'd think he was a charity worker. But then, I suppose that's what I am, a charity case, so there you are. . . . Now what did I read the other day in the paper, oh yes, a fellow is suing his father for the way he was brought up. Can you imagine such wickedness? That's right, he's asking several million in damages, I don't remember precisely how he claims he was damaged, but he said he had been scarred for life and would never be the same. And the lawyer says they might accept a settlement, but that would depend on the extent of the father's admission. . . . Can you believe it all? I suppose it will all come back to them, though, in the next life. I believe you know that there will be a next life, and that is why I try to leave a nice smell behind in this one. I say, Mr. Scroflone, do you believe in Hinduism?"

"Ma'am?" He swallowed; he looked quite frightened now.

"The ancient Indian religion, you know, the worshippers of Rama, if I'm not mistaken. Now my mother was always a Jew- ess, but she liked to keep an open mind about philosophical matters, metaphysics if I'm not mistaken, she was interested in metaphysics and some of the old religions, the oldest I believe is the Zorro, the Zoroastrian cult, that's where they simply leave the bodies out to decompose in towers. Do you know anything about it?"

"I—sure, I've heard of that one. That's an Eastern religion, isn't it?"

"Yes indeed, good for you—now at least *you* don't think I'm stark raving mad. Although I well might be. Now my mother, as I said, kept an open mind, she believed this was all too much" —here Grandma gestured toward the garden, then to the heavens above in an inclusive, delicate sweep of her arm—

"all too much to simply disappear; we carry the world about with us, and when we pass on, the world is reborn in someone else—the whole world, you understand, Mr. Scroflone, the whole world; every tree and river and animal and book—yes, this she believed, although as I said she was a Jewess. But the Jewish religion, as perhaps you're not aware, has a mystical side to it, and there are many old wise men who believe things just as peculiar as you will. I attended a lecture once by a fellow who was very learned in these mystical matters, and he said you had to have a full stomach to study these things, speaking figuratively, of course, meaning that you couldn't begin to understand the mysteries until you had mastered the more basic knowledge—the Torah, the Talmud and other writings. So I suppose I really wouldn't be qualified to be a mystic. Which doesn't surprise me in the least.

"Oh, but I do go on, don't I? Now then, Mr. Scroflone, how much exactly do you need? Joseph, pay attention, I'm doing this for your benefit, as usual."

7

I may be questioned as to my own source of livelihood at this time. I had not completed any real work in months; ideas for feature articles—mostly on the food of Italy, with Mr. di Barnaba as my cultural liaison—were entertained halfheartedly. But little was carried through. The managing editor of *Bon Vivant* asked whether I had found work elsewhere. I told him I was experiencing family difficulties, but had been researching a long article on the cuisine of Sardinia. He assigned me a review of a Moroccan restaurant that had recently opened in Malibu. "I hope it's exotic enough for you," he said. "And please—no culture-hounding. Keep the background material to a minimum." He had little faith in my expository approach to gastronomy; he said that if I ever decided to write a cookbook, he would hate to be the editor. "Who do you think you are, Henry James of the kitchen? Simple and comprehensible, Lorditch— that's the key to food writing. What does it taste like, how is it made? I don't want to know anything else—don't tell me anything else. Save it for your masterpiece." Yet he liked my articles in spite of himself; he would read them aloud under the guise of criticism: " 'A yolk-bound rhapsody of subtly saliferous sorrel.' OK, Shakespeare, not all gourmets carry dictionaries, you know. And anyway, this description doesn't exactly

138

make my mouth water—though I work up an appetite trying to pronounce it. Run it through again—and this time make like Hemingway, why don't you?"

The Sands of Time was on Pacific Coast Highway, just south of Malibu pier. It was one of those quake-inviting structures built on stilts, overhanging the water, so that in case of catastrophe you had your choice of death by landslide, if you were sitting at the rear of the restaurant (which rested partly on land—that is, a small cliff by the highway), or if you were fortunate enough to be occupying the choicer seats at the front with an ocean view, death by water.

I had brought my grandmother along, for she happened to be alone that night, both my uncle and Mr. di Barnaba being otherwise engaged in "business dinners" (an unusual appointment for the Italian, who until recently would have scoffed at such an idea, and in fact continued to do so, despite the fact that he was now for some reason unable or disinclined to beg off). It was our first evening alone in quite a while, and I wanted to take advantage of the opportunity to learn more of the details of her "secret life" with him.

I sensed further developments—romantic and otherwise—beneath the placid surface of her consistency. A man—perhaps much more than a man—had come into her life. What was she feeling? What bridal hopes, what widow's fears? And what did she really think of him? Would she ever truthfully say? Or would she simply let loose a chatter of multipurpose aphorisms, to cover more profound misgivings? Yet she knew she could be frank with me. ("We have an understanding," she would say. "You don't need flattery, and I don't expect it anymore. That leaves the way open for more important dialogue, I hope." She paused. "Now please, don't say anything nasty or vulgar"—as if, coming from me, these must be the consequences of honesty.) I liked to think that if she had anything to disburden herself of, she would disburden herself of it on me; there was really no one else.

I hoped the circumstances tonight would be congenial for a

familial tête-à-tête. She didn't exactly relish the thought of being propped over the ocean, I knew; for though she had traveled the ocean liners of her time, this structure was a freak, a California monstrosity. The lighting—"atmospheric" to me, "suggestive" to her—was achieved by scented oil-lamps hanging from the low ceiling—which was further depressed by billowy, bedouin-looking tapestries, giving one the impression of being inside a tent, with the vast black desert outside. The unconventional decor did little to put Grandma at her ease; nor did it afford the least reassurance of tables or chairs: the patrons lounged among giant pillows and ottomans, in various postures of leisurely surrender to the local god of Hip.

"I say," demurred Grandma, "are we to lie on the floor? Now I was in Cairo, but I don't remember it was done like this at all. . . ."

"This is Moroccan, Grandma. They're a more horizontal people."

The hostess, loosely swathed in nearly translucent muslin (or a synthetic imitation thereof), approached us. My grandmother gave her a cautious look—cautious because she herself, in spite of our doubts about the respectability of the establishment, did not wish to seem too quick to judge or take exception; she wished to appear aware (though if this were the case, she was quite mistaken in her belief) that the hostess was of "another culture"—that is, a cruder one, where such provocative displays of corporality might very well be tolerated, for all my grandmother knew, with impunity, as "part of the custom." (She had forgotten, if she had ever known of, the veil of purdah.)

I told the hostess of our reservation, making no mention of the magazine, though this would have guaranteed us the best location and service. Nevertheless she led us to the front, overlooking the water. Waiters, their legs bundled inside fat folds of bright silken bloomers, slid by on curly-toed slippers. The hostess gestured to a pile of cushions by the window. "Enjoy," she said vaguely, and left us.

140

Grandma took it all in, silent, almost respectful, for the sake of a more tolerant perspective; yet it was clear she missed table and chair.

"Should I help you down, Grandma? Just pretend it's your sofa."

She answered, "That's what I was afraid of. I would never sink my sofa on the floor." She strove to veil her criticism with a bland smile of attempted sympathy for the poor souls whose backward culture could produce such an inconvenient interior design. She nudged a pillow with her foot, then knelt to it, gracefully but reluctantly, as if bowing down to the toilet to be discreetly sick. "Oh my, it feels rather comfortable," she said in surprise as she sank several inches into the material.

"Use the other pillows to prop yourself up, like this." I helped to buttress her. She weakly resisted my efforts; she wanted to do it herself, though the large, bulbous cushions were cumbersome for her to maneuver.

"Take off your shoes, you'll be more comfortable," I suggested. But the idea of comfort through such graceless means was repugnant to her. Her little feet, still with their shoes on, stuck out from the pillows like a child's from an overstuffed easy chair.

"I say, this is a ridiculous arrangement, why can't they have sitting-chairs? I would certainly mention that in your article. Is that the table?" She indicated a low, round, inlaid table before us.

"I guess so."

"Well, it looks like a coffee table to me. . . . We're not expected to dine off it, are we?" But here she quickly caught herself up, and superimposing upon her displeasure the necessary if transparent lamination of worldliness, the proper perspective for a woman who has traveled and wants to be known to have traveled (even though perhaps she has not liked or even understood all she has seen), she added, "That is, if you're actually *in* the country I'm sure it's understandable enough, but over here, well, you'd expect they'd make

141

things a little easier . . . not very sensible at all. . . ."

A waiter swished by and, pausing briefly, laid over the table a large, engraved brass platter inset with colored glass and enamel.

"That is a nice platter, clever craftsmanship," Grandma allowed. "Are we supposed to eat off it?"

"I'm sure they'll bring us plates." I was not at all sure; in fact I had been told at the magazine to expect something quite different. Yet I had to seem confident for Grandma's sake; as far as she knew, I was the only thing this evening between her and a human sacrifice.

"Perhaps you should mention it to them, Peter—it might not be the custom there."

"Grandma, don't be a worrywart. You're supposed to take a night off. Relax. This is Los Angeles, not Casablanca. Nothing terrible or treacherous is going to happen." (To myself though I reconsidered this statement.)

"Well, all right, I suppose, yes, well, I'll leave it all up to you this evening." She seemed to welcome my chiding; and feeling the burden of responsibility shift from her to me, she assumed a gayer tone. "I'll let you handle the menu, then. But please, don't order anything alive." She giggled to herself at her bold imagination. It was time to take advantage of the change in her and order drinks: a gin and tonic for her, and for me a Pimm's Cup.

Our waiter was not familiar with this drink. "Pisscup?" he asked innocently. My grandmother put her hand over her mouth, and delightedly, with her eyes, sought participation in the fun.

"No no, Pimm's Cup—Pimm's Cup," I enunciated for the sake of decency—as if this in itself would resolve his fundamental misunderstanding of the liquid consonants in our language. "The bartender will know," I assured him. Yes, he probably would—and duly urinate into a highball glass.

Grandma recollected, " 'Pimm's Cup'—well, I say, now Cousin Irwin used to drink a Pimm's Cup. After golf he liked

142

it. And he was very particular about the celery, celery and cucumber and a slice of orange, if I'm not mistaken. . . ."

"Well, we'll see how they make it here."

Grandma wrinkled her nose pessimistically. "Well, I suppose they can't go wrong with a gin and tonic. That was why it was such a popular drink in India, I imagine." Here she allowed herself a twinkle of mischievousness. My grandmother had a sense of the charm of outdated—and therefore harmless, she conceived—colonial racist attitudes, such as the condescension of the British toward the Indians. These attitudes were much closer to her world than to ours, and she could not conceal a certain sense of comfort, even of righteousness perhaps—not malicious, but naïve, quaint, like the terms of racial identification she often employed: "Negress," "Jewess," "Chinaman," etc.—that she felt their usage entitled her to. Thus she was able to satisfy herself that she was indeed not of this world, not subject to the current prevailing trends of thought—by virtue both of her language and of certain outmoded sensibilities and misconceptions that her language served—features that by now had taken on the properties of historical documents, unimpeachable and self-justifying, and had thereby ceased to carry any particular force of good or ill in the "real" world. Absolution from the accusation of prejudice was her privilege, bestowed by time; and it solved once and for all the aggravating problem of having to conform.

The waiter soon brought our drinks, and the busboy set down in the middle of the brass platter an Aladdin's Lamp burning fragrant oil.

"OK, Grandma, you get three wishes," I said. She smiled, took a sip of her drink, and looked out at the dark ocean below us, as if from there would soon surface her dark mysterious desire.

"Well, now," she began, blinking reflectively, "I wish for health, happiness, security." She paused. I knew these were not her real wishes.

"Actually I wish he would stop it."

143

"Who?"

"Both of them. They're acting like two children, it's simply disgraceful, and of course I'm left holding the bill as usual, it's I who have to pay for the indulgences of others. I should have learned better, I should have learned to watch out for myself—well, that's that, I don't want to bore you, it's a nice restaurant and I'm so happy and touched you brought me here, Peter dear."

But this was not nearly all. Unseen djinns lurked around us in the blackness, waiting to understand better the request she did not really know herself.

"Wait," I said. "First I want to know just who you mean—Joseph and Mr. di Barnaba?"

"Yes, yes, of course, Joseph and Tullio, the two babies," she said, with a knowing maternal petulance—which, from a certain satisfaction in her tone, she apparently felt to be more a privilege than a burden to carry—as mothers invariably do.

"Honestly, you'd think, wouldn't you, the one would knock some sense into the other. At least that's what you'd hope. But he's really no more sensible at all, it's all talk, talk talk talk. He should have been a lawyer—then at least his mouth could have made money. This way, the money drains off at the mouth. I am so relieved you are the quiet sort, Peter—perhaps you'll be sensible enough to conserve your resources. As two glaring examples have not. Then again, they were not even theirs to conserve." She gave a bitter laugh, and sipped her drink.

"Are you worried about the restaurant, Grandma? Is that what you mean?"

"Restaurant? What restaurant? Do you see a restaurant? I certainly don't. I see nothing but an abandoned storefront."

"Well, Uncle Tiger showed me some plans, some blueprints—"

"Plans!" she scoffed. "Blueprints! Blueprints for our destitution, that's what they are. I can't say I trust Mr. Scroflone anymore either. I thought he was a generous, kind man, but I do believe he's leading us all downhill on the road to ruin—oh

144

dear, help me, Peter, whatever shall I do with such a wicked brood. . . ."

She began to knit her fingers. She looked about her at the strange surroundings, more threatening now in her new anxiety . . . a hostage in a bedouin tent, amid carnivorous savages. . . .

"Grandma, please don't sound so desperate—"

"I *am* desperate, I *feel* desperate. What do you expect me to feel? They're taking my money and ruining us, and the lawyers, oh, those lawyers! They're crooked too—"

"Richardson, you mean?"

"No, I don't see him—even the others warned me against him—"

"He's Joseph's lawyer, you know."

Her hands collapsed in her lap. "Oh, isn't it awful." Her eyes, hooded with worry, looked searchingly at me. "How did he come to be so wicked?"

"He's not 'wicked.' But he doesn't know what he's doing—he fell in with a bad crowd." I sounded like her. "But don't panic prematurely—maybe the restaurant will make money."

"Well, you can be sure we'll never see a penny of it," she sighed prophetically.

"And what do the lawyers say?"

Her eyes wandered distractedly out to the water, and the lights thrown across the bay. "Oh, they want to see papers. I say I have no papers—Joseph and his associates have them. Would it look bad, do you think, if I asked them if I could see them?"

"Not in the least—after all, you are the principal investor. You have the right. You should demand to see them. You should have done so at the very beginning."

She fixed me again. "Well, why didn't you help me then?"

I, in turn, looked to the blackness outside, "We were all led along," I said. "I thought you were doing what you wanted to do."

"I wanted to do it for him," she replied, meekly, almost

abashedly, as if made aware now of the wages of selflessness. "For him, and for you."

I was silent. She began again to knit her fingers.

"Oh Peter, I wanted so much to be able to leave you what I could, it was all set aside, if only this stupidness had not interfered. It was wicked, truly wicked—"

"Don't. You had other obligations. You're a mother," I reminded her.

"And I am a wicked grandmother. I have allowed terrible brigandage of my loved ones, I see now that I have let dishonesty prevail through my own weakness—" Her hands were fluttery, wild things. "Oh, evil woman, wicked woman. . . ."

"Grandma, stop. Don't torture yourself. You don't even know what's really going on. None of us does. That's part of the problem. As I say, it's very possible that it is all a legitimate venture—"

"I should hope so! With my money yet!"

"Well, that in itself is no insurance. But I'm sure it will eventually succeed. It's the only place like it in the area." This was undeniable. But the prospect of commercial success seemed to do little to assuage Grandma's painful doubts. In her eyes she had once again failed—failed to be as strong, as immovable, as steadfast of tutelary purpose as the ideal family martyr she somehow conceived she'd been born to be; and from the frustration of this destiny arose what she felt to be (and with unsurpassable vanity, really, when one considered the ideal to which she aspired) her "wickedness."

She considered the matter now with her characteristic gnomic resignation. "Well, it doesn't matter now, it's too late for anything but a prayer. But don't worry, Peter dear, I have not been so absolutely prodigal as you may think. I have thought to tuck a little something away where even I have forgotten to look. You see, I am smart enough to trick myself sometimes. You shall not want—no grandson of mine shall ever want." Her hands, quieter now, tapped accompanying reassurance on the counter. She sipped at her drink, and found it was empty.

"Nor shall you, Grandma. Do you want another?"

"Trying to get me drunk, are you? What's wrong—haven't I already talked enough?"

"Not nearly. I want to know about Mr. di Barnaba."

At that moment the tardy waiter brought our menus—palimpsest-like tablets with the writing fashioned to look as if burned in wood—and Grandma was for a moment distracted. "I say, are these menus or plates?" She squinted, trying to decipher the fustian script. "I'm afraid you'll have to translate for me. Why can't they print it in English?"

"It is in English."

"I beg your pardon," she bridled. "I believe you are mistaken, dear Peter. I happen to be familiar with the English language."

"I don't doubt it for a moment, Grandma. But what language is 'New York sirloin tips *fra diabolo*'?"

"Well, I don't make that out." She suspiciously scanned the hidden writing, and passed her hands over the sheets as if they were in braille.

"Grandma, you need new glasses. How long since you had your eyes checked?"

"Oh, that's all right, Albert's glasses suit me fine. . . ."

"Albert's glasses?"

"Yes, they're nearly the same as mine, what does it matter anyway," she grumbled. "He was nearsighted just like me."

"You're wearing another person's glasses?"

"Oh, don't make such an event of it, please. They help to magnify, that's all," she explained placidly.

"Grandma, you can destroy your eyes that way. I want you to take those glasses off immediately." She did not. I moved to take them myself; she shied away, hissing "leave me alone," and in the process knocked over her glass, spilling ice over the platter and cushions.

"Waiter, help! My grandson is attacking me!" She held her glasses defensively to her head, and bent down toward the floor. "Help, help."

I retreated quickly. "Grandma, sit up please, and don't be so ridiculous. Look what a mess you've made."

A mystified busboy approached with a towel. "Spill the drink?"

"Yes we did. On her." I pointed.

The busboy crouched by the low table to sop it up. Our waiter came by to remove the glass; moments later he reappeared with a fresh drink.

"But I don't want another drink," said Grandma, already drunk. The waiter had left. "Why did you order another drink, I don't want one, I'll probably spill this one too."

"I didn't order it, he brought it."

"Well, I don't want it." She frowned, and took a sip.

I read the menu. There were several unusual dishes I wanted to order: a chicken-and-egg pastry, 'lamb braised in honey,' 'couscous with fruit'; but I was not sure Grandma would appreciate them. Also, we were expected to eat with our fingers, and, I observed, there were no plates; you held a wide towel across your lap. This would all be disconcerting novelty to Grandma, but if she were drunk enough, she'd laugh it off. My grandmother's first impulse was always to enjoy what there was to enjoy, and learn what she could in the process. Lawyers and accountants, however, had recently done much to stifle this disposition in her, in favor of a more cautious approach—presumably, that enjoyment not based on real property assessments and tax deductions was a foolish thing indeed. But liquor helped to enhance her fundamentally joyous nature, and loosen up the strictures of legality. *Nunc est bibendum,* Grandma.

"I say, have you decided what we're going to eat? I trust you, Peter, not to order a whole ox on a spit. Not that I am unfamiliar with that dish. I once ate ox, you know, but I'm sure you've already heard the story many times. . . ."

This story I could always hear again. "No, I don't remember. Speak, memory."

"Oh, I've surely told you that—when we were on a cruise in the Black Sea, with all the German princes on board, and those wonderful horsemen, the Cocks, Cockers, Cossacks, that's it, I believe they're called, if I'm not mistaken. . . ."

"Cossacks, that's right."

"Yes, well, the Cossacks had an equestrian show on the beach for us. It was magnificent." Her eyes glazed over now. "They danced on the horses as they were galloping, and passed, you know, under the underside of the horses, and did tricks with swords, and all sorts of acrobatics. And then they served us a magnificent banquet, still on horseback. That was when I had ox. They cooked it on spits in the sand. My my, what wonderful . . . and peasants came out in boats to say goodbye, and we threw them coins. . . . That is no more."

"Well, certainly not in Russia. But the Cossacks, Grandma—they actually served you on horseback? I thought they were pretty wild fellows. I'm surprised they didn't put you on a spit and cook you."

She laughed. "Yes, well, I suppose they were commanded by the Czar to be nice." (Again we have an illustration of the manifold function of the word "nice"—describing here the pleasant effect of the subjugation of Cossacks into waiters.) She was apparently pleased at the nostalgic orderliness of it all; in her day the Nice could actually expect and receive compliance from the Wild, whereas nowadays it was the Wild that prevailed over the Nice.

"Oh, what a wonderful cruise. We went to Yalta, and saw the Czar's palace there, and Batur, where the oil is, and Tiflis and we traveled by motorcar in the mountains—it was new in those days, the motorcar. This was Imperial Russia, mind you. And we saw a puppet show in Petersburg. I say, is that Joseph?"

I looked behind me. My uncle and, following him, Mr. di Barnaba, were being led to cushions in the corner of the room, just under the picture windows. My uncle looked impatient; Mr. di Barnaba, mildly amused. Grandma appeared for a moment not to recognize, or to recognize only at great pains, the robust stranger accompanying her son. Then she said, "Oh dear." But at once, remembering herself, she thought to add, as if speaking of long-lost friends, "Why, this *is* a surprise, we must call them over."

A flock of waiters had already amassed in their corner. I could hear my uncle squawking orders: ". . . reservation . . . Mr. Richardson . . . bigger table . . . you don't have tables? . . . heard of such a thing. Mr. Richardson is expecting tables." Then he saw me. "Look, look, here's my nephew. What are you doing here? Hello, Peter. Shifa, this is my nephew." He introduced me to the hostess. "So who are you with?"

"I'm with your mother."

He laughed as if he would rather ignore this. "This's great, just great, bring her over, we'll all sit together." He wore a Cheshire-cat grin of foolishness, promising a night of the same. I thought of Grandma and the Cossacks; here was one that got away.

Mr. di Barnaba seemed pleased to see us; nor did he appear particularly embarrassed at the exposure of his "business dinner." After all, it was not so far from the truth, for if dinner with my uncle could not be considered strictly a business appointment, it was, for Mr. di Barnaba, I suspected, also far from pleasure. It was one of those unavoidable necessities of life, useless but undergone so as not to offend.

There were enough cushions in the corner to accommodate all of us, and still save a place for Richardson, that Elijah of the law, who my uncle said planned to meet them there. He just had to finish some important business first.

"Joseph, why is it we have never met this intriguing man?" asked Mr. di Barnaba.

"He wants to meet you—all of you. You'll see him tonight."

"Is that a promise? I have been waiting." Yet expectancy was absent from his tone.

"I think he's a figment of Joseph's imagination," said Grandma.

"I think he has become a figment of all our imaginations," observed Mr. di Barnaba, glancing meaningfully at my uncle to include him in the joke. And the Tiger in turn liked to show that he could take a little teasing—even if it was based on a misappraisal of this great man.

"I don't care what you all think. He's been a great help to us."

"Is that so," said Mr. di Barnaba.

"Well, he hasn't helped me," muttered Grandma. "No lawyer has—they're all pettifoggers. No offense to your friend, my dear."

"Mom," whined her son, "when will you catch up with the times—"

"I'm as caught up as I care to be, thank you. Besides, there's nothing old-fashioned about watching your pocketbook. Nowadays more than ever—I should think you would have learned your lesson by now."

"Please, friends, this is a social occasion," interceded di Barnaba the peacekeeper. "Let us not bring our own petty quarrels into this exotic atmosphere." He looked above him at the tumescent, pendulous ceiling, as if this were exoticism. "Such a happy coincidence surely was meant to be." But he did not sound so sure.

"Yeah, how did you end up here, of all places?" my uncle asked me. "Mom hates to eat out in places like this—how'd you ever get her to go?"

"It's free," I whispered to him. "I'm reviewing it for the magazine."

This pleased him greatly. He gave an approving chuckle, apparently proud that for once I was showing some business sense.

"Well, you make sure she eats right," he said, with affectionate concern. Then, in lower tones, to me: "She hardly ever eats a bite, poor thing—not like us Lorditches." He nudged me.

151

His attention was drawn to the others, and he said, with a hospitable authority, as if we all were his guests at table, "Everybody relax, this is a casual place, you're supposed to lounge. Mom, take off your shoes."

"I will not."

"Aw, come on, it's allowed. It's *de rigueur.* Shifa," he called to our hostess, "tell my mother she's allowed to take off her shoes."

Grandma was terribly embarrassed. "Joseph, stop it. Honestly, my son is impossible," she explained to the hostess. "I'm terribly sorry—I wouldn't think of doing such a thing."

"Oh, but it is quite all right," replied Shifa. "We encourage you to feel at home. Enjoy."

"Thank you, but I prefer to keep my shoes on at home," replied Grandma curtly.

"So, as you like." The hostess smiled, obviously humoring the old lady. "When you are among family you need not worry."

"Family," muttered Grandma. "That's when I *begin* to worry."

The hostess smiled broadly at the rest of us, as if to acknowledge what a fine old specimen we were fortunate enough to have preserved. "Would you like to order anything to drink?"

"We sure would," said my uncle. "I'll have a beer, a Heineken. My mother will have—what are you drinking, Mom, gin and tonic?"

"No more for me, thank you."

"She'll have another." Grandma did not refuse. "And Mr. Barnaba—" Thusly would my uncle forever call him, whether deliberately or not, and di Barnaba, his pride notwithstanding, had finally gotten tired of trying to correct it. "Mr. Barnaba, what are you drinking—wine?"

"That will be fine. Red, please."

"And for my nephew—"

"Another Pisscup, please."

My uncle frowned. "Look at him—see what a gentleman he is."

"Thank you, and enjoy your meal," said the hostess, gladly drawing away, as if veering from a drunk on a bus.

"We will. Peter's reviewing this place for *Bon Vivant* magazine, so it better be good tonight," gaffed my uncle. Fortunately, I think she was beyond earshot.

"Uncle, relax," I said. "I'd like to stay for dinner."

I saw that my chances for a tête-à-tête with Grandma were now destroyed. Still, I hoped I could gather information just by observing her and Mr. di Barnaba together. They were sitting across from me and my uncle. It was hard to tell whether Mr. di Barnaba was pleased or not by the coincidence of our meeting. The posture of mediator he had at once adopted was a convenient shield for his deeper feelings; but this was due more to a habitual reflex gesture of his innate discretion than to any studied attempt to dissimulate, I thought. Whatever he had expected from this evening, he now seemed content to serve as the inert stabilizer compound for the unstable element that was my family.

My grandmother, on the other hand, was anxious; even the dosage of alcohol she had taken could not conceal this. Her hands were never still; they fingered her eyeglasses, the rim of her drinking glass, the menu, the tassels on the cushions, the string of lacquered peach pits she wore as a necklace. Her eyes were wary. Could she detect, through her maternal and grandmaternal instinct, hatching plots of which I was unaware? Her failing eyes seemed to possess another sense, for which exactitude of optical vision was not required, was even superfluous—they were no longer merely sensory organs; they had acquired the power of emanating moral expression. They warned, they forbore, they prevailed. But although the general idea of their message might have been intelligible to me, its substance was not. It spoke of sights I would never see, experience I would never feel, vast restless continents of changeful

153

territorial demarcations, the rise and fall of nations—events in the unrecorded moral history of a woman on the fringe of time. She needed a biographer. Unfortunately he would never have received her cooperation. She could not even tolerate the handful of short stories I had written years ago, broaching, very superficially, the subject of herself and her ancestors. "This is *not* true," she had pointed out, offended. "The grocer never said that—we could be sued. You must not write untruths. Just ask me and I will tell you how it was." Fiction, for Grandma, was lies, therefore libel; biography—the assimilation of one person's life by the understanding of another—was blasphemy. Who will sing you then, Grandma, your works and days, your words, hopes and fears? You who never yielded up or failed to live a day of your life, how can you consent to vanish forever when your time is up?

Don't worry, Old Girl, your Boswell will come someday. . . .

Mr. di Barnaba was speaking to her now, evidently relating something of interest, for his hands were fashioning sentences; but he spoke so low I could not hear what he was saying. It did not look like "business." My uncle stared at them with displeasure; used to being the cynosure, he was irritated when events outside of himself presumed to attract attention.

"I wonder where Richardson is," he reflected not quite to himself.

"Oh, I say, that reminds me, Joseph," said my grandmother, turning from Mr. di Barnaba, to whom she had been listening perhaps not as attentively as he had supposed, "the lawyers have asked me to see your papers."

"Papers? What papers?"

"The papers, you know, the papers to the restaurant—official documents."

"I don't know what you're talking about," said my uncle sullenly. "What for?"

"They would like to review them. They've asked me several times."

He was evasive. "They'll have to talk to Richardson."

Grandma bridled. "I say now, these are our lawyers, you know—all of us—who are officially representing our interests in the matter, and they have requested to review certain documents. And who, if I may ask, is Ed Richardson?"

"Richardson is *my* lawyer," said my uncle possessively—as if this remarkable personage were his exclusive resource in case of litigation with his mother.

"But the other lawyers are your lawyers too, are they not?" interjected Mr. di Barnaba.

"I don't know them—I never met them."

"Well, I have never met Ed Richardson myself," added Grandma. "And neither has anyone else, for that matter. I don't even think he exists," she huffed—not really doubting it, but simply put out that the rudesby had never taken the trouble to introduce himself. "At any rate, Mr. di Barnaba is right, ours is the same side after all. There is really no reason why you cannot cooperate."

"No business, no business tonight." My uncle raised his glass in a toast to no business. He reflected a moment. "I don't want 'em snooping around."

"Joseph, be reasonable," soothed Mr. di Barnaba. "They probably want to make sure everything is in order, that there are no minor infractions—"

"I'm legal," my uncle snorted. "What do they want—I've got nothing to hide." He paused to reconsider, then went on, "Who needs 'em?"

"*I* need them," stated Grandma. "Heavens, I wish I didn't. But as long as I have them you might as well cooperate. Otherwise . . . otherwise they might be suspicious."

"So let 'em be suspicious—what do I care? I've got nothing to hide," he repeated.

"He doth protest too much," quoth Mr. di Barnaba.

"What's that?"

"Nothing, just talking to myself."

"Yeah, well, as I was saying, no business tonight. I want you to stop worrying, Mom." But he himself looked terribly worried. His face was beginning to droop in that expression I recognized so well—all the thwarted desires and unfulfillable hopes, past and future, were scrawled in hurried incompletion, never intended to be read clearly, across the troubled, cracked and slightly yellowing parchment of his face. To begin to make sense of it, you had to be an expert in the codology of despair.

"Come on—it's a party, isn't it?" He raised his beer glass high, then drank a long, sloppy draught. "Aaaaahhhhhh. Come on, Mom—cheer up."

His toast did little to cheer her. She closed her eyes in exasperation, then, opening them, made a show of examining the Aladdin's Lamp on the table. I asked her again what her three wishes were.

"I wish we would eat," she grumbled. "At this rate we'll be here all night."

"Yes, Joseph, perhaps we should order," said Mr. di Barnaba. "I'm sure there will be enough for Mr. Richardson if he does turn up. We are all hungry. As you know, and speaking of lawyers, an empty stomach is bad counsel." He raised an eyebrow to toast in turn his own cleverness.

My uncle mumbled something. He did not wish to appear to sanction the proposition that Ed Richardson might once again fail us. He was not pleased, and to cover his losses, he ordered heavily.

I had suggested some specialties I wanted to try: the chicken-and-egg pie, the honeyed lamb, and the fruit couscous.

"That sounds terrible," he frowned. "But go ahead, I don't care—nobody else will eat it."

"Well, I can't eat it all myself," I said. Nevertheless, he ordered all the dishes I had mentioned, then asked the waiter for more suggestions. When consulted as to his preference, Mr. di Barnaba politely deferred to our choices; Grandma, at this point, was not particular. "As I once overheard a hungry fellow say on the boat, 'If it's dead and cooked, I'll eat it!' " She laughed, and looked toward the waiter to share her joke; but he only said uncomprehendingly, "Thank you very maach," and took away the menus.

"Well, if I were reviewing this restaurant, I'd give the waiters a zero for intelligence," said my uncle.

"I don't think they speak much English," I said.

"That's another zero. I don't think they speak much of anything. Dumb," he concluded.

"And your waiters at the Caffè, Joseph? Will you give them an intelligence test before you hire them?" asked Mr. di Barnaba, slightly teasing.

"If I do, it'll be a fair one—I'll have to pass it first."

"That's being a little too fair, don't you think?" I said. He ignored my joke, but Mr. di Barnaba gave a snort of acknowledgment.

My uncle continued, "All my waiters will have to be bilingual, I've decided."

"Well, then, you will have to give a Ph.D. exam."

"You think I'm joking. Everyone thinks I'm joking—well, you'll see. I'm not talking about completely fluent, you can't expect that. Just bilingual enough to give it atmosphere, a word here or there—like you, when you first came to this country."

My uncle's tone was not deliberately cruel, though the words themselves may have sounded that way. But in his own mind he was simply appealing to Mr. di Barnaba's experience—that is, what he thought to be his experience. That it was a careless and offensive thought, and a mistaken one, was not of present concern to him. All that mattered was that Mr. di Barnaba be made to appreciate the considerations entering into the selection of staff for the restaurant.

"Well, I was fluent," answered Mr. di Barnaba, adding, with an ironical smile, "A perfect candidate for a waiter's job. Perhaps I should have become a waiter instead of an architect—then you wouldn't have to think twice about hiring me."

"Don't be ridiculous. A man of your experience—" my uncle began, but he did not finish. For it suited him more to imagine

Mr. di Barnaba's experience as manifold and yet indefinable; that way he could make of it what he would.

"Yes, too much experience and too little knowledge," Mr. di Barnaba went on. "But perhaps better like that than the other way round." He glanced at Grandma ironically, for he knew she liked him just as he was. And why shouldn't she? A man with too much knowledge to add to her own experience would make a burden heavy for her eighty-one years to bear. And really, after all was said and done, what good was more knowledge at her stage of the game? It could bring no deeper convictions than those she already held, tempt no fresher curiosity, promise no greater wisdom. It would have been nothing but a superfluous pedantic supplement to the already crowded text of her life. But another's experience, on the other hand, was a diversion, a relief from the task of judgment; being not her own it remained forever new and fresh: a bit of entertainment, a slice of someone else's life, contiguous yet discrete, posing little threat of disruption to the course of her own. In other words, my grandmother desired no longer to know, but only, at a distance, to suppose, to imagine, to feel what was, what forever might have been.

Mr. di Barnaba, I had come to realize, was perfectly conscious of his effect on her; and it was not only his fund of experience, and his manner of relating it, that produced this effect, but also his confident posture (both physical and social), his "bearing," his obvious respect for the sturdy vessel, himself, that contained such precious riches—a handsome pagan bronze amphora, whose rarefied contents were not for everyone to enjoy. I wonder how much even Grandma enjoyed them. She made a show of always being reluctant to accept gifts; like Sinon in the *Aeneid*, she was suspicious. She would often intentionally misread compliments as disguised mockery. They embarrassed her; and her evaluations of her own character were inevitably brutal. Given this tendency, it would have seemed only natural for her to pooh-pooh Mr. di Barnaba's attentions, urge him to find a more deserving object, and grow irritated if he persisted. Yet this did not happen. She tolerated the ministrations which, under other circumstances, one would have expected her to flee. This may have been, as I have said, because of his manners—because the despised gifts came in such a charming container, welcome to her in this land of plain wrapping.

But I think it was something else too; I think she intended to help him. Help him how? With what? To what end? Only in her benevolent, inaccessible heart, if anywhere, deeply held and guarded, were the answers. She may even have lost track of her reasons, or her pride may have been reluctant to yield them up to her sense. I had known and studied her long enough to understand that this was one of the paramount objects of her life: to help the weak, the needy. She saw anyone needing her help as weak. There was a certain grudging reluctance in her establishment of herself in the stronger position—a position she perhaps partly disbelieved in, was not comfortable with, yet accepted; and she resented, and found fault with, her defenseless protectorates—her late second husband Albert; my uncle; me; perhaps now Mr. di Barnaba—for their reliance on such an unworthy power as Cissie Samuels. One sensed that if the roles were reversed, she'd have chosen no one rather than rely on herself; she knew better. But she resisted the temptation to question or judge; and things and people being what they were, she accepted her duty.

Much of this was simply a question of temperament; she needed to please endlessly the few whom she loved, and she figured she could please best by "helping"—that is, by managing. Did that mean she loved Mr. di Barnaba? Was she "helping" him out of love? Would marrying him, in her eyes, legally and morally enable her further to do so? Certainly in a financial sense it would, if she felt he was in trouble that way. But he owned a house in Pacific Palisades; he could not be that badly off. Was it mortgaged to the roof? Was he in danger of dispossession? Had he ever thought to invest? Did he have any stake in his father-in-law's estate? How about his deceased wife's? These were questions Grandma must have asked herself, and him, and to which, having possibly received upsetting answers, she would have thought of her "help" as the only answer, the solution to his distress.

But if Mr. di Barnaba was distressed, he did not appear to be; or else he was virtually embracing his predicament. He continued to wear his cuprous sheen of good health and self-satisfaction. If creditors were banging on his door, he did not let it disturb his sleep. He did not look—to anyone except Grandma perhaps—like a man in need of help, especially from an octogenarian dowager.

Watching them together now, I had to wonder about it all: on what their relationship was founded, if it was founded at all; what were the expectations—for despite their age and experience, there still had to be expectations, where there was any feeling at all; and about that feeling—what was it? Was it growing? Would it last? Was it love?

They seemed to be supportive of each other. She listened to him, he was patient with her. Was he protective? She seemed more protective than he; perhaps she sensed he needed it more. It was no trouble for her to give, it was something she was used to—her family had required it of her. But was Mr. di Barnaba in turn sensitive to what she was giving? Did he need it? Whatever his feelings, he seemed receptive to the offer; he had the sense to know he should be, that this was important to her. Her aphorisms were acknowledged, even encouraged with a knowing nod and a smile. If he was not in her world exactly, he was not far from it.

The waiter now brought the first course, the egg-and-chicken pie, encased in a flaky pastry crust and dusted with sugar. He handed us each a large white towel to drape over our laps; there were no plates or silverware.

"Isn't that the craziest thing you've ever seen!" cried my

160

uncle, smacking his slobbery lips together in anticipation. Mixed together with his appetite there was, I sensed, a long-awaited, forbidden childish joy at the absence of restrictive implements coming between him and his food.

Mr. di Barnaba arranged the napkin in my grandmother's lap, and she groaned ever so politely. "I say, how are we to serve ourselves . . . or are we?"

The rich pie steamed before us, like a delicacy on a windowsill, inviting pillage. My uncle found it easy to pillage. His hand reached for the hole in the center, and he extracted a piece of chicken and held it to his mother, like an obedient trained hunting dog; she shied away, wincing. "Joseph, really, you'll get us thrown out."

"Whad'you mean?" he snorted, bolting down the morsel himself. "That's what you're supposed to do. They gave us no plates on purpose—that's how they eat in Morocco. Come on, everybody."

Everybody was hesitant. The pie looked still too hot to handle. But my uncle fingered it with delight. His towel was already spattered with gobbets. I dipped my fingertips into the pie, then brought them gingerly to my lips, juggling the food with my tongue and gasping. It was a unique combination of sensations: sweet, savory, crisp and very hot. I urged Grandma to try, but she said she would not eat with her fingers. She felt it was unsanitary.

"But aren't your hands clean?"

"Yes, of course they are—and I plan to keep them that way, thank you, not gummed up with food like some beggar-woman's."

"Ah, come on, Mom, don't spoil the fun," said my uncle—as if he were asking a playmate not to ruin his birthday party.

Mr. di Barnaba, without further ado, scooped up a bit of the pie and, before he had tasted it himself, brought it to her mouth; and she, like a trusting infant, ate.

"Mmmm, it is quite tasty, though I never would have

161

dreamed from the way they serve it." A fleck of egg stuck to the corner of her mouth; Mr. di Barnaba flicked it away with uxorious dexterity.

"See, what'd I tell you?" said my uncle. "But you had to be fed before you'd believe me."

"Yes, well, I know, I'm just a baby, in my second childhood. Well, then, what does that make you, my son?"

Her son apparently did not appreciate the thought. His eyes drifted from the table, following the attractive hostess, Shifa. He continued to shovel portions into his mouth. Mr. di Barnaba looked concernedly from mother to son—but after all there was not much he could do; the mother was barely in his domain, the son was not.

I said to my uncle, "Don't bother looking for Richardson—he's not coming."

"How do you know? He said he would. He's probably working late—he'll be along."

"That's it."

"Listen, I don't want to hear any more of your sarcasm. I'm tired of it." He looked tired. He added gloomily, "You've got to get this chip off your shoulder and face reality."

I did not answer, and he looked away in disgust, turning his body to an angle where it would be less exposed to me and my sarcasm. I think he would rather have had a different nephew: someone more suggestible, less afraid of the world, less critical, more ambitious; someone who could have sympathized more with him, understood better his plans and the magnitude of his aspirations; someone bigger, in all ways, to make him great. Yet I do believe that in many ways—ways in which I would even have preferred not to—I did sympathize, I understood better than anyone, for I had made rather strenuous efforts in this direction. I don't know, though, whether it has made us any bigger or better.

"Children, children," began Mr. di Barnaba, "children of all ages, let the petty demon of quarrel not prevail here tonight.

Imagine us in a tent in the desert—would we be fighting like this?"

"Worse," I said.

"Perhaps—but then over important things, like water, or who gets to ride the camel to the oasis. Be thankful. Have you ever ridden a camel? Cissie, you must have."

"Yes, I believe I did, in Luxor once," she recollected.

The nonchalance of her historicity delighted him. "In Luxor once," he repeated, as if quoting the beginning of a fairy tale.

"It was not terribly comfortable, I'll have to admit—I almost became seasick, or camelsick, rather," she laughed. "We had waterboys, carrying water in tarred goatskins. They lived in the ruins of the temple, what is it called, the temple of, oh, a very famous god. . . ." She shut her eyes in concentration; she shook her head. "What is happening to me. . . ."

Another course was brought—the honeyed lamb shanks.

"Oxtails?" said Grandma with vague distaste.

"No no—lamb flanks with honey," corrected my uncle. "Well, how do you handle this one?"

The waiter, who had overheard us, bent down to my uncle and whispered, "Pick with the fingers."

"Jesus, I could have told you that," returned my uncle, pleased that he could continue to eat this way and be vindicated. My grandmother hung her head in shame; the beast in us came out tonight. I felt sorry for her, and with her too I could sympathize. What had begun as a quiet evening with her grandson had been perverted, in the usual fashion, into another family spectacle. It must have seemed to her (and the sense of this had certainly oppressed me at times) that she could never escape; she was bonded to us like a bailsman to his pledge. And love was the force that bound her.

Mr. di Barnaba, under these circumstances, must have been something of a consolation to her; and it was a relief that he did not appear to take her son too seriously. With an Italian gentleman there to pass it all off in a few pithy, well-turned phrases, her despair over her son (and possibly her grandson, also) must have struck her less acutely. Especially if she could bring herself to believe that their association might be mutually beneficial—that Joseph Lorditch might actually be able to "do something" for her betrothed, present him with a suitable offer of employment, and that Mr. di Barnaba would assent to this. As a mother, she would have felt the same encouragement as when a son is removed from bad influences, and voluntarily seeks out better ones; or as a wife, when her husband finds a better job.

Such a job, she considered, might be provided by the Caffè Ice Cream. Now whether Mr. di Barnaba felt the same was doubtful; like everything else he encountered, he seemed to take the Caffè half-seriously. Not that this was a particularly inappropriate attitude toward the venture, for he knew it was still in the "planning" stage. This meant that my uncle was talking a lot about it. It will be remembered that Sheba Enterprises and Vox-Tone (a miniaturized electronic bullhorn for the stricken or the dying) had also seen their "planning stages," and yet never seen the light of day—under which, no doubt, like dreams, they would have vaporized. Still, these "planning stages" were hard for us to ignore. The plans were always with us, we grew familiar with their insane details; and, as with the specter of Ed Richardson, we began to wonder—not so much about the possible existence of these things, but rather about their vivid hold on Joseph Lorditch, the desperate quality evoked in him by all their delirious possibilities.

But to return to Mr. di Barnaba: what were his expectations, what was his purpose? I was reminded of Emerson's snake in the graveyard: "not to eat, not for love." But perhaps that was unfair. He displayed genuine feeling for my grandmother—and he certainly loved food. Yet for all his appetite, all his easy avowal of impressions and confessions, there lurked a snake on his property. Perhaps not a snake; perhaps a small rodent, a marmot or ferret—one of those wriggly things you always suspect but are unable to catch at anything—yet the eggs keep

164

disappearing. The creature is rather cute; one would like to resist suspicion. Then one day the animal is confronted with its quick little face smeared with blood, and the remnants of some secret prey. It looks at you unashamed, as if you were the culprit. And you tell yourself it is just acting according to its nature.

Endowed with an understanding, catholic mind, Mr. di Barnaba might have found it not impossible to countenance the unseemly; perhaps he felt he was better equipped, with all his experience, to appreciate it, to put it in its proper perspective. He cultivated with little effort a healthy tolerance for my uncle's excesses of body and mind, and liked to show that he could weigh the man with a lighter measure. Likewise with my grandmother's worries, and my own protestations against my "vulgar" local environment. And he applied an easy standard also to himself; he judged not too harshly, if at all. Why should he? He was liked, he liked himself, he was not called upon to make decisions (unless by himself). For these reasons, his enjoyment of his life had been allowed to grow into a virtual celebration. In short, he had been providently spared (like my uncle, although their circumstances were vastly different) that counterpoise of a more troublesome reality from which life derives its heavier and more somber qualities. His criteria of performance—as opposed to the rhapsodic ideals of which he spoke—were not too exacting. He lived, one would presume from his actions, not to expect, but to enjoy. To quote one of his classical favorites: *carpe diem, quam minimum credula postero.* "Think about tomorrow as little and as seldom as possible, my lad."

I wished it were possible to believe, as I watched them now like two smug, senescent lovebirds, he feeding her bites of honeyed lamb sandwiched between flat Moroccan bread, that he was following his own best advice—that he was content in the here-and-now with the pleasures that an eighty-one-year-old woman could provide. But his patience, his thoughtfulness, his sympathy, his tolerance—it seemed to me that all of those qualities he was happy to make so apparent were employed in the service of yet another not quite so beguiling: his certitude.

He was waiting. He must have guessed he wouldn't have to wait forever.

The void of the ocean beyond the window, the frail string of twinkling lights along the bay, modestly delimiting, with their delicate, sure arc, the extent of nature's beastly blackness—tokens of man's meaningless presumption, Mr. di Barnaba would have said, venturing into the darkness that he cannot light—these gave to our little assemblage an insular warmth which, in spite of my misgivings about family solidarity tonight, went a good way to making the evening bearable for me. I ended up writing a good review, demurring only on the fruit couscous, which contained kumquats, which I abhor.

My uncle, however, swallowed them whole. "What's wrong?" he asked. "How else are you supposed to eat these things?"

8

My uncle, I learned, had begun to look into architects. He wanted for the Caffè an Italian architect, preferably "someone who knows the tradition, who I won't have to explain everything to. Don't worry—I know lots of architects. I'm not talking about a Michelangelo—just someone who can get the job done. I want lots of glass and brass. I can already see the whole place in my mind. We'll have a bandstand—maybe a gazebo-type thing, I don't care—where we can put the band. Did I tell you we're going to have a band? Yeah, just like the Piazza San Marco. All Italian. I want only Italian musicians. Barnaba'll be able to find 'em. I'm sure he knows lots of Italian musicians— he's just the type. Doesn't he play an instrument? I don't care— I don't want him. He's got to worry about the flavors. Flavors and maitre d', that's his job. But I'm talking about the architect. . . . I want a zinc-topped bar. I want a cappuccino machine, big, all shiny copper and brass, with spouts and eagles, the size of a car—I don't care, the bigger the better. We'll be doing a lot of coffee."

"I thought it was an ice cream place," I seemed to recollect.

"Sure it is—that's our specialty, but we've got to have coffee too. I'm not calling it the Ice Cream Caffè for nothing, you know."

"Uncle Tiger, I have to tell you—I don't really like that name."

"Why? What's wrong with it?"

"Well, it sounds foolish." Actually it sounded infantile.

"What foolish? That's what it is—it's the Ice Cream Caffè," he repeated proudly. "Because we've got both, don't you see? We've got coffee *and* ice cream—the best in the world. That's the whole point—the name says what it is. Maybe I should call it 'The Best Ice Cream Caffè.' Why not? Sure." He liked the sound of that.

"I don't know, Uncle," I demurred, "I think you should think of something a bit more—"

"I'm not *talking* about that," he rasped. "What are you going to say—'sophisticated'? Screw that. This place already *is* sophisticated. You can see that before you even walk in. I'm not worried about *that*." (As things now stood, "this place" was still a derelict beer-supplies shop on Sepulveda Boulevard that needed a wrecking crew more than it needed an architect.)

If my uncle "knew architects," he also let it be known that he "knew business." He fancied he possessed an uncanny sense for deploying the talents of others: thus Mr. di Barnaba was the "flavorer" and, though he was never to assume this role, the maitre d'; Big Steve was the manager; Uncle himself was "owner" and idea-man; and Ed Richardson was, of course, the consultant.

"Richardson's drawing up the charter," he told me one day.

"Charter? Why do you need a charter? Are you a society?"

"What society? We have certain beliefs in common, and we have certain common goals," he explained, as if he were undertaking to found a small nation. "Besides, Richardson says it's a good idea."

"Yes—for him."

"Don't be so cynical. Richardson's an experienced business lawyer. He knows all about restaurant law, all the ins and outs. He's very important to us, don't kid yourself."

"Are you planning to get sued?"

"Don't be ridiculous—but don't you know about this business? It's full of crooks."

"I believe it."

"You've got to have a lawyer. People can do anything, they're capable of anything. You've got to have a lawyer. You've got to be prepared. I'm always telling you this, but you never listen. You don't know what goes on out there." He pointed to the garden. "It's a jungle, Peter. I've seen things . . . you can't imagine. Anyone can sue you—literally anyone. Some guy could walk into that garden and trip or have a heart attack and sue your pants off."

"Sue Grandma's pants off, you mean."

"Or yours—you never know. You're just a sitting duck unless you have a lawyer. And especially in the restaurant business. Say someone accuses you of poisoning him—what are you going to do? Say somebody chokes on his ice cream—I'm telling you, it happens, there's guys that do this for a living, they're all in it together and they back each other up. Crooks."

"They choke to death for the money?"

"I'm not saying to death, just enough to sue, they just choke and sue."

"But Uncle Tiger, no one's going to sue you if he swallows something the wrong way, or coughs a little. That's their fault."

"The hell they won't," he thundered. "I told you, they're all in it together, these guys. They'll say anything. They'll say I put a fish in there to make him choke. Anything for the money. It staggers the imagination."

"It certainly does."

"That's why I need a crack lawyer like Richardson to tear apart their lies. This whole thing is very complicated—you don't know. You've got to be very careful and go step by step, or you could have a real mess on your hands."

I suspected we already did.

But I never really thought it would happen; I never expected the fantasy to be carried through. It was, after all, just another of his wild schemes, an "idea" just like the rest. It wouldn't dare happen; it would be too crazy, too complicated. And in Culver City? Never.

One day toward the end of March, my uncle informed us that the opening was in a week. I was sure he would have a heart attack. According to him, he had about twenty meetings a day. How many people were involved? It seemed to me that only a month ago he had still been trying to find an architect. Perhaps he had decided to go ahead and design it himself. I can just see him drawing up the blueprints: "I'm not *talking* about that. We don't need a door there, we already got a window. Wiring? You're not listening! Building codes? Don't worry, I know Mike Salzman."

Opening night at the Ice Cream Caffè was like something you might have experienced in Naples on New Year's Eve, according to Mr. di Barnaba. The celebrants in that city—anyone, that is, who can boast worldly possessions to waste—throw furniture and kitchen appliances out of the windows. Ruffians of all ages carrying blank pistols shoot deafening miniature skyrockets in the air and at each other. The waiters in the restaurants festively drop their plates at midnight to participate in this sport. Whores, festooned with paper streamers, run through the streets, pursued by the Italian navy, and others. Everyone eats sweetmeats. The bay is illumined like a sparkling wedding cake by thousands of tiny explosions; it sounds like war. Nowhere is there anyone who is not celebrating. Restaurants, caffès, whorehouses and jails are filled with the roaring and singing. It is like a city released from siege. And indeed, that is what it is: a city released for a brief moment from the siege of time and its own sad history.

Imagine, then, this Naples transported to Culver City—or to one building in Culver City. And in that building imagine a constellation of weirdos in which Achekosa, Big Steve and Joseph Lorditch figure only as a minor star cluster—forms of life alien, unrecognizable, no doubt illegal, eccentrically orbiting in a brass-and-glass cage, emitting lethal doses of cosmic radiation.

170

We could barely get into the door that evening. "Make way, everyone," clamored the gruff, avuncular voice of welcome. "It's Mom and my nephew Peter. Here's Mr. Barnaba too, our special consultant. Mr. Barnaba, your flavors are going great guns. That prosciutto-and-melon ice was a great idea—it's all gone already. Make way, folks! Just remember, it's my family you're trampling. Right this way, Mom!"

"I say, you have a popular establishment tonight," exclaimed Grandma. "This looks very promising—or is it just the free food?"

"Oh yeah, we pack 'em in," answered my uncle. He turned to me. "Richardson's here. I want you to meet him. There's lot you two have to discuss."

"I don't believe it. You mean I actually get to see him, after all these months? I feel somehow as if I know him already."

But tonight Uncle could turn a deaf ear to my sarcasm. "Don't worry, you will, you will. He's watching for you."

"Uh-oh. I forgot to bring my wallet. Will he take a check?"

"Very funny, Mr. Weisenheimer." He turned to Mr. di Barnaba. "What about it, Mr. Barnaba? Does it get the Italian stamp of approval?"

Mr. di Barnaba looked about with gentle incredulity. "As far as that dubious imprimatur goes—it passes with flying colors, Joseph." He glanced at a woman wearing nothing but feathers.

"Lots of people for you to meet here tonight, Mr. Barnaba. Lots of people for you to know."

"Friends of yours?" asked Mr. di Barnaba.

My grandmother muttered, "Honestly, such people, I don't know where on earth . . ."

"Have some ice cream, have some ice cream," cheered my uncle to no one in particular, and disappeared.

"I say, where is the ice cream? Joseph? Oh really, such a crowd. . . ."

An Ivy League type—or rather a USC epigone of that school of dress: penny-loafers, flammable synthetic slacks, two-button tweed jacket—elbowed into me. "Some crowd, I'll say," he re-

marked, achieving in his tone a mysterious allusiveness, as if
we shared a common perspective on things. "Can't see the
forest for the trees."

Can't see the tweed for the acetate, I was about to reply—but
some presiding angel of charity in my heart bade me spare this
Beau Brummel of the Southland, and I smiled. His response
was, "Looking for the ice cream? I know what you mean. Go
for it." He said this last without thought, like a nervous tic. I
waited for him to pass me, then followed in his wake.

I noticed several attractive women in the crowd, gaudily
dressed. Opera music bellowed from speakers in the ceiling.
Some form of Italian was being spoken impatiently from behind the counter. I wondered where Uncle Tiger had found his
Italians. I doubted they were friends of Mr. di Barnaba. They
were probably lieutenants of Scroflone.

"So what's cooking now," said a voice near my knee. It was
the Javanese midget, blinking spasmodically, no doubt con-
founded by the delirium of having recognized someone. I was
impressed that he was able to distinguish my knees from
among all the others. It was probably an acquired skill, I
thought, like lipreading. He was spooning ice cream into his
agile round mouth.

"Hello, Mr. Achekosa. I see you're getting right down to
business."

"Oh sure, you know me. So what's cooking with you now."

Oh God, he was at it again. He sounded, when he spoke, as
if he were reading, at sight, a list of American idioms for which
there were no remote equivalents in his own language. He
blinked delightedly, endeavoring to squeeze every last iota of
fun out of his miserable joke. Did he try this on everyone, or
was I his only victim?

"Actually, I was just looking for the ice cream myself," I
answered.

"Mmmm, good, good," he exclaimed, raising the goblet of
ice cream towards me like a holy offering to the god of Height.
"Taste? Your uncle a genius. That ham ice cream is something

else." Of course he would think so. "Melon-and-ham ice cream —it's Italian. At least that's what your uncle say," he laughed.

Well, as the Italians say, *porco Dio*! I was curious to hear how Mr. di Barnaba could explain his role in this, but neither he nor his betrothed was anywhere in sight. Perhaps they had already been trampled.

Begging Achekosa's pardon, I left him and sidled as best I could up to the counter. I must say it was nicely done. The zinc covering glittered, reflecting tulip-shaped milk-glass light fixtures that bloomed from polished brass poles above. A massive cappuccino machine, baroque in complexity, with nozzles, tubes and levers sprouting from its inner works, hissed and rumbled at one end of the counter. A vast expanse of mirror on the wall behind the counter doubled the already formidable array of deep copper dishes running along its base. The dishes, holding the ice cream, were labeled with elegantly scripted placards: "Cioccolato," "Nocciola," "Panna," and, sure enough, the incredible "Prosciutto e melone." A hairy hand dipped into this last, and emerged with only the dripping remains.

"*Prosciutto e melone non c'è! Non c'è più! Mi scusi signorina ma non ne abbiamo!* There is no more!"

Groans of disappointment arose all around. "Now I'll never believe it," someone said. "I'm glad!" someone else said. "We'd probably have gotten trichinosis!"

That's the least of it, I thought to myself. I ordered a goblet of my favorite, hazelnut (or, as my grandmother would say, "filberts"). On the question of presentation they had not scrimped either; the goblets were cut crystal. I assumed half of them would be gone by the end of the evening. (I was taking one myself.) Nor had they cut corners in the production of the ice cream. At first spoonful the consistency was just right; and that taste of roasted hazelnuts coated my tongue in rich rhapsodic fantasy. . . . A dream of Italy melted in my mouth.

"Say now, take it easy, you know that stuff's expensive!" roared a voice in the crowd, followed by cetaceous chortles that

173

could only have issued from the Big Man himself. He cleaved through the crowd as if it were sea-foam, breached at the bar, and bellowed, in tune with the music: " *'Se quel guerrier io fossi . . .'* Wonderful stuff, eh? Nothing like good opera, and good food to go along with it—if I say so myself! Ha! What's that there? Hazelnut? My favorite—goes down like butter. And I should know, I eat a lot of the stuff—butter, I mean! Seriously, what do you think? A little crowded, eh? Well, they'll all be coming back, we hope. If you treat 'em right they'll always come back." He appeared to reflect on this. "Jeez, I hope they like opera. We're getting a string quartet next week—Joe tell you? Where is that bum anyway? Have you seen Richardson?"

"No—never in my life."

"Well, you'll know when you do. Enzo! *Dammi uno scoop di nocciola—no, due scoop!* My friend here's got the right idea. Where's your grandmother and her escort?"

"I came in with them, that's all I know."

He looked me up and down. "Well, you ought to keep better track of your sainted grandmother than that. You wouldn't want to lose her—none of us would." You can say that again, Big Man. "She's quite some lady." He paused. "I don't know about her escort, though. I'll tell you in confidence, Peter—" he came close "—I don't think he likes the way we work. He didn't like any of our flavors. The guy doesn't know the first thing about flavor coordination."

"I could have told you that."

"Well you should have—it would have saved us a lot of trouble. Remind me to tell you about it sometime. You're a writer—maybe you could do an article. Enzo! *Ma dov'è? Disgraziato, sbrigati! Ah finalmente*, Enzo. My ice cream boy Enzo's working on Italian time. I tried to tell them before they started work, I said, 'Everything's Italian, boys, except the time and the money.' Well, I'm glad they got at least one right. Listen, do me a favor—you happen to see anyone trying to pass *lire,* tell me about it. *Ciao*, chum!" He reared away, clutching his goblet as he furrowed the unstill waters around him.

Pocketing my goblet, I went in search of Grandma and Mr. di Barnaba, and on the way I had a chance to observe some of the guests. I saw a man with a fabulous mustache, whose eyes were not quite parallel, listening to a Mexican menu being recited by a very tan woman.

"Because I hope you like *cilantro*," said the woman.

"I do indeed," said the man.

I saw a woman silently crying as if she were overwhelmed by laughter, or laughing as if she were weeping. Her companion looked smugly on.

I saw double-knit in various attitudes of leisure.

I saw a little girl chanting mockingly in singsong, to the tune of "Twinkle Twinkle Little Star," "Why why why why why why why? Because . . . I . . . said . . . so." Her mother saw me watching, and looked embarrassed.

I heard a woman finish a sentence with the words, "Don is a beautiful person, for sure."

Framed gilt mirrors hung on two walls; white stucco *putti* climbed out from the spaces between. The floor was tessellated in black-and-white linoleum. The tables were marble, or a convincing synthetic facsimile, and set in wrought, twisted wire— reminiscent, to me, of the furniture at Wil Wright's. The chairs were fashioned to match, with wicker seats. Deep red banquettes ran along the walls under the mirrors. At one end of the room was an intimate alcove, where candlelight illuminated scenes by Piranesi.

And the ceiling—here was the *capolavoro*. There hung overhead a cloud of contorted *putti* in all imaginable poses of disportment—some homesick Italian's turgid conception of heaven diabolically fashioned in plaster. One stood in this room at one's own risk, feeling overhead the constant threat of crushing death under these *enfants terribles*. What had my uncle wrought? Had he been bamboozled by some senile, pederastic immigrant artificer of turgidity, grotesquely possessed by the ambitions of a Michelangelo—all the agony without the ecstasy? Whoever he was, this unsung demon had willfully colored in the eyes and rosy cheeks of the lads, to make them look more lifelike as they gamboled in chubby infantile torsion. Feet, elbows and buttocks protruded at impossible angles, just begging to be grasped and torn from their bodies before they tore off your head. If I had been at best indifferent to children before entering this room, my feelings had now resolved themselves in the negative as I stood under the claustrophobic nightmare. I realized it could not be my uncle's idea alone, but who could have conspired in such madness? I could well imagine what Mr. di Barnaba thought of it; yet undoubtedly my uncle had "consulted" him beforehand. Had he just stood by passively while the monstrosity was erected? Perhaps there was, after all, a cozy kitsch corner in that expansive heart of his.

He and my grandmother now appeared in the room, and came to stand beside me. "Really, he's gone all out on this one, hasn't he?" said my grandmother. "I must say I never expected such a . . . such an affair . . . and the people, the guests seem to like it, don't they?"

"It is a fantasy we are all trying to believe against our better instincts," observed Mr. di Barnaba as he squinted incredulously at the ceiling.

"Oh, I'm not sure it's such a fantasy," countered Grandma. "It looks very real to me."

"Oh, it is real. That is what is fantastic about it."

I whispered to Mr. di Barnaba, indicating overhead, "You mean you had no idea?"

"No idea, no idea at all. Of course, I saw the plans, but I did not believe them."

"Who'd he get to do it?"

"He ordered it."

"Ordered it? What are you talking about?"

"He ordered it from a plaster iconographer up in Daly City.

176

The man evidently has tons of such things in his warehouse."

"A plaster iconographer? You mean these were made to order, someone actually manufactures these things commercially?"

"Of course. My lad, 'There are stranger things in heaven and earth. . . .' And your uncle has dreamt of all of them. You underestimate his powers of 'research.' After all, haven't you heard of *Plaster Monthly*? Don't you subscribe to *American Iconographer*?"

"And who painted them?"

"Aha, for that I know many artistic Italians."

"And you played along?"

"Played? I beg your pardon, it was hard work. I had trouble even talking to the painters—they were Sicilian, and consequently terribly stubborn. Furthermore, they didn't like me. They would not communicate. They thought I was trying to trick them. They did not believe anyone would want this done. But I gather they were duly charmed by your uncle."

"But how did it all get done in such a short time?" I wondered. "The whole thing took barely a month."

"Your uncle had much good help." Mr. di Barnaba looked inscrutable.

"Scroflone?"

His eyes narrowed. "And others. Do you recognize most of the people here?" I did not. "There, you see. And there are many more whom you will never see. Some of them you would not even be able to imagine. Yes, my lad, business is a complicated proposition. But your uncle, I am beginning to realize, is skillful at this sort of thing. He knows very well how to bridge the gap of fantasy."

His words were full of rather melodramatic implications. I wondered how there could be others besides Scroflone. I had formed by now an almost fond conception of the Big Man, which I did not want belittled by the suggestion that he was not in fact top dog, but was answerable to others—who furthermore were not, I feared, liable to be concerned for my uncle.

177

Big Steve himself was not really dangerous, but perhaps the others were.

I asked my informed source, "And what about Richardson? I heard he was here—I still don't believe he really exists."

"Yes, in fact he does, I can assure you—if I can trust my own senses. I just saw him eating ice cream and talking with that little man—Arenusa, what's his name?"

"Achekosa?"

"Yes, who seems to love his ice cream. He was practically inhaling it."

"He loves pork, is what it is. By the way, have you tasted the melon-and-prosciutto—oh, that's right, I remember now, you don't like ice cream."

"No—but I invented that one." He smiled. "In fact, that's one of the reasons I can't eat it. It makes me nauseated to know what's inside. Yet it seems to have gone over well. I am pleased. 'No accounting for tastes,' as your uncle would say."

Grandma began to complain of the crowd, and Mr. di Barnaba agreed to leave after he had tasted the coffee. He whispered to me a last criticism:

"I wish they had selected better music. Well, I did what I could. I suppose Verdi is what's expected, but I really prefer Mozart. How unpatriotic of me, isn't it! *Don Giovanni* over and over, that is my idea of a celebration. *Notte e giorno faticar*," he hummed, and led my grandmother toward the counter.

I had turned to follow them when I saw someone squeezing his way into the *putti* room. He was noticeable for wearing the only down ski vest in the room. He had longish hair the color of margarine, sideburns and mustache a shade darker, a neck like a loin of meat, and assertively stupid, small eyes. I recognized Mike Peterson of Mariner's Village—the bully who had knocked me down at the salad bar. I told myself I would make it my business to stay away from him tonight, although we were in rather close quarters. I could not imagine why or how he came to be here. He did not appear to know anyone. He

178

had an uncomprehending yet petulant look set in that assemblage of crude squiggles that passed for a face—which seemed to me to have been designed by nature, or whoever fashions such monsters, as an aid in the extermination of Jews. Not that in Mike Peterson I could necessarily detect any signs of anti-Semitism, or even consciousness of the Jewish race. But whether or not he knew it, and whether or not he was ever to realize his natural calling, he had been born to harass them. It was written on his face. Anything else he could have done in life would have been beside the point.

He noticed me watching him. "Hey really good party," he said, quite friendly. (He pronounced it as "rully gud," hardly moving his lips when he spoke.) I nodded; I admit I was scared of him. If he pushed me into the cappuccino machine I could be scalded to death.

"Have you had the ice cream here it's rully gud."

"Yes I have, I had the hazelnut."

"Rully, go for it."

"Can I ask you, do you remember knocking me down?"

"What, man?"

"I said do you remember knocking me down under the salad bar at Davy Jones' Locker in Mariner's Village one evening not too long ago?"

"Wow. No. No man, not at all. I in no way remember. Somebody knocked you down?"

"Yes, I distinctly recollect, and I thought it was you. Perhaps I was mistaken."

"Must of been, 'cause I in no way remember you. I don't even know where that place is, I never go there. My brother lives there, but I don't go there at all."

"Funny," I mused, "I thought I saw you there."

"No way."

I asked for it now. "That *is* peculiar, because I seem to know your name. Your name is Mike Peterson."

He didn't like this at all. His upper lip seemed to swell in

179

offense; his eyes became slightly hooded. He assumed the sheepish, frustrated, impermeable look of a dense child confronted with thoughts.

"That's too bad, man, because you're gay," he finally decided loudly. "You're gay and you know it, and don't give me none of your shit, you little faggot. I could beat the queer puke right out of you now, so just shut up, you better shut up."

Now, although I am generally squeamish, courage does not desert me in a crisis. "Take it easy, Mike, you're attracting a crowd," I said. I don't think he liked my attitude.

"Little faggot."

"Now now, let's not make foolish accusations. I believe you're mistaken—perhaps you're a little confused yourself."

His eyes twitched and constricted like reptilian cloacae. "Outside. Now. I'll do you a favor, you little piece of shit."

"Go get some ice cream, Mike, before I decide to hurt you."

"Oh man," he sighed, almost with pleasure, "you don't know how bad you want it, you filthy little buttfucker." I almost had to laugh at his use of this word, which recalled to me the sixth-grade bathroom. Not that I wasn't trembling—I knew he wanted to kill me, and would have if he'd had a gun or knife. But he didn't, so he didn't touch me. You see, he was basically a coward.

By this time everyone in the *putti* room was looking on. One of the Italians came from behind the counter. "OK, *basta basta*, who're these guys, let's break it up to get out of here, come on come on come on—"

Peterson sent him flying. He grabbed him by the face and threw him up and away; little Enzo's back caught against an exposed limb of one of the *putti* and the impact brought them both crashing to the floor. There were screams and laughter. Guests huddled against the banquettes; they could not escape, since Peterson was barring the way. The opera music did not stop. "*Sempre libera . . .*" I was backing against the counter. Peterson, wheezing deeply, did not take his eyes from mine.

"Little faggot," he kept repeating, letting me know he wasn't through with me; he hadn't even started.

But before he could advance against me, a pair of silent, massive arms appeared from nowhere around his neck, lifting him up helpless in a full nelson; a silent, massive torso inched him around from behind. Peterson bucked several times, but it did no good; he was engulfed by leviathan flesh, which absorbed his strugglings as a jellyfish on the beach absorbs a thrown pebble. The flesh turned him toward the door and waddled him out. And I heard Big Steve in a soft, welcome, appeasing voice: "Let's take a walk outside, sport, where I can snap your nasty spine in peace and quiet."

"That crazy man, he broke a *bambino*," cried little Enzo, somehow unhurt, and already bringing out the broom and dustpan—implements evocative of his own mortal frangibility. I was still shaking. I felt, after all, somewhat to blame; in my own way I had provoked the monster, and into the bargain had been publicly declared a homosexual. I knew well the signs that he had misconstrued: a certain arch, haughty posture of mine in the face of insult or danger, and a snotty, derisive attitude of superiority, which are devices of some homosexuals. And so it could only look to observers in the room as if the preceding scene had been a rather overcompensatory rebuff to some homosexual advance on my part. I could not expect people to know, with even my limited experience of the fact, that Peterson was mistaken. I hoped Big Steve could finish him off outside; otherwise there was no way of knowing what further damage he might do to my reputation, and me. He might possibly pursue me into *Bon Vivant* magazine and ruin me there; he might even "reveal" that I was Mr. di Barnaba's aging catamite. It would clearly be better for all of us if Peterson were disposed of.

Unfortunately I could not count on this. Big Steve later told me he had taken the offender outside "to make sure he wouldn't come back. And when he walked away, he must've been feeling pretty sore. I would have liked to give him a heart punch, but then he would've died on me, and I don't need *that*." It must have been frustrating for Big Steve to have to restrain his heart punch; I know he would have given a good one.

My encounter with Peterson put a damper on the rest of the evening. I was about to leave the scene as unobtrusively as possible when my uncle's voice called out to me, "Where are you going? What's wrong?"

"I'm leaving. I've had enough for one evening."

"Wait a minute. We got rid of that guy. What was his problem, anyway?"

"Don't you remember? He was the guy who attacked me at the salad bar in the 'Locker Room.' "

"What? What are you talking about?" My uncle frowned, following me outside. "What do you mean?"

"That guy, Mike Peterson, the guy who pushed me under the table. Made a big scene, said he was trying to protect you. The night you wore the pink coat. Don't you remember?"

"Just wait a minute. Now how did he get here? You didn't invite him, did you?"

"Of course not. But he's got it in for me."

"Well, just hold on," said my uncle, trying to get a grasp on the situation. "Now if you didn't invite him, somebody else must've. . . ."

"Did you?" I realized this was not an impossibility. It was just his style to take a liking to someone like that, then to appear utterly surprised and disillusioned by the consequences.

But now he seemed truly shocked at my suggestion. "What do you think I am, crazy? That guy was a vandal, a criminal. You bet we're going to prosecute. He ought to be locked up. He could have killed little Enzo. He almost ruined my opening night." He paused, considering this. "Do you think he's following me?"

"Why would he be following you?"

"I remember now, I've seen him before," my uncle went on.

"He's no good—he's what Mom would call a 'vulgarian.' He's not the sort of person we want in our place. Where have I seen him?"

"I told you—the night we went to the 'Locker Room'—that crazy night—you probably don't remember anything about it. Fortunately for you—you were pretty wild."

But my uncle preferred not to acknowledge that evening. "Now listen. You better watch it. This joker, whoever he is, obviously has it in for you."

"That's what I just told you."

"I'm not talking about *that*. Now listen. We're going to have to protect you. You never know when this guy might show up again."

I protested, "But aren't you going to *do* anything—aren't you going to arrest him?"

My uncle's voice became tense. "Now just shut up and listen. We're taking care of that crumb and that's all there is to it. But you better watch out—you never know what could happen—he could have friends. Well," he answered himself, "we've got some friends too. We've got more. We've got friends you wouldn't believe. But just keep it under your hat. Don't tell Mom."

His manner was perplexing; he was not drunk, just very excited. The world of great possibilities had once again opened up before his eyes. What did he see? What didn't he see? Worldwide franchises perhaps, international intrigue, agents from Sheba Enterprises infiltrating the inner sanctum of ice cream technology . . .

"Uncle, just what is happening here?"

He looked childishly stubborn. "What do you mean?"

"I mean who is Big Steve, really, and why don't I ever see Richardson—"

"Richardson wants to meet you, he said so. He's a very busy man."

"And what does Mr. Achekosa have to do with this, and how did you get it all done so fast, and where the hell did you find those countermen, and that *putti* room—my God, that room, what's going on?" I was practically screaming; I was very upset. I felt we were all preparing for some hideous, ridiculous, altogether avoidable fate, the kind exemplified in "scoop" headlines: FREEZE BOGUS ICE CREAM RING: 27 DIE; or, UNCLE SUSPECT IN "FAT MAN" TERROR; or, GANGLAND GRANDMA LINK IN PORK-POISON DEATH. I could hear myself trying to explain, each explanation sounding less and less likely as I vainly tried to exculpate the family. My protestations of innocence played right into their hands: ("And this fat man, you say, this Mr. Scroflone, he was a friend of your grandmother's also, and came often to the house for 'tea'? He said he needed 'help' from your grandmother, and she, without hesitation, provided it?" "Yes, that is correct." "And you furthermore claim, Mr. Lorditch, that you never saw the putative 'lawyer,' Mr. Richardson—although you had often heard about him, even felt as if you knew him—and he in fact had also expressed a wish to meet you, yet this meeting never occurred?" And so on and so forth, unto the mercy of the court.) I had an acute sense of the "before" contrasted with the "after." "Before" being before Grandma had become implicated, before we were guilty by association—conspirators, swindlers, enemies of the people— when we were merely faithful customers at Scroflone's restaurant, supporters of the order; and the "after" proceeding rapidly from this, bringing upon us the recognition of our baser nature and our submission to it, our willful conspiracy of evil purpose and, worst of all, the inevitability of the "after," as I saw it now as if in retrospect—the grim truth that such people as we, criminals at heart, were meant for ignominious issue, it was beyond dispute, a law of nature, and we fit unwittingly into some ruthless greater wisdom. . . .

But my uncle remained apparently unperturbed. "Listen, what do you care? Stop asking so many questions—what does it matter? You've got to have friends, that's all I say. You saw how Big Steve stood by you." (And where were you, Uncle?)

"That's 'cause he's your friend—and he's my friend too. And friends can do stuff for you. Just remember that."

"I will. I'll remember all they did tonight. But tell me now, how are you going to protect me?"

"Just never you mind. It won't be that obvious. Leave it up to me."

"That's just what I'm worried about. What gives you the right to protect me? And don't I get to know about it? Did you ever think of asking me?"

"Listen now, don't play lawyer with me." He looked at me with affection in his tiring, watery eyes. "I'm your uncle, aren't I?"

I found out afterwards what had happened to Grandma and Mr. di Barnaba during the fracas. Unwilling to bear the crush at the counter, they had left to go for a walk down Sepulveda Boulevard—a street, as it happens, preeminently unsuited for walking, the sights being principally gas stations, commercial storefronts, industrial parking lots and, as background to this, like bobbing hobbyhorses, or those tireless drinking birds that are activated with a cup of water, the perpetual oil pumps that forest Culver City's brown hillocks. I don't know how far they walked, or how for that matter they managed to remain unmolested while I was inside the *putti* room in fear for my life. Credit it to that charmed impunity with which Grandma seems to have been blessed throughout all her travels and adventures.

When they returned, they found that much of interest had developed in the meantime.

"You were accosted!" cried Grandma. "Where is the man? He's a common criminal! Was he arrested? Why not? Where is Joseph? Does he know anything about this? What does he plan to do about it? Nothing, I'm sure. Where is he?"

My uncle was in back, talking with a group of men. Grandma walked briskly up to them.

185

"Joseph, what is the meaning of this? I hear Peter was accosted by a ruffian. This is disgraceful. What do you intend to do about it?"

"We're right on it, Mom. Here, I'd like you to meet some of my associates. Adam Feldman, Hunter Lee, this is my mother—"

"Delighted, I'm sure. Now I say, has this man been arrested, do you know who he is—"

"Yeah yeah, we already knew him from before," said my uncle, reluctantly, as if forced to acknowledge a familiar nuisance who had been dunning him persistently, the mention of whom now embarrassed him in front of his "associates."

"What? Knew him? You mean he was a friend of yours?"

"No, not a friend, just some jerk from the Village, the kind that hangs around—"

"And you let him 'hang around' in here, is that it, until he beat up your nephew—"

"He didn't beat him up, Mom—fortunately, he didn't. You weren't even here, you didn't see it—"

"I am not concerned with what I did or did not see, I've heard well enough what happened, and you ought to be ashamed at your conduct."

"*My* conduct? Look, Mom, this guy came in here, everyone thought he was just going to be peaceful and try out the ice cream—which we all have been doing, with great results, I think you might like to know," he put in, for the benefit of his "associates," who were now casting about uneasily for some possible pretext on which to excuse themselves from a sticky family argument.

"There was no way we knew what was coming," continued my uncle. "I think the guy was really crazy, he gave no indication that he was going to make trouble, and all of a sudden there was a scene. I think Peter was as surprised as anyone." He looked hopefully in my direction for support. But Grandma was not about to let him off the hook.

"No, not as surprised as I. I'm more than surprised, I'm

disgusted. Disgusted and disillusioned. And on your opening night—it's simply disgraceful."

My uncle's face drooped now with the particular type of shame that is a child's unspoken answer to the question, "Well, are you proud of yourself now?"—an expression conveying abject regret, recognition of his parents' moral superiority, and hatred of their authority: an expression understandable in a child of twelve, but thoroughly grotesque in a man of fifty-four.

"And what is that—what is that mess?" She pointed to Enzo behind them, sweeping together the remnants of the shattered *putto*; and Enzo, noting the reference to himself, laid aside his broom and came forward to my grandmother to adduce his own testimony:

"I got thrown into the ceiling. See where that broken plaster is? There used to be a statue and he take me and throw me like I was a ball on the ceiling. I would have broke my back. We got to get that guy, huh, Mr. Lorditch?"

"He threw you onto the ceiling?" My grandmother's attitude was that of a weary, disbelieving investigator who finds herself more and more caught up in the details of an incredible but worthless case.

"Yeah he take me and throw me up and I hit that statue and we both fell down."

"Well, are you all right? Do you have any breaks? This is terribly serious."

"Oh sure, I'm fine. I'm so lucky but I'm fine. But we got to get that guy before he does some more damage."

"Yes, it appears we do. But now I say, perhaps we had better get you a doctor, Mr. . . . ."

"Enzo."

"Mr. Ensor, perhaps you should get some X-rays taken, I don't like the sound of that at all."

"No, no, I'm OK, maybe I have some bruises tomorrow, that's all. I know how to roll with the punches—believe me I had lots of practice, I got used to it," he laughed.

"Well now, and Mr. Scroflone, where is he?" dogged the indefatigable octogenarian investigator. "Is he handling it? I certainly hope someone is taking command, or I will have to. One can clearly see that we have a mess on our hands." She turned sharply to her son. "I don't know how you always manage without fail to get yourself into these scrapes—although by now I suppose I should be used to it, since it's always I who have to pay. And I'm terribly sorry to have to say this in front of your friends—" she nodded to Feldman and Lee, still looking on— "but what other chance do I have to see you, you never call, and you don't want me to visit you, honestly, and what's more, I shouldn't know even then what's really going on. Not that I do now." She turned smartly on her heel and walked away from him. She came over to me.

"Now I say, Peter, no one seems to be in command here, it's such a pity, but really after all to be expected, considering the people involved. If you're going to do something, you've simply got to do it yourself, as my mother always said. I don't know where Mr. Scroflone is, I had meant to talk to him about this, but as usual I'll have to go ahead on my own. That's all right, I've become very good at that." She gave a bitter laugh. "Now I think it would be a good idea—wait, let's go outside, there are all sorts of ears in here. . . ." She drew me outside. "I think it would be a good idea if you had a bodyguard. I know what you're going to say, but I don't care, I've had too much difficulty in my too-long life, and I'm not about at this stage to risk my favorite and only grandson simply because of the selfishness of certain parties, I'm sure you know who I mean, who shall remain anonymous. . . ."

9

In this way I obtained a bodyguard. His name was Sergio. He was Chicano, born in the Barrio, and although I would have thought it unlikely, we soon succeeded in reaching an understanding.

Sergio seemed to know what he was doing. He was 225 pounds, stood six-two, and his chest was the width of a small car. His hands were the size of plates. He had a soft, mild voice, and spoke very slowly.

"Mr. Lorditch," he would say, almost apologetic, but determined to speak the truth, "I know you hate me followin' you around like this, but you know it's for your own good. Your uncle, he's mighty fond of you, he told me he hate to see anything happen to you. I told him, ain't no danger of that while I'm around. No, sir."

"That's OK, Sergio," I would answer, "I don't mind. It's someone to talk to, right?"

And really I didn't mind. Sergio made for interesting company. He had already done time for armed robbery, and up until we hired him from a federally funded agency representing the "socially reformed," he had been working as a guidance counselor for juvenile delinquents on Whittier Boulevard. He still checked in at the community center on his days off. I

189

suppose he could identify with these kids—although he had grown up tougher even than most of them—so that watching to see how they would turn out, if they would turn out at all, was a matter for him of retracing the course of his own coming of age, with all the breaks and pitfalls of that period of his life now dramatized, magnified, heroized perhaps, in his eyes, by the long, generous telescope of retroactive wisdom.

"Yeah," he would sigh, "I had some fine little criminals this week. Told some stories that'd make a sailor blush. You know I think they makin' 'em smarter than in my day—maybe not as tough, but smarter, and dirtier too. If I'd been as smart, maybe I wouldn't of ended up now where I am."

"You might have been a lot worse," I said. "I'd say you speak pretty well for yourself, Sergio."

"Maybe I do." He smiled. "I guess I'm gettin' my life in order now. I sure got enough to think about."

With a wife and four children to support, he had more than enough. I guessed that his wife worked also, though he never said. I knew that Sergio was not above moonlighting—sometimes as a security guard, sometimes as a bouncer—to pull in extra cash, which went for medical insurance premiums. One of the children, the youngest, still practically an infant, had had to have an operation for a herniated navel. ("That belly button just popped on him one day.") The eldest daughter had recently broken a leg. I offered to help him out with these expenses, but he refused. I think it was a matter of pride with him that his premiums were so high; he saw them as measurements of his inexhaustible patriarchal love and responsibility, for the privilege of exercising which no price was too great.

I often wondered, in view of the rather desperate excitement of events in his family, whether he was bored with his job with us. Nothing ever happened. He drove with me to the magazine offices, when I had to deliver an article; he drove with me to the Italian deli; he drove with me occasionally, when I met my uncle there, to Mariner's Village—the only place, if any, where

190

I needed protection. Sergio would follow a pace behind me until I persuaded him to stop that. But he persistently held doors for me, and was never first to enter the car. He accompanied me to the bank, and inside, where he stayed especially close. In restaurants, amid company, he was a silent force until spoken to; even then, his answers were exemplars of laconic fortitude. He was always very careful to show that he knew and valued a bodyguard's place. He took his job not only seriously, but honorifically. Yet there were occasional clues that he was a bit confused as to its purpose.

"You know, Peter," he said one day (I had prevailed upon him to stop calling me "Mr. Lorditch"), "sometimes I get the feeling I should be guardin' your uncle instead of you. Seems like he needs it more."

"I know what you mean, Sergio. But you realize it'd be a much more difficult job. In fact, it would be impossible."

"No kidding," he mused. "You know, I worry about your uncle. He's a kind man, but he's going to get himself hurt."

"What makes you say that?"

"Well, you see, he don't know his limits. He just does everything as much as he can. Like I say, he's a kind sort of person, he don't want to hurt nobody—but he's gonna end up hurtin' himself. In a way, I hope it's just himself—like, I mean, I hope it ain't anybody else big, 'cause they gonna hurt him worse. Much worse. That's what I'm mostly afraid of. I like your uncle a lot. He's got gold for a heart, but it's all covered over so no one can see."

The thought was touching and—from someone in his line of work—not a little disconcerting. "Do you think he's in danger, Sergio?"

"I ain't sayin' danger yet—though if he keep on doin' how he doin', there could be danger. It don't take much for danger to walk into his life right now. Door's wide open. I seen it happen like that before."

"Physical danger, Sergio?"

191

"No danger I ever seen that wasn't physical."

"Then perhaps you're right—we ought to take steps to protect him."

"But see, that's what I'm sayin'—you can't protect your uncle. He won't let you. Sometimes he's like a kid like that—I don't mean him no harm, it's just how I see it. You know the way a kid don't know himself what's good for him, he don't even know really what he want, and so he just goes snoopin' around and leave himself open to a lot of—you know, influences. And sometimes those influences they're not so good."

"Who do you think those influences are?"

"Oh, I don't wanna name no names. Could be anybody, you know, who wants somethin' out of him. And there enough people like that around."

"Do you think they would hurt him?"

"Could be, you never know. People when they want somethin' hard enough they could do anything to get that thing. I seen it happen before to worse men. But like I say, your uncle's biggest threat right now is himself. You got to keep him away from himself."

"But if he won't listen to anyone—"

Here Sergio gave a smile of compassionate resignation; he flexed his hands out in a gesture of helplessness. "Ain't nothin' you can do, is there? If he's gonna be that way, if he ain't gonna watch out for himself, now who else can? I mean, say I could be the best bodyguard in the world, but if he won't do his share—" He paused. "I mean, how you gonna protect someone who wants to destroy himself?"

He looked at me as if he expected an answer. Sergio cherished that bluntness of sincerity which, welcome and essential though it is at times, afflicts those who have just recently discovered the value of honesty—for whom the sensibility that informs an honest attitude was not until now familiar, had never been for them a prolonged burden of conscience, or even a passing concern. Sergio furthermore betrayed the zeal of the neophyte in psychological inquiry, who has just discovered that

192

one's weaknesses can actually be dominating forces, not only over oneself but over others—that people are strange creatures exhibiting wondrous peculiarities having nothing to do with nature or God. For all their novelty, these discoveries, I could sense, were already somewhat onerous to him; he didn't really understand or welcome them. And yet they were terribly pressing, they could not be ignored, in that they appeared to him as newfound truth.

"How you gonna do that?" he repeated. "I ain't learned that yet. That's something no bodyguard can do, I'm afraid. No bodyguard could guard your uncle."

"No, I guess not," I agreed. "Maybe it's better for both parties concerned."

He considered this. "I guess that's right. Sure wouldn't like for nothin' to happen to him, though."

"You're beginning to worry me," I said. "Do you happen to know of any specific threats?"

"Don't need no specific threats. Life's just one big general threat."

I laughed. "Well, that's the way I feel all the time."

"And look at you—you got protection."

I allowed that that was the case, but through no wish of my own.

Sergio went on, "What I mean is, your uncle, whatever he does, it's contributin' to somethin's gonna happen to him sooner or later. He don't necessarily have to go out and provoke somebody—just leave the door open and someone's gonna walk in."

He had a way of putting things. It came, I suppose, from the attitude of hard-boiled, though much concerned, pessimism of the "school of hard knocks." Sergio had lived among blacks, in and out of prison, and had clearly picked up from them both mannerisms of speech and a sureness of perspective on his fellowman. The result was somewhat as if Juvenal were speaking in the voice of Richard Pryor. Yet Sergio had a gentle manner all his own. With his build, to be sure, he could afford to be as gentle as he chose. But his assurance came from more than physical confidence; it came from that same sense of respect, that slightly mystified consideration for the individual that I had noted before in his attitude toward my uncle—a philosophy granting that people were frail things, subject to "influences," vulnerable, venial, ultimately unknowable; but that even if you could not know them, you had an obligation to protect them. It was, I suppose, the bodyguard philosophy of life.

Although Sergio knew his function, knew his "place," he was not wholly satisfied with the limitations therein. He was often frustrated, as fanatics are prone to be, when he found he was unable to accomplish all that was ideally possible in the realm of his profession. Sergio could not really accept that it had been given him to save not my uncle, but me. He was sure (and he was not alone in this) that my uncle's need was greater; the bodyguard's instincts, experience and theory all agreed in identifying Joseph Lorditch as a marked man. Why, then, was the bodyguard attached instead to this man's nephew? It was an insult to the profession.

"Truth is, your uncle is self-destructive," Sergio explained to me one day (apparently forgetting he had already pointed this out). He did not appear very comfortable, though, with the thought—it ran counter to the premise of a bodyguard, which operated on the assumption that people considered their bodies worth guarding. "Maybe I'll get my friend Ricardo to talk to him," he offered. "Ricardo and me, we're old buddies." Perhaps they were prison buddies.

"Maybe you'd better not, Sergio," I demurred. "It might get him worried. He's got enough on his mind right now."

"He sure does—that's his problem. We got to get that man to *relax*. I was figurin' maybe if he had someone around, he'd have more time to relax."

"No, I don't think so. I think it would just aggravate the problem."

"You mean make him more nervous. Well, if you say so. You

194

know your uncle better than I do. I was just thinkin' about his peace of mind, is all."

It was something to think about, although my uncle evidently did not bother himself too much about it. He would have thought a bodyguard for himself unnecessary and even ominous; as he saw it, he was surrounded by friends and associates—so what need for protection? Everyone was working for him, or at least with him—even those who did not know him. His numerous contacts were like benevolent, protective feelers, testing, in his interests, the outside world, which was not yet acquainted with his name. Perhaps indeed there were, lurking somewhere, forms of life hostile to his purpose; but these were only ugly, deformed creatures of darkness, obscure, venomous and useless things, harmless enough to him as long as he kept close to home.

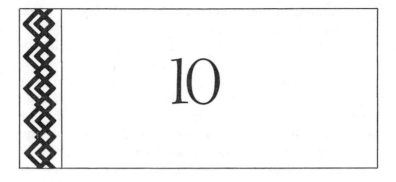

10

Trouble was, he didn't. Starting from Mariner's Village, he had waded out over his head. He could swim, but not all that well. Isolated from his own congenial hermetic ecology, he was flailing, grabbing at flotsam, at anything that might buoy him in his distress, preserve him from the lethal stonefish of wills not his own.

He turned for a while to creatures of the restaurant; yet these passing acquaintances afforded him little satisfaction. The idea of passing acquaintances was alien both to his vanity and his purpose. For, just as he would have found it impossible to conceive that anyone actually known by him was of only limited importance, neither did casual relationships do much to further the cause of "business." He was much less likely to extract favors from acquaintances than from friends—not to mention the incalculable beneficences raining from the hands of those he was fortunate enough to hold as "close personal friends." No, the idea of lukewarm relationships was repugnant to my uncle. Even an enemy could prove more useful than an acquaintance, through the possibility of cooperation that the enemy encouraged among his opponents, and the hope that he might some day be converted to the ranks of the righteous; but an acquaintance promised little excitement of movement in either direction, and as such, was useless.

This rather Machiavellian scheme of relationships was brought to the test in my uncle's dealings with people. He knew no one of or to whom he could not rave, for better or worse. He was pleased by what he imagined as the resultant clarity of position. "You've got to know where people stand," he explained to me. "It's better to know someone hates your guts, and you hate theirs, than to have to imagine what they might be thinking. I have no time for that crap." He swept "that crap" away with an impatient thrust of his arm. "You're only going to have so many friends in this life, Peter—you may as well get that straight from the start." (Was this in apparent contradiction to his belief that "you've got to have friends," and presumably as many as possible?) "There're only so many fresh fish in the sea—the rest of them stink. So don't you worry about the rest. Let 'em stink—what do you care? You got your own worries—you can't worry about other people's problems. Besides, it's not your business."

"No one ever said it was."

"Good. So that much is clear. As for the others, like I said, it's always better to know they don't like you. I want to know my enemies—I don't care who they are. Long as I can see their faces, they can't hurt me."

He persisted in these fallacies in spite of my objections. After all, what did I know? Besides, to him they were not false; as principles, he conceived that they had worked so far to his advantage. In them, I imagine, he found whatever strength, reason or solace he could derive from the underestimation of the world.

It was now the beginning of April. My uncle had much to worry about; he had an actual enterprise on his hands (although whether or not it was *in* his hands was debatable), but he was still answerable in theory to his mother—should she ever happen to be curious about the return on her investment.

197

One would reasonably expect that such responsibilities would sober him up, but they only caused him all the more desperately to seek an outlet from the grim aspect of his nemesis, reality. Sheba Enterprises, Inc., had begun to loom large now as a conceivable tax shelter for the limitless funds he imagined were pouring in from the restaurant. (Just how well it was really doing, no one yet knew—with the exception perhaps of Big Steve, who wasn't telling.)

His manias were worse than ever. He no longer seemed to experience hangovers; his waking hours were one long drunkenness. I guess he was also disconcerted by the thought, whenever that process fleetingly occurred, of his mother's upcoming marriage, now only weeks away. She would leave him; she would be another's; the other was imponderable; he was Old Europe; and he hadn't even helped in the restaurant, not really; he didn't care, and neither did she. Suspicion assailed him. It was no wonder he was the way he was. And yet, in spite of his limited capacities, he was at the Caffè every day from early in the afternoon till late at night, greeting, talking, raving—entertaining the multitude of customers patronizing in a constant flow, he said, until closing time at two.

And I have to report that the times I went in there, with Sergio close by my side, the place was well filled. I don't know where they came from, but it wasn't Culver City. It was a slick crowd, much neck jewelry and print clothing and Mercedeses—preponderantly Marina, a touch of Beverly Hills, even Baldwin Hills—for there were some fashionable blacks there who always ordered the most extravagant ice cream dishes, together with coffee and mixed drinks.

I was perplexed by my uncle's drinking, because I seldom saw him actually take a drink. I suspected he put it in his coffee, or perhaps he sneaked it behind the bar—although this sounded too sleazy, and too difficult, to suit him. I felt that with him it was more a state of consciousness, drunken consciousness; it was beside the point whether or not he aggravated the condition with a drink. Sergio took exception to this:

how could I say that, when it was obvious that the man was an alcoholic, and needed help? The first thing was that he should stop drinking, go to AA and learn what was the matter with him.

"Maybe it's your grandmother," he said. "I bet he feels overwhelmed by her, like he's pressured to succeed. Maybe also he's tryin' to challenge the image she's got of him."

I told him I thought he had begun to drink in college, with friends.

"Sure," he said, "it probably started way back then. I'm sure the pressure was on—she wanted him to be a lawyer, didn't she?"

"I don't think so. She never liked lawyers. She'd rather he was an alcoholic than a lawyer."

"Peter, that ain't funny. Your uncle's sick and an attitude like that isn't going to make him better."

"Neither is psychoanalyzing him," I said. Maybe I shouldn't have put it quite that way—but I've never had much respect for that vulgar discipline, especially when it presumes to apply to something ultimately beyond its grasp, like human suffering.

"Well, that's just great—you're just going to let him pickle himself, is that it? I can see why he drinks—'cause no one cares. And I bet your grandmother doesn't even know how much he drinks."

"Everybody knows, and cares, and we've been trying to do something about it for years. But it's not as easy as that. One doctor thought it was chemical, in the blood—something about not enough oxygen getting to the brain. Alcohol makes it worse, of course, but it isn't the prime cause. The prime cause is organic."

"And you don't think he'd be better off if he stopped drinking?"

"Of course he would, probably—but how can you tell him he can't have a beer? One beer? What can you tell him? No, because he has a mysterious disease?"

"Yes you can. You've got to. People with diabetes or hepati-

199

tis don't drink—not if they want to get better. You've got to make him understand."

"The sentiment is admirable, Sergio, but with my uncle there are certain things you have to preserve, certain illusions you can't totally destroy or you would destroy the man."

"But man, he's destroying himself."

"Maybe that's true—but in a way he doesn't have anything else. He doesn't have anything but his dreams, and finally one of those is coming true, it seems. It might be a very small dream, but for that reason it's coming true. And he believes in it very strongly, and he wants to follow it through."

"And you're just going to let him follow it right through and kill himself? Talk about killing with kindness—"

"It's not kindness that's killing him. As you said, it's himself, it's in his character. It's everything that he's built up and let crumble. It's his refusal to see himself. He sees everything in terms of himself, but he doesn't see himself. We could never make him believe he's sick. To him this is impossible. It would be too inconvenient, it would upset all his plans, it would threaten, maybe even stop the future. His life is lived in the future. I know that sounds terribly sick and misled to you, but if you look back, it's the way he has lived his whole life. And after all, looking forward to the future is not so sick; we all do it, in fact all successful businessmen—"

I stopped. I had begun to sound to myself like my grandmother. The truth, for those of us who are its victims, does not always reveal itself opportunely, in the service of necessity, or under the guidance of benevolence. It need not even be completely true; the sting of a half-truth is often painful enough. I experienced, in epiphanic brevity, a vision of how our family all resembled one another: our idiosyncrasies, indulged to the point where they acquired a sacred intractability, as if thereby setting a standard which we really did not expect to be able to keep, but the reminder of which we guarded always close to our hearts, as a sort of negative paragon of impracticality and delusion; our expectations, our common ideals of the highest and most improbable order, of a uniquely anachronistic stamp, doomed to disappointment and perpetual obsolescence in the real world—ideals of honor, of beneficence, pledged to eleemosynary compassion, to that perennial fight against what my grandmother typified in her language as "the wicked," what my uncle would have called "the others," "other people," threats to his world, his field of operations, which Mr. di Barnaba contemned as "modernity," and which I in my snobbery passed off as the "vulgar"; our conceit of superiority, often disguised as a false humility, a sort of moral *noblesse oblige* of character, by which the rest of the unfortunate world must somehow benefit by suffering under, yet without ever really understanding why; our championing, by the same token, of the underdog—midgets, German cripples and noble Italian indigents, and our generous inclusion of them in our world; our never-ending battle against the cruel forces of reason, always scorned by us as "mere reason," the last refuge of those less blessed than we in tradition, less abounding in idiosyncrasy; not to mention the mild strain of madness that ran through the family and seemed to have reached its fullest expression in my uncle. All these things, our common traits, passed like coded shibboleths of a vanished people through my mind, baffling me with their obscure language with which I was yet so familiar— for it was my own.

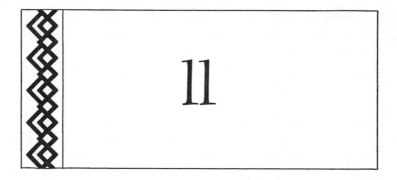

This brings us, by way of somewhat sad reflection, up to the happy present, and my meeting with the rabbi of Beth Israel to arrange the details of the wedding. Actually our encounter was less felicitous than it might have been, because Sergio insisted on accompanying me. "You never know what fanatic types could be hanging around there," he warned me. And who is to say—perhaps he was right; at any rate I introduced him as one of my grandmother's executors.

Rabbi Medford, we learned through the same introduction, was also the "executive director" of the temple, which was really, he explained, a "temple foundation." "We are a very powerful and benevolent organization," the rabbi informed me.

Medford brought us into a room where all the lights were recessed into the ceiling. Their beams projected onto the walls, illuminating mounted and lacquered documents originating from the mayor, the president, and various "honorary" organizations and committees. (Most of these documents were of the type beginning "Whereas . . ." continuing with a litany of the rabbi's attributes and accomplishments, and concluding, "Therefore . . .") Displayed with these were photographs of the holy shrines of Judaism and Diaspora—the Wailing Wall, the Old Synagogue in Prague, a teeming street in some ghetto; reproductions of art masterpieces—Chagall's Wedding and Temple Windows, and his painting *The Town and I*; and lesser works—a palette-knife painting of an old bearded Jew laying *teffillin*, another of a Jew weeping against a turbulent carmine background. Thumbtacked onto a cork bulletin board were a child's crayon drawings.

The rabbi's desk was sparse and orderly; the few objects on it were indeed of the "executive" type, austere yet trendy: a digital thermometer; a transparent, cubical, magnetic paper-clip dispenser; a black, concave pencil tray holding several colored pencils; a cassette player in a perforated black leather case; and on top of this a pink rubber elephant.

"So you're going to marry?" began the rabbi, glancing inquiringly back and forth between me and Sergio.

"No, it's not me, it's my grandmother," I answered.

"Your grandmother?" Now the rabbi leaned forward. "Forgive me for asking, but she must be . . ." He searched diplomatically, but could come up with nothing suitable. "This is not her first marriage, I take it?"

"No, she has been married twice before. She is eighty-one. I wanted to bring her, but she thought it would not be in good taste."

"Good taste? What do you mean?"

"Oh, I don't know, that was her phrase. She thought I should talk to you first. She's a rather shy lady."

"She can't be too shy, to be getting married at—what did you say it was, eighty-one?" He looked at the "executor," as if for official confirmation of this fact. Sergio pursed his lips, and nodded officially.

"Rabbi," I said, "she asked me to talk with you about the possibility of holding the wedding here, in Temple Beth Israel." I was surprised at the strange, deferential tone in my voice.

"Is she a member of our congregation?" asked the rabbi.

"No, she isn't. In fact she's from New York. She's visiting out here." I don't really know why I lied, perhaps to avoid the complications of a truer explanation.

"Visiting? And she decides to get married?"

"Well no, she didn't just decide. She'd been considering it for some time. I suppose now seemed as good a time as any. I mean, she had planned it; it was just a question of when and where." I was conscious of omitting much, for the sake again of what the woman in question would call "good taste."

But the rabbi was becoming interested. "You mean she came all the way out here to get married?"

"Yes and no. I mean, she didn't plan it, it just worked out that way."

"But you said she did plan it. You just said that, didn't you?"

"Oh yes. The wedding, yes. The general idea of the wedding she had in mind. She just hadn't considered certain specifics—location and date, I mean. She's eighty-one," I reminded him. He was looking suspicious, but curious.

"Now Mr. Lorditch, your grandmother is beginning to intrigue me," he said. "It's a pity I haven't yet met her—I would like to do so as soon as possible. It would make me a little more comfortable with the whole situation. I'm sure you must realize that such an arrangement we don't see every day. She seems—she must be a woman of great spirit."

"Yes she is—and great determination," I added.

"Yes," repeated the rabbi, folding his hands before him, and pausing, as if to let the air settle before his next question. "And the groom?"

"The groom?"

"You do know the groom, I hope, Mr. Lorditch?"

"Of course I know . . . Mr. di Barnaba."

"Mr. di Barnaba?"

Sarcasm was now detectable in his voice—and the ensuing silence almost comical. I said, "The groom is a family friend we've known for years."

"Permit me to ask, Mr. Lorditch, how old is the groom?"

What did he expect me to say—twenty-five? "Close to my grandmother's age, I'm sure," I replied coolly. "I've never asked. Both parties are of a certain age, I'm sure you'll agree, Rabbi."

"And Mr. di Barnaba is a converted Jew, I take it."

"No he isn't. Come to think of it, I don't think he is a Catholic either." But my purpose was not to sabotage my grandmother's wedding, and I added, more softly, "That is, Rabbi, I'm sure he would opt for any ceremony my grandmother wanted. He's a very reasonable man, and has left the decision entirely up to her. And she has decided most definitely in favor of a Jewish ceremony. She is a religious woman," I assured him solemnly.

"And yet she is marrying a non-Jew. An elderly woman. All very confusing, very confusing," the rabbi mused, rubbing his neatly cropped beard, as if about to enter into a state of Talmudic reflection. Which was as it should be, for my grandmother is an intricate text, legible to few, if any. The pious Medford, at least, was never to read her. All the better—I'm sure he wouldn't have liked what he found. A daughter of the Jewish people yet!

I began my pitch again. "My grandmother wants very much to be married in your temple, Rabbi. If it is a problem that Mr. di Barnaba is not Jewish, I can assure you he is willing to convert."

"It is not only if *he* is willing to convert, Mr. Lorditch." The rabbi smiled a bit wearily. "This is a two-way street, you know. It also depends on whether *we* are willing to have him. Do you happen to know whether he is thinking seriously about conversion? From your tone I think he is not. It is hard enough to be a Jew; it is even harder to become one—and when, as you have suggested, he has no particular religious convictions. Many people would say, 'Why would you want to do such a thing?' The important thing is whether the man is truly sincere in his heart." The rabbi leaned forward and clenched his hands more firmly together. Evidently he had reached a crucial point. Now he enunciated each word, and for the first time I noticed he had quite a Brownsville accent—at least what I conceived a Brownsville accent to be: "Mr. Lorditch, you cannot play Russian roulé [*sic*] with religion."

If I had been in doubt of it before, I was now certain that Rabbi Medford lacked the light touch. I pretended to ponder this grave, mispronounced truth for a suitable interval, and then, when I had been thoroughly chastened, I meekly answered (a meekness, for the record, solely in the interests of my grandmother), "I understand, Rabbi, I understand."

The meekness was just the right ploy. The rabbi concluded generously, "But I would like to help you and your grandmother. I want very much to see this marriage, and even to instruct the groom, if he wishes to convert—"

"You mean, then, that conversion is obligatory?"

"No, not obligatory. But I think the groom should know what he is doing, don't you?"

An admirable sentiment—as if such a knowledge were possible in our family!

"But I can't help feeling," added the rabbi, "that I must know more about your grandmother. Why don't you bring her to me—let's see . . ." He took a small black ring binder—"The Year at a Glance"—from his desk and flipped through it. "Next Tuesday. We can have a nice talk. She can bring Mr. Barabbas, if she likes."

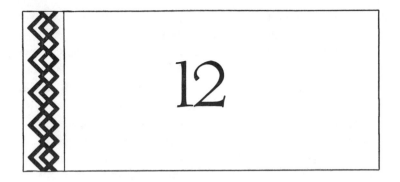

12

On the morning of her wedding, my grandmother was up very early. I could hear her rummaging in the kitchen, puttering through the living room, and the sounds of something—God knows what—being dragged over the carpets. I had awoken early myself, as if from a disturbing dream; but I could remember nothing, and just lay there for a while, feeling slightly apprehensive. Then it occurred to me why; it was the day my grandmother was to be married. This was suddenly a shocking thought to me. Was she actually going through with it, would the act be done today?

Yes, it was finally May 11. Morning fog, not uncommon for that time of year, was rolling in from the sea, flowing into the canyon, creeping up the hillside to the top of our hedgerows. I have always felt a certain security in fog. Perhaps it is in the light it casts: a protective background softness, like the undercoat of an old painting, embalmed, mute—yet, in its discretion of color, richly declarative of the mastery of hidden technique. Or perhaps in fog is my romanticized ideal of England—its insular placidity, its endurance. Fog seems to me the natural privilege and spiritual expression of that brave nation. Or maybe it is simply that fog causes me to experience the delight of the unexpected; I wake, and it is there, like snow—another one of those romanticized elements the notion of which I have rarely had the opportunity to compare with experience. For fog is an event to us in the Southland. It appears on only a few days in May or June; and when it does, it is such an assertion of nature that one looks on it with the same awe as at the appearance, in these parts, of thunderheads, lightning, or hail.

I lay there then, with my fog and my thoughts, listening to the stirrings in the house. She had probably been up half the night, worrying and fidgeting. Finally I threw on a robe and went out to the living room. There she was, wandering about in her slip, holding a crepitating transistor radio in one hand. Her hair was in disarray. She looked at me with a vague, absent-minded grimace.

"You're not going like that, are you?" Her voice was weak and cracked.

"Of course not. Have you been up all night? Put on a robe at least, it's chilly, you might catch cold."

"I'm afraid my radio is broken again," she answered.

"Well, it's time we got you a new one. A wedding present."

At the mention of the word, her eyes rolled up and she growled through her teeth—which she had not neglected to install, even this early in the day.

"Grandma, you really ought to put on a robe, it's not sensible—"

"Yes yes yes, well I've got to make breakfast now, and where's Paul, he said he would be getting up early today. Honestly, I don't think he understands a word I say anymore, I'm afraid he's becoming senile—"

"Oh, he'll be out. Remember, he's got to take Mr. di Barnaba over to the temple."

"Yes yes, Mr. di Barnaba." (She seemed vaguely to remember the name.)

"Let me make you breakfast," I volunteered, all generosity today.

"No no no, you ought to get dressed yourself. I'll make what I usually have, thank you, I prefer that anyway." She was referring to that unconscionable promiscuous sludge of cottage cheese, jam and whatever leftovers there were—and there always were—wiped onto crackers or bread, the staler the better. I chose not to be in the room when she ate this food.

I went to rouse Paul. Knocking at the door to the den where he now slept, I heard, coming from within, the familiar imprecation "Gottdammit." Paul, I should mention, had recently taken it into his head that our house was haunted—although somehow he was the only one who noticed this. From the sound of his displeasure this morning, I assumed that Mrs. Wheeler, the deceased wife of a former employer of his, and his current visitant, had given him a rough night. Paul's theory was that Mrs. Wheeler was jealous of Grandma.

"Paul, are you up?"

"Ya ya ya, just give me a moment here when I fix everything once. This damn fog don't give you no chance to see nothing in here. Ach, I sure hope it burns off so we can see what we're doing." He groaned. "What a crummy day." This last comment was probably meant to be overheard by Grandma. Fortunately she was in the kitchen.

"Remember, Paul, Mr. di Barnaba should be at the temple as soon as you can pick him up." (Mr. di Barnaba wanted to go over one last time with Rabbi Medford certain details of the ceremony.)

"How soon is that," Paul snapped back. "Ya ya, I know how soon Mr. Barnaba he talking about—not so soon—at ten o'clock he gets up. Well that's okey-dokey with me, I got lots to do today."

"Well, I'm going to get dressed," I said. "Grandma's having her breakfast. Make sure she has all her clothes laid out for her—the ones she chose yesterday, remember?"

He grunted. I guessed he was now strapping on his leg.

I went back to my room to shower and dress. It had grown lighter outside, but the fog was still thick. Lights were glowing faintly still across the canyon; and on the enormous apartment building straddling the cliff, bright lights beamed through the fog onto the pillars of the central parking structure, in an eerie configuration that looked like a spaceship about to take off. I heard a lone dog barking in the canyon: it sounded muffled and plaintive, like an omen.

I had chosen for the wedding a white suit, white shoes and a bright red tie. Grandma had said she wanted me to wear clothes that looked gay.

Soon Paul was at my door. "I'm ready to go for Mr. di Barnaba now—you better make sure Mrs. Samuels is ready, I think she is feeling nervous. Calm her down please when I'll be back."

"I'll try," I said. "And you remember where the temple is? Wilshire and Crescent Heights."

"Ya ya, no problem, I got it all stored up here." Paul tapped his skull, indicating the repository of knowledge. I remembered he used to have a head of black hair; but now it was a mottled silver, and thinning over certain bony spots, which stood out with a nervous, angular effect, suggesting the result of fruitless years of misguided intellectual inquiry—which in Paul's case was especially alarming, since his talents certainly were not of a cerebral nature. Yet Paul's brain, when it was unoccupied (which was increasingly rarely) by ghosts and *volkische* nostrums from the Old Country, was still quite keen when it had to be; but Grandma no longer gave him credit for this, and chose to remark only on his more peculiar ideas, which were to her contemptible. In Paul's defense I ought to say that some of Grandma's own superstitions were equally outlandish, though they did not appear to her so much as even questionable. For example: She always slept facing north, careful not to have placed her shoes anywhere above the level of her head. If she gave any sharp object as a gift, she also gave a penny along with it. She placed a dried green bean underneath her favorite chair. And in a little toy safe she kept sandwiches, just in case she should suddenly find herself destitute, with nothing to eat. But I think she had forgotten about the sandwiches, and they were not exactly edible. Yet in spite of all this, she wanted no part of Paul's superstitions. Hers were, after all, hers—grounded in her tradition, validated by her experience, sanctified by her continual practice, and—as far as that went—more "sensible," in other words, more comprehensible to her. Whereas Paul's were alien—German, not Jewish.

Paul, on his way out now, stopped in the doorway. "I had me a bad night last night," he sighed. "Them ghosts . . ."

"Mrs. Wheeler again?"

"I don't know who was there, but they sure was makin' one hell of a racket."

"Maybe you were frightened by the fog."

He resented the imputation of what he would have called "sissiness." "That was sure no fog what was makin' *that* ruckus." (Paul's language, in syntax and vocabulary, sometimes showed the influence of his beloved Westerns.)

"Well, I suppose Mrs. Wheeler is back again," I said. "Taffy was probably with her." (Taffy was Mrs. Wheeler's cocker spaniel, who, according to Paul's account, had died in bed with her.)

"I don't know about no Taffy," Paul said with a sour, tired look that bespoke his weariness of the dead and their pets. "But whatever it was, they sure kept me up all night. And now I got a wedding to plan."

This, of course, was a slight exaggeration—the planning stage was over, but it was clear that Paul, in spite of the inconvenience involved, would have liked to have had more of a hand in the tactical preparations. Not that he did not fundamentally and repeatedly hold that a woman of my grandmother's age and experience should remain a widow. This was the respectable thing to do. My grandmother might even have agreed with this view, and perhaps on some theoretical level she did. I would have found it not at all surprising to hear her say, with characteristic firmness of axiom, that older women—especially of a *certain age*—do not marry younger men, of whatever age—and *especially* younger Italian men, and *quite especially* if they are charming, urbane and still handsome. No, the woman who made such a choice would be, in Grandma's opinion, not a very *nice* person. Meaning: she would show herself as a woman lacking in discrimination, discretion and basic modesty—a woman of a certain ostentatious vanity, with a taste for piquancy bordering on the vulgar; a woman, in short, of a rather common mold. Clearly many principles in my grandmother's cosmology of morals opposed such a marriage, and the woman who would make it. Yet the woman was herself.

"Oh, and Paul, did you double-check with the caterers?" I called after him. "They're supposed to deliver at Mariner's Village at noon."

"No, well, you got to do that, Mr. Lorditch. They not opening till nine. I told them already once what time, and I said we'd call back today just to double-check. But you got to wait now till nine."

"All right, all right. Drive carefully."

I came back inside and found Grandma gone from the dining room table. Crumbs and smears of her makeshift breakfast were left on her plate. She was out on the patio, still in her slip.

"Grandma, come inside! You'll catch cold out there! You've got to get ready now, come inside! It's almost eight."

She smiled at me with a look of sublime oblivion. Was she losing it now, of all times? What if she suddenly forgot who Mr. di Barnaba was? I realized she would probably go ahead and marry him anyway, out of a polite fear of embarrassing him.

She made no move toward me, but turned and looked up into the jacaranda tree that overhung the patio. "Do you see our lovely parrot? Sssh, don't disturb him."

I whispered, "Grandma! Come inside!"

But she repeated, "See the parrot, pretty polly parrot? I heard him talking just now."

By this time I was quite annoyed; I stepped over to bring her inside, but she was adamant, she wouldn't budge. She just kept staring up into the tree, whose upper branches were obscured by fog. I looked up to where she seemed to be looking, and saw

212

a blotch of red. It appeared to be moving back and forth. Suddenly it uttered a shrill cry, like a baby's.

"Hear him?" said Grandma, pleased. "Pretty polly." Two squawks answered her, and the red blotch moved down a branch. Then, a liquid warble that sounded like a broken recording of reveille.

"That is my friend, the pretty polly," Grandma explained. "He is a wonderful singer, isn't he?"

It sounded undoubtedly like a parrot. But how could it be? Where had it come from? It was all alone in the tree, but it seemed quite at home. It was certainly not shy. But then it had no right to be—it was loud, and very red. It was apparently fond of Grandma, and playing up to her. She seemed to see nothing unusual in any of this.

"How did it get here?" I asked. "How long has it been here?"

"Oh, this is my friend," she answered. "We've known each other a long time, haven't we, polly?" The bird emitted another infantile shriek. "Yes indeed. Now don't get excited, we're right here." Then she bent down and, reaching behind one of the flowerpots on the ground, brought forth a can filled with birdseed. She scattered some of the seed over the patio. "There, there, come and feed."

"Grandma, what is this? How long have you been doing this? Why didn't you tell me before about this bird?"

"Why should I tell?" she said mildly. "This is my friend— he's going to bring me luck today. Look, he sees the food. My friend polly, we've been friends for a long time now, haven't we, red bird?"

The bird plopped down onto the patio, not far from us. It was a large bird, larger than any pet parrot I had seen, and it walked unsteadily—pigeon-toed, if you will. It waddled up to the grains and pecked at them, clearly uninhibited by our presence.

Grandma, watching the parrot, looked touched. For a moment I wondered if she had lost her reason. Certainly the picture she presented was one of almost mythical senility: old lady wearing only a slip, standing on the patio holding a can of birdseed, raptly watching her friend, a large red parrot. This woman was to be married in a matter of hours!

"Grandma, you've got to get dressed now," I said sharply. "Paul has already left to take Mr. di Barnaba to the temple. It's getting late."

At the mention of Mr. di Barnaba, she seemed to snap back. "Yes yes," she said almost wearily, "I'll get dressed now. And you, you're done up rather nicely today—for a change. I can't think I am the cause of such a special event. It must be for a young lady. Goodbye, my friend," said Grandma to the parrot, who had stopped pecking and was watching us now. "Perhaps I shall see you again sometime."

For some reason this struck me as a strange thing for her to say. I took the birdseed from her, placed it back behind the flowerpot, and led her inside.

She had chosen to wear, for her wedding, a simple blue suit with bonnet to match. She had considered pinning a brooch to her lapel, but as the one she had in mind, a penguin, was a gift from her late husband Albert, she decided against it. It would not be in good taste today.

"Do me up in back, will you, my dear?" she asked me. "Am I too gaudy-looking?"

"Not at all—you could never be that," I reassured her. "You're quite conservative."

"Do you think Mr. di Barnaba will approve? Oh, I suppose he'll be dressed to the nines. . . ."

"Grandma, he'll be delighted. You know anything you do is fine with him."

"Oh, I wish I could be sure of that." She hesitated. "I am never sure."

"Hold still, I have to get this hook."

"Yes yes, and my hair, is it all in place? I have such a mop—"

"It's fine. Hold still."

She gave a long, distracted sigh. I hoped she wouldn't fidget like this during the ceremony. After all, she'd been through two of them already; she might get bored. And Rabbi Medford certainly wouldn't help, with his dreary, high-handed seriousness. One might well be impatient to get through it all and on to the reception.

It was to be held in Mariner's Village. My uncle had already "set it up." That things had been allowed to develop unchecked in this direction was partly my fault, I admit, since I had been put at least nominally "in charge" of the wedding arrangements; although I must admit also that I was intrigued by the frightening possibilities in the very idea of my uncle's "planning," and I was looking forward to this spectacle with a sort of morbid curiosity. Festivities (in the wording of the invitation) would center on the Schooner Lounge, by the swimming pool (which was actually only the largest of four swimming pools in the Village). The "lounge" was really nothing of the sort; with a five-hundred-person capacity, it was more the size of a ballroom, including a bar, buffet section, sitting and dancing areas, and "gaming rooms" (backgammon, pool and a miniature bowling alley) in the back. The whole place rented for fifteen hundred a day—terms which, my uncle emphatically hoped, would be concealed from the bride-to-be. This price did not include the cost of the catering, which was to be provided by Pheasants 'n' Things of Beverly Hills. The owner of this establishment, needless to say, was a friend of Scroflone's; but whether our Italian connection had exerted himself here to effect any reduction in the horrific price was unclear.

And then there was the band. Grandma had said she wanted a "nice traditional" band. My uncle and I had been to see several agencies, and had paged through countless folders advertising the services of the Qiana generation. They all looked—and, I guessed, sounded—the same to me, and in the end I left it up to him. I was curious to see what he had finally come up with—no doubt some hideous, half-circumcised cross between the Zimmel Brothers and Wayne Newton, singing God only knows what kind of music ("Lublin on My Mind"?).

I was also curious to see where the hundreds of people

needed to fill the place would come from. My grandmother, while she was well known in all the tea shops and delis of Santa Monica, did not exactly command a cult following. She could be expected to draw about twenty, tops. Mr. di Barnaba's case was similar. Although he had lived in the Pacific Palisades for a number of years, I doubted that he had any close friends. He displayed an almost British reserve in company. As for me, I had invited only a couple of people from the magazine, to taste the food. It was clear that the majority of the guests—and a sizeable majority it would have to be—would come from my uncle's crowd.

These speculations occupied me as I fiddled with Grandma's collar-hooks. When I had finally got the top hook threaded through its loop, she pulled away and examined herself in the mirror. She was concerned about her hair.

"Oh, what a mess, it's sticking out at the sides. I'll have to have a larger bonnet, but then it won't match—oh, what'll I do? And it's already so late. . . ."

"Relax, Grandma, it isn't eight-thirty yet. Just take your time. Your hair looks just fine. I think the bonnet is perfect."

"No it's not," she snapped. "It's not perfect at all. I look like a hag." She plucked out the hatpin and flung the bonnet on the bed. Then she realized what she had done. "Oh, what am I thinking of!" she cried, retrieving the article of bad luck. "You see how I am coming apart!"

"You are not. Please just relax. I want you to relax and fix your hair."

"Yes yes, my hair . . . my hair is such a mess . . . a French twist, that's what I'll do with it. . . ." She began to wind her hair and fix it on her head. But her bony fingers fluttered about without doing much good, and soon she was quite exasperated. "Oh, I'll never get it right," she moaned. "I'm just a mess, a mess, I'm in no shape to take a husband, I pity the poor man. . . ." I tried to reassure her, but she wasn't listening. Her mind was on the struggle with her hair (she was probably trying to duplicate a hairdo of the twenties, which she couldn't

216

quite remember). Suddenly she burst out with a short laugh: "Perhaps I should go as a Chinaman, with a cap on top and my hair down behind."

"That's a terrific idea, Grandma, but I'm not sure you look the part."

"Inscrutable, yes . . ." she muttered. "Well, I could use a little of that. I'm a sucker, as it is." She took a hairpin and stuck it into the arrangement on top of her head. On top of this she fixed the bonnet.

"That's that, and I'm not worrying anymore," she declared. She dusted her nose with a powder puff, then rubbed her hands vigorously. "Impossible things," she said. "They don't obey me any more." She looked at them thoughtfully for a moment. "They don't deserve a ring," she said. "By the way, did you ring up the caterers?"

"Paul said they wouldn't be open until nine, and we should call them then and make sure."

"Nine? Why that's almost time for the wedding—oh, what does he know, I can't trust him with anything—"

"He said he had already talked with them."

"Talk talk talk, yes, he's very good at that, I know. That and fifty cents will get you a ride on the subway. He did go to pick up Mr. di Barnaba, you say?"

"Yes, he'll be back at nine."

"Well that will be none too soon—my word, we've got to be there early to prepare, I told the rabbi . . . and the caterers, where are they? . . ."

"Relax, Grandma. I told you, we'll call them before we leave. And besides, they don't deliver until twelve-thirty."

"Did you see about the flowers?" Grandma asked.

"Yes yes, that's all fixed. All you have to do now is get married."

"Yes," said Grandma, "though I was worried for a while that I'd have to get married without you."

I spoke up in my own defense. "Now wait a minute, you see how early I'm up today. How could I miss such a spectacle?"

217

"Oh yes, a spectacle indeed . . . well, I do hope at least it is *not* a circus."

"Don't worry, Grandma—and even if it is, you'll be the central attraction."

"Thank you very much."

"Grandma," I said, "your bonnet is crooked."

But, holding her hands to her bonnet defensively, she moved swiftly out of reach. "That's all right, I don't need any more redecorating. I'm too old for that. Such vanity is silly and unnecessary for someone of my position in life," she intoned—and turned to reexamine herself in the mirror. "Now I was going to have my eyeglasses fixed, you know they don't work at all, and now it's too late, I can't even find them, what am I going to do, the rabbi, I won't be able to see a thing, stupid, stupid woman, wicked. . . ."

"But you can see all right, Grandma—you just saw the parrot."

"No I didn't—not really," she confessed.

"What do you mean? You pointed him out to me—you knew just where he was."

"Well, I heard him, and I could see the outlines, and there's really no mistaking him—it's the unfamiliar I have trouble with."

"The unfamiliar? But you know everybody, Mr. di Barnaba is familiar, and the rabbi is familiar, you've met him, and we'll all be there—"

"Oh, but that's different," she went on, "it's an unfamiliar surrounding. I don't really like that temple at all—"

"But you wanted to have the wedding there. You chose it."

"Well, it was the only one I could think of. There aren't so many here. After all, this is not New York."

"But Grandma, there are other temples. You chose that one—I thought you liked it."

"Oh, it doesn't really *matter*—let's forget it." Such a dismissal was Grandma's prevaricating way of indicating that it *did* matter, as in: "it doesn't really *matter* that the stew is salty"; "it

218

doesn't really *matter* that the tea is cold"; or even, once, though she would always deny it afterwards, "it doesn't really *matter* that he [Mr. di Barnaba] is of Mediterranean extraction."

"But Grandma," I said now, "if you won't be able to see—"

She replied curtly, "I'll manage. I've managed for years and years. Boy, how I've managed."

"OK, Grandma, now think where your glasses could be."

"Oh dear, I can't think, I'm so upset. . . ."

"Please try. Are they under the bed?" No, not under the bed, or inside the pillowcase, or on the dresser, or in the medicine cabinet. Had she flushed them down the toilet? But I wasn't really worried, I knew they would turn up sooner or later—they always did.

This time they were in the refrigerator.

"How did I ever? . . . Now isn't that something, what was I thinking of all the time . . . I suppose I'm losing my mind. . . ."

By this time we were ready to leave; we were waiting only for Sergio—and Paul, who was soon enough heard muttering in the hallway.

"Mrs. Samuels I got him all set up down there," Paul said, referring to Mr. di Barnaba. "You should see how he looks nice—all in his fancy suit. You got yourself a real doll-boy." Paul made a loud, rather disgusting kissing sound with his lips. Grandma made a nasty face in response.

"Mr. Lorditch," Paul said to me, "you got to call that Jewish cantor's now, see once how everything is fixed up with those guys."

"Cantors? Oh, you mean the caterers."

"Ya, well, whatever they call themselves, they openin' up now. So you better make sure they deliver to the right place. We don't want no mess-ups today. You get them now on the telephone, Mr. Lorditch."

While I was on the phone with the catering people, Paul was helping Grandma tie her glasses around her neck. Things were becoming confusing. "Hello, Pheasants 'n' Things? How's my parrot—I mean my order. The name's Lorditch. . . ."

219

Grandma and Paul came out into the living room. "Well, I suppose we could go now," said Grandma. "Now's as good a time as any."

"Wait a minute," said Paul, "where's that what's his name, that bodyguarder."

"Oh, that's right, I say, where is Sergio? He can't be holding us up now. . . . What a silly idea that was, we really don't need him at all. He's just a big pain in the *derrière,* if you'll pardon my French. He hangs about so—he's a nice enough fellow, but he's rather a nuisance. . . ."

"Well, a lot of good it does to bring that up now," I said. "I'm the one who has to suffer. But don't worry, I'm sure he'll go over big at the reception."

"Listen, that's all right," said Paul, "this way we don't got to pay for no security guard—this one's a two-in-one shot." He liked the idea, and winked. Then he turned to me. "So what did those cantors say?"

"Everything's shipshape, Paul. Delivery at twelve-thirty."

"Is that enough time for the wedding?" he asked.

I hadn't really thought of this. "Well, if it runs over—and it shouldn't, if Mr. di Barnaba has done his homework—if it runs over, we could always send someone back early to the reception, to receive the food. I could go—I don't care."

"Why?" asked Paul. "Don't they got someone there to deliver?"

"Yes, but I think one of us should be there to supervise, just to make certain that everything we ordered is delivered."

"Oh, Joseph can take care of that," said Grandma. "After all, he did arrange the reception."

We looked at her. It was true, the basic plan had begun with my uncle's idea. But it was the execution of the idea that I was concerned about now—and execution had never been my uncle's strong suit. I felt sure that if this were left to him, we would have another "salad bar incident." In fact I was surprised that, after that fracas, they had let us rent the banquet room. The ubiquitous Richardson must have interceded on my uncle's behalf.

"That's all well and fine, Grandma," I said, "but I'm sure he doesn't want to worry about all the details at the last minute. I'll do it—I don't mind." I did mind, of course; but the thought of Uncle "supervising" was too terrifying.

"So what's the big deal, I'll handle it," said Paul. "I know how to deal with those guys. The important thing is, don't let them know they can take advantage with you. Once they talk to old Paul, they'll see how good he does business—and that's no monkey-business either." He winked.

"Why, that's very nice of you, Paul," said Grandma. "But I really don't see why Joseph—"

"No, Mrs. Samuels, Mr. Lorditch Senior, he's no business-man, better he don't worry about that stuff, leave it to me."

Grandma rallied. "I beg your pardon, he *is* a businessman— and a very good one, it so happens," she sniffed.

"Ya sure, I mean only he's not so good on the practical side like I am. Leave it to old Paul, you won't have to worry."

The persuasive practicality of Paul won out in the end, and it was decided that he would leave the wedding early. At that moment my bodyguard arrived on his motorcycle, charging down the driveway and stopping about an inch from the garage.

"Oh, I say, he drives like a madman," hissed Grandma. "I can't see why we have to tolerate such a person . . . not really very nice at all . . . just a terrible burden. . . . Why, hello, Sergio," she altered her tone abruptly— "we've been waiting, but I'm glad to see that you're here."

"Oh yeah," said Sergio, strutting up, pulling his pants loose from where they bunched around his crotch. "Hi, everybody. Yeah, you see there was an accident comin' out of the Valley—"

"You were in an accident?"

"No, but I passed through an accident. Traffic was clogged up from Mulholland to Moraga."

221

"Oh dear, I hope it wasn't a serious one."

"Yeah, it was. I think some dudes was wiped out," he replied. "They had a nambulan', and the Highway Patrol was there, shooin' everybody on—you know the way people like to look, I'll never understand that part of people that likes to see sufferin'. Lots of glass, there was glass all over. Saw some blood, too. It'll all be on the TV tonight, you ought to watch it."

"That sounds simply awful, but I suppose we really ought to go now," said Grandma, with a preoccupied, misgiving look at Sergio—who, if it happened that she was late for her wedding, would be held accountable. Sergio moved his motorcycle and we got into the car—Paul and Sergio in the back, and my grandmother in front. I was driving. As we pulled out of the driveway, I noticed Grandma glancing back at the house with a wince of regret—in which pregnant look also was expressed the painful acknowledgment she had finally had to make to herself, that when she returned, although the house itself might still be there, might still be the same, things would have changed; and her fortress would lie no longer in her undisputed demesne.

When we left it was still foggy; but as we drove inland it grew sunnier, although it was a hazy, halftone sunshine. The Saturday joggers were out in numbers along the grassy median strip of San Vicente. A man ran with his legs flapping out sideways from the knees at an awkward angle. Running seemed an agony, but he kept on straining with his eyes shut.

"That fella's going to have himself a heart attack, you wait and see," warned Paul. "Running like a crazy man. All the joggers business is a bunch of bunk. Give me a nice walk quiet in the country, with flowers and trees, that's good enough for me. When I used to be a young man, there was sure walks enough. I remember such beautiful forests in the country around Solingen, the air was like wine. You don't get it like

222

that no more. Nobody knows how to live no more," he concluded.

I looked over at Grandma. Her face wore that mask of martyred placidity indicative, in her, of her ongoing conflict with a mild feeling of disgust—deriving, in this case, from the arrogant and mistaken attitude that Paul's opinions and notions were merely expressions of his ignorance. This was really a tragic misunderstanding, since, in its own way, Paul's motley folk experience was every bit as rich and instructive as her own, and simply another example (although a humbler one) of the undocumented relics of an outdated moral history that had surrounded me since childhood.

We made the turn onto Wilshire, passing the Veterans' Administration Hospital and its vast grounds and cemetery. Over to the right, just off the freeway, they had recently completed the new annex to the hospital, twice as big as the original building. It was disturbing to think that nearly everyone who entered the hospital, and many in the cemetery, were crippled or disabled in some way. I had never seen a soul stirring on those grounds—except one, when I was in eighth grade. Our school bus used to pass an empty field next to the VA, and in that field, at the same time and place every afternoon, stood a man with his back to us. The man's motions were always the same. He wagged his head from side to side, in rhythm with his pelvis. His hands were engaged somehow, somewhere out of sight. We would cheer every time we saw him, but he didn't seem to hear us, or if he did, it made no impression on him. We called him Field Man. He must be dead by now, I thought.

We came to the wide bend at Warner, and then climbed the short grade to Crescent Heights, where we turned into the temple parking lot. The lot was empty, except for a Mercedes parked near the rear entrance. We pulled up there, and Grandma immediately said, "I think we should go in the front entrance, don't you?"

"Well, this entrance is right here, we might as well go in here—"

"We might as well *not*. I am *not* going in by the rear entrance on the day of my wedding."

"Good taste," or superstition, or some premonition more profound—call it what you will, I deferred to it. I wasn't about to argue with her today. We walked the long way around to the front entrance. The sun, by now, was shining bright. It had that relentless quality I associate for some reason with dental appointments in the early afternoon, as you ease your head back fearfully into the headpiece that will hold it during your besiegement. . . . The dental assistant brushes by, smiling with a vengeance, about to conspire in the invisible torture of your mouth; and you are conscious that the sun, through louvered blinds, is also smiling mercilessly. . . . Perhaps a sunny parallelogram has already crept through the blinds, and blazes on the sickly linoleum. . . . Even the cars—which you cannot see from the crazy angle at which you are sitting, but which you can hear—even the cars seem to sparkle, from the swishing clear sound they make as they pass along Wilshire. . . . And you are aware, with a feeling of privileged security mixed with misgiving, that your class is still in session, but you alone are here. . . . And as the gleaming assistant now arrays on the tray by your side the aching tools of unseen exploration, you are impressed with the particular helplessness of your redundant fear: they are going to do it again. The accompanying music in the background is of the kind that people have accidents to on the freeway . . . and the dentist, scrubbed and cool as ice, eases his vicious probe into your mouth and says: "Okey-dokey, Petey, now bite down—oh, come on, I bet you can even bite your girlfriend harder than that. . . ."

It was that sort of sunshine. We came up a blazing marble walk bordered by cypresses on both sides; it was so bright, the cypresses looked black. The walk led to two wooden portals with carved spiral handles and Hebrew lettering in intaglio. Grandma waited for me to open the door.

Inside, all was darkness as our eyes adjusted. The interior

smelled fishy—probably a carpet cleaner they were using, or Medford's breakfast of Lithuanian redolence.

"Ecco! They are here!" called a voice from within. I could not see at first where it was coming from, although there could be no mistaking whose it was. Then, squinting beyond a partition in the entranceway, I could barely make out two figures standing on the dais at the front of a large auditorium. I blinked several times, and could finally distinguish, curving outwards from the base of the dais, in a scallop-shell configuration, plush upholstered seats, as in a movie theater. At the edge of the dais, slightly off-center, was the red wedding canopy. It was supported by four thin rods, and appeared collapsible. In back of the dais hung a huge midnight blue curtain, lit by spotlights that highlighted its velveteen undulations. A great bronze chandelier—radiating lights at the ends of spikes—hung suspended from the ceiling by a long, braided metallic rope. Oblong stained-glass windows were set in at either side of the platform. These were the only clues that the building might serve a religious purpose.

We approached cautiously along one of the aisles. "There's no one here," whispered Grandma.

"Don't worry, they're coming," I said, though I was not at all sure myself.

"Hello. You're early. We are still rehearsing some of the passages," said Rabbi Medford, about as charming as a priest. He was wearing a light blue suit and a knit skullcap. With his neatly trimmed beard he looked, in contrast to my last visit, rather dapper and dignified. His presence onstage seemed to entitle him, in his own mind, to an official manner not without overtones of gentility.

"Well, don't let us disturb you," said my grandmother. "Better soon than sorry, I always say. And how is your student doing?"

We all looked at Mr. di Barnaba. He was, as usual, the personification of Charm. His charcoal gray suit—an almost Edwardian cut, with short, narrow lapels and a graceful cutaway, which could only have been made in London—fit him perfectly, and brought out his robust shoulders and chest, yet without suggesting what his bride would call "vulgarity." One was reminded that he had been, in his youth, an excellent fencer. He wore a burgundy necktie similar to my own, and his bronze face further glowed with an inner joy, which I almost expected to burst out any moment in cries of ecstasy. Such a man, I realized, they do not build today; they lack the raw materials; and there is little demand anymore for such products.

To my grandmother, however, he must have appeared not so very strange, since she was quite literally from another century herself—the nineteenth, with its ruinous formalism. It is harder to say for Mr. di Barnaba. His was a bit of all time: the sanity of Periclean Athens; the nostalgic bitters of Rome's Silver Age; a certain passionate fever of his own country's Renaissance; the sentimentality, clearly, of a Romantic. But there was one age that Mr. di Barnaba would never understand, let alone become a part of, because he simply had no feeling for it, did not wish to educate himself in its culture, kept himself always at the furthest possible distance from its seething masses and senseless violence: it was his own.

"Golly, you sure looking nice and fancy, Mr. di Barnaba," said Paul, and turning to me, he whispered, for my benefit, "You see, that's how a real gentleman dresses like. That's how you get the ladies."

Rabbi Medford said to Grandma, "Your relatives?"

"Yes, Rabbi, I believe you've met my grandson Peter. And this is our friend, Mr. Delgado, and my, ah, my 'valet,' Paul Kirschner."

"Pleased to make the acquaintance, Rabbi," Paul said in his most respectful tone, reserved for celebrities and Jews—though in fact he had already met him earlier that day. The rabbi, obviously trying to be as accommodating as possible today, directed a tight smile at our motley assemblage. He turned back to the groom, who was studying the little booklet he held in his hand.

"Just once more, I think, Rabbi," whispered Mr. di Barnaba.

Grandma spoke up suddenly to us: "I say, it's not bad luck for me to be here early, is it? And where is everybody, they're not going to arrive at the last minute, are they? Oh, and my son, where is he? I hope he hasn't botched it up. . . ." She began wringing her hands, and turned to Paul anxiously. "Did you check on him?"

"Ya, Mrs. Samuels, he's supposed to be fixing up the reception over there at the Marine Land. Maybe he got a little tied up. . . ."

"Tied up! But it's my wedding, he knows what time he's supposed to be here—"

"Relax now, Mrs. Samuels, it's not ten-thirty yet, he'll get here soon, you wait and see."

"He's drunk!" she muttered under her breath. "Drunk on my wedding day! Wicked!" Her hands flew up to her bonnet, as if only this fragile headdress were preventing her distraught brains from spilling out. We persuaded her to sit down; but still she fidgeted in her seat.

Up on the dais, the rabbi and Mr. di Barnaba went through the final recitations.

A quarter to eleven, and still no guests had arrived. The rabbi closed the booklet and pulled a gold wristwatch out of his coat pocket.

"A disaster, a disaster," Grandma muttered to herself. "I am so ashamed."

Just then, I heard behind us a raucous greeting—Scroflone's voice, lumbering nearer. "Hello hello, hope I didn't miss anything. You haven't gone and gotten married without me, have you, Cissie?" Then he was standing right over us. "Can I kiss the bride?" he chuckled, and his blubbery lips came dangerously near.

"Oh, hello, Mr. Scroflone," said Grandma absently, succeeding nevertheless in averting her cheek from the importunate fat. "Have you seen Joseph? I don't know where he is, he's simply terrible."

The cast of Scroflone's dripping face duly altered itself from outsized joviality to whopping concern. "You mean that turkey isn't here yet? I know he left an hour ago."

"I can't think of where he could be—the ceremony begins at eleven sharp."

"Oh, don't worry, he probably went to pick up his crowd," threw off Big Steve, looking around the deserted auditorium, as if to measure whether it would hold all the people who would soon be descending on it. He noticed me, and gave me a stiff smile. "Hello, Peter—looking sharp."

"Hello."

"I like that suit. You look just like F. Scott Fitzgerald. John Travolta, I mean." Scroflone himself was wearing a massive pinstriped affair with a double-breasted jacket—clearly a winter suit, and apparently his idea of formal attire. He wore a pink handkerchief in his breast pocket, which was monogrammed "SOS." He eased his way, barely, into a seat.

Three women came in together. They all wore slacks, and one of them, the one with the darkest tan, wore a low-cut white blouse that set off her dark, horizontally striated throat, across which dangled several trinkets on a gold chain. The women plopped into the rear seats. My grandmother put her glasses on and took a long look at the new arrivals, but apparently she did not recognize them either. She wrinkled her nose and mumbled something under her breath. A moment later two other women walked in, also unescorted.

Big Steve could no longer stand this parade of glory. "I see you're popular with the young set, Mrs. Samuels," he joked, his eyes riveted to the back seats.

"No no, I don't recognize any of them," said Grandma icily.

"They must be friends of Joseph's."

"No doubt."

"I wish they were friends of mine," he quipped. He was looking desperately for someone to recognize. Several more women came in singly, and then the one with the deep tan, who had been seated, stood and came over to us.

"Are you Mrs. Lorditch?"

"Yes, I am Mrs. Samuels."

"Oh, I want to congratulate you. I've heard so much about you. Congratulations."

"Why, thank you," said Grandma, always affable in the public eye, no matter how "vulgar" it struck her. "Now I don't believe I know you."

"No, we haven't met, that is until now—" she laughed— "but I feel as if I've known you my whole life. My name's Wendy."

"Well now, Wendy—I say, I hope you'll come to the reception."

"Oh for sure I will. That should be lots of fun." She smiled as if it would kill her.

There entered an ape dressed in long tennis whites. The arms were prehistorically hairy, with the sort of hair meant for the beginning of the Ice Age, not Southern California. White duck trousers, creased to perfection, concealed what I imagined must be veritable pillars of pilosity; but at the chest, the hair burst forth in all its Neanderthal profusion, as if the shirt could really not contain the tendrilous Congo that erupted at the openings between buttons. The face was miraculously clean-shaven—a process that no doubt had to be repeated twice a day—except for the requisite mustache that drooped over his upper lip. His teeth, when he smiled—which he did unconscionably often, for he had many friends here—were Pepsodent-white, and apparently made of milk. His hair was rather short, pincurled and pubic.

They all seemed to be arriving at once now—all but my uncle. He shouldn't be hard to spot in this crowd. Where was he? I wondered if he'd be wearing the pink coat.

When he finally did appear, however, at a little after eleven, he was wearing a yellow seersucker suit. I had never seen it before; he must have bought it for the occasion.

"Hello hello hello," he said gruffly when he reached us. "See

229

all the friends I brought you?" He bent over to kiss his mother, and for a moment held her head forcefully in his hands. His jaw was set; he was obviously trying to assert control over himself, but it was difficult, and his face showed the strain.

"Joseph, who are all these people? I don't know a soul—where are my friends?" said Grandma.

"Everywhere—everywhere, Mom," he assured her, and sat down between us.

But in fact, she was not terribly well represented; I could see only Mrs. Marsh and Mrs. Podspur, sitting at the edge of the auditorium and looking impervious to it all.

"Look, Grandma, there are your two English friends."

"Oh, where?" she said, immediately rising. "I should go over and greet them."

"No you shouldn't—it's their business to come to you today. Stay here." But my remonstrances were in vain. They had noticed her standing, and waved diffidently; already she was eagerly moving along the aisle toward them, as if at the beck of the sole acquaintances who could save her from dreaded anonymity on this most important occasion.

By this time the rabbi and Mr. di Barnaba had left the platform, and although the auditorium was by no means full, there was now a sizeable representation—of whom, I was not sure. We occupied the seats of honor, front row center. Mr. di Barnaba, I noticed, was sitting with an elderly Italian gentleman, in back and to the right of us. He was not supposed to mix with us until after the wedding was sanctified. I noticed him looking about curiously; no doubt he was as surprised as we were by all the unknown female guests. He must have been cherishing these last moments as a widower—though he did not dare show it. For he was, as my grandmother would agree, a most tasteful man.

"Well, Tiger, what kept you?" asked a man behind us whom I had never seen before. "We were beginning to worry. All the retinue, but no Tiger." He winked.

"Business," said the Tiger.

"On your mother's wedding day? Shame shame." The stranger made no attempt to introduce himself.

"I'm not kidding," continued the Tiger. "Lots of business you wouldn't believe. You wouldn't believe for instance this Vox-Tone thing—"

"I believe it, Joe, I believe it—but not now."

"No. But later—you'll see. Sky's still the limit, Art, sky's still the limit," promised the Tiger. The man then sat back, apparently satisfied with this peculiar assurance.

"Who did you invite?" I asked my uncle. "Do we know any of these people? I feel like I'm in the 'staff only' section of an airport lounge."

"Well, why the hell not?" he said, his breath all over my face. It smelled of a mixture of spice, soap and old shoes. "Puts a little life into the thing. Better than a bunch of old farts doddering around—know what I mean?" He pointed his finger in a didactic pose. "Just remember. The Tiger knows how to have a good time. Ed'll tell you."

"Ed Richardson? Where is he?"

"He's coming." At my suspicious look, he paused. "No no, he's coming, you'll see," he assured me, seeing no humor in the suggestion of the nonexistence of this extraordinary personage. My uncle liked to cultivate and preserve a sense of mystery surrounding what he conceived to be the important. Very likely this was because he feared he appeared to others a clown; and so he wanted to show that there was much more to him and his ideas than people thought. Perhaps also it was his way of telling himself he was accomplishing something truly rare and vital, something that required an atmosphere of silence and mystery for its enactment. I think it was his illusion of the unique, coupled with a misguided, almost alchemical quest for the universal, for the sake of the "useful product," that led to his inevitable disappointment. Instead of trusting in the things he knew, he trusted in the things he didn't—for these alone could never betray him.

The rabbi reappeared now, wearing the shawl. He signaled

231

to us, and I rose together with Grandma, who had just returned from Marsh and Podspur. "All right, here we go," I said, holding her shoulder. "Just take your time, and don't worry. I'm right here with you—we all are."

Mr. di Barnaba was coming up the center aisle. Rather, he was pacing statuesquely, head held high, shoulders back, as if representing his barony in a ceremonial processional of nobles. We followed him up to the front, where I left Grandma. The rabbi led them to the dais. Faint organ music drifted from somewhere behind the blue curtain.

Once they were under the canopy, the rabbi arranged them one on either side, and began his address to the audience. (He was of the Reform School, which has done away with much of the ceremony surrounding marriage procedure, in favor of a few pithy words from the presiding official.) I believe I have mentioned earlier that I never met a man with less charm than Rabbi Medford. This shortcoming was especially glaring now that he stood on the same platform with, and in such stark contrast to Mr. di Barnaba. Medford was humorless, self-important, preachy, complacent and unconscionably dull, with a consistency and relentlessness that, when applied to an act of holy matrimony, were virtually the kiss of death. It was almost as if he were possessed by the demon of a frustrated lawyer, who had set the rabbi's soul on fire with forensic platitudes. There was not a single syllable the rabbi could utter without miraculously rendering it the most boring sound on earth. And his words were at one with his appearance. He was not an unattractive man, but he lacked striking features. His complexion was healthy and unmarked. (Pockmarks or liver spots would at least have lent him an air of suffering.) His beard, as I have noted, was trimmed and un-Talmudic. His body was round without being stout, and the only remarkable thing about it was the awkwardness of his hands when he gestured to express supposedly awesome and unmanageable ideas: "the prosperity [hands] of the Jewish people"; "a rich inner life [hands]"; "the marriage of spirits, the wedding of worlds [hands]."

He finally got around to marrying them. He read from the Bible, then from a smaller book, and had them repeat after him—first the groom, then the bride. Mr. di Barnaba got through the Hebrew passages smoothly enough; in fact it even sounded more convincing with a mild Italian accent—suggesting a Sephardic Jew from the Levant. Grandma had a bit more trouble. She tended to anglicize her pronunciation of the Hebrew, and slipped up on a couple of words; but she repeated them until she got them right.

Then it was time to exchange rings. Mr. di Barnaba, with a rather theatrical gesture, drew his from an inner pocket of his suit-coat, and threaded it onto his bride's knobby finger; and Grandma . . . Grandma couldn't find her ring. We had forgotten all about it.

"Jesus," groaned my uncle, "didn't you remind her? How could she forget the ring?"

"She told me she would be wearing it," I said. "She probably dropped it when she was looking for her glasses this morning."

"But how could she wear it? It would be much too big for her. What happens now? Does this mean they can't get married?"

There must be some allowance in the Talmud for this kind of thing, I thought—an appendix to the procedure: "In case of loss of ring . . ." The groom seemed to be taking it all in stride; and as for Grandma, she had put her hands to her head, and seemed to be giggling. Either that or she was finally cracking. She laid a hand on her cheek and shook her head. But, providently, the rabbi had a ring (he had several). He took one off his finger and gave it to Grandma, who gave it to Mr. di Barnaba. Now either Medford was improvising, or he was really up on his Talmud—if in fact such a contingency is covered there (I don't see why not). Anyway, she slipped the rabbi's ring onto her groom's finger, and they were man and wife.

I wonder what my superstitious grandmother thought of that.

And sooner than I'd expected, it was done—no seven times around the canopy, no smashing of the glass, no cantor. Her new husband kissed Mrs. Cissie di Barnaba nobly on the cheek.

‹ My uncle kept saying, "Isn't that something? Isn't that something? She's some Old Girl. Can you beat that?"

Access to Mariner's Village is achieved along a ramp, leading off Tahiti Way, called the Captain's Row—actually a simulated drawbridge ornamented with chains hanging from pilings, and wooden planks that clatter evocatively as you drive across. The sweep of the long driveway is broken by bumps placed at regular intervals, but this is fine, as it gives you a chance to notice the marine motif that begins immediately: hawsers, netting, cork and colored-glass buoys hanging from the overhead shelter covering the guests' parking spaces. We parked in one of these, and walked ahead to the reception area, where Paul would be waiting for us. We came to the end of the driveway, fashioned as a roundabout, and stopped for a moment to gaze down at the carp pond. The carp were sizeable, and basked lazily in the sunlight near the surface. Grandma was especially taken with a huge golden one. She had seen them in Japan when she was a girl, she said, but never so big. "They are raised to have their markings on their backs, so you can see the patterns when you look down at them. The Japanese make a hobby of carp-watching," she informed us. "At least they used to."

From a balcony above us, someone began throwing crumbs of bread down to the fish. They swarmed for the food, making kissing noises with their mouths as they fought for the bigger pieces.

"Look at how fat they are," remarked Mr. di Barnaba. "Such feeding has become a habit, no longer a treat. The greedy devils can hardly move. What is that line from Coleridge? 'We deform and kill the things whereon we feed.' "

His timely quote went uncommented upon, however; I think it was a bit grim for the occasion. Our brief reverie among the fish was broken as a voice boomed behind us:

"Well, look who's here! What's the matter, you folks party-shy? Come on, Mrs. di Barnaba, your guests are waiting on you." Scroflone's bulky shadow, and my uncle's dumpy one, joined ours over the railing.

"Let them wait, then," I heard Grandma mutter. Then, in her public voice: "Yes, we're coming, we were just watching the fish."

"Pretty things, aren't they? Some big fat raccoon's going to have a nice feast," Scroflone said.

"I didn't know there were raccoons in this area," said Mr. di Barnaba.

"Well, if there didn't used to be, there will be now. They love fish," chortled Scroflone. "Look at the size of those babies!" They swarmed around our shadows now, as if we were the food.

"He's wrong," said my uncle, rather forcefully. "Big Steve, you're wrong. There're no raccoons here. I've never seen one, and I live here, I should know. He's wrong."

"OK, OK, old man, I stand corrected. We used to have them over by Tujunga, is why I mentioned . . ." Then a more compelling thought occurred to him. "Hey kids, I'm hungry. We've got a reception waiting on us. Mrs. Barnaba, Mr. Barnaba, after you!"

"Excuse me, but it is *di* Barnaba," corrected my step-grandfather, ever so politely; and then he added, more softly still, with a smile smooth as a sword, "Past history, you know."

My uncle led the way to the reception hall, following the carp pond out past Davy Jones' Locker and into the central patio area—a cluster of sundecks, adults' and children's swimming pools, and the clubhouse complex. I noticed the same

235

gold-tile fish at the bottom of the children's pool, but now they were shimmering happily under the splashings of frantic playmates. We worked our way around the latticed plastic furniture on the sundecks, and came to the clubhouse entrance.

Already the music had started up, and there were guests inside. Paul, who had left the wedding early, stood by one of the long white buffet tables, with his hand on his chin, as if surveying damages. He had changed into his official white uniform, the livery of his sacred office.

"Ach, so there you all are, good. Congratulations, you two, you make one big happy couple, both of you." He contemplated the newly marrieds proudly for a moment, then he drew me aside. "Listen once here, Mr. Lorditch. These guys here—" pointing disdainfully to men in green livery who stood behind the buffet tables— "these guys tell me two of the dishes went rotten and they had to throw them out, they stunk so bad. They said it was like poison food. I said OK, you're better safe than sorry."

"Which dishes were these?"

"I think it was that fancy Italian stuff what your uncle ordered—canal, canal. . . ."

"Cannelloni?"

"That's it. So it was poison, phooey. You better watch now they don't charge you for it." Paul was always conscientious about saving money and accounting for our expenses, although he tended to overestimate both his responsibility and his efficacy in that regard. But he was obviously very proud now of having uncovered this double crime of treachery and wastefulness. We left him to surveil the activity of the caterers; Grandma and Mr. di Barnaba had already begun to mix, and I set off to observe the guests.

There seemed to be a disproportionate number of single women—even more than at the wedding. They obviously had nothing to do with my grandmother, or anyone else. They had come just for the reception, and were looking for their male

236

counterparts, some of who were now emerging, scrubbed, medallioned and Qiana-ed, from the weight rooms and saunas at the back of the clubhouse. In small pockets, some still alone, the guests were milling about to the music of the band, nibbling at the more accessible tidbits on the buffet tables, and trying to talk above the sound of old Beatles and Petula Clark tunes played to the accompaniment of a stuttering, slightly funereal-sounding accordion. This type of music, wherever it occurs, is perhaps the most useless in existence; one feels that the arranger, given the elaborate and almost pedantic whims to which he has succumbed to distort the original material beyond recognition, could more easily and felicitously have composed his own material. The music made little impression on the crowd here, who were no doubt more attuned to disco, and were kept here only by the lure of free food, drink and hope of male Mariners. I caught snatches of conversation:

"... only the cutest guy in the *Village* ..."

"... outrageous new Mercedes ..."

"... don't give a hoot what he said, I just know what I feel. It's a gut reaction, Don ..."

"... I like to call it 'screen presence' ..."

"... for sure I'd go for it, Judy ..."

"... rully ..."

The person who spoke this last word was bobbing her head enthusiastically. I realized only afterwards that she had in effect spoken a complete sentence, conveying the idea of her own emphatic approbation or encouragement.

There was no sign now of the newlyweds; perhaps they had already fled. I did come across my uncle, propped against a polished-brass ship's throttle with a drink in his hand. His clothes, the pose and the prop together looked like an advertisement out of an exclusive New England mail-order catalogue offering clothes to appeal to the executive's sense of staid eccentricity. But my uncle's drooping face and portly body complicated the impression: he looked not at all healthy.

237

"Where'd you get the suit?" I asked.

"Oh, this, I've had this for years. Brooks Brothers. Canary yellow."

"Well, you certainly do stand out."

"You know me, I like to have *style*." He emphasized this last word with a grand gesture of his drinkless hand. "What do you think of this place? Pretty nifty, eh? The Tiger came through all right, what d'you say?"

I demurred, "I guess it has what you say—style."

"You bet it does—style and class. And not lacking its share of jolly girls," he added, casting a leer in all directions. He took a sloppy swig. "What happened to Mom and Mr. di Barnaba? I don't see them."

"I was wondering myself. Maybe this thing is not at all their 'style.'" I realized then that I probably shouldn't have said that. He was proud of his idea, especially as it seemed at last to have taken shape—although unassisted by the two people for whom it was ostensibly intended. But, as he would say, "Who cares? It's a party, isn't it?"

"What style?" he answered now. "They love it, it's just their style. Maybe they went out to—consummate the marriage. You never know. . . ." And with this, he roguishly swaggered forth toward the food, and the jolly girls.

Sergio and I were standing at the end of one of the long buffet tables, by the chicken-liver mousse, when I was bumped from behind. It was a mild pressure—I cannot say truculent or provoking; it was simply determined, it wanted to get to the macaroni salad next to the mousse, and I was in the way.

"Excuse me genelmen pardon me," said a deep voice, in tones of restrained violence suggesting elemental impulses of dumb brute strength that it was, however, too "polite" to indulge—except when absolutely necessary. The voice I knew. I turned—not to make way, but just to see, already with a curious anticipatory tingle, who it was. It was Peterson. As usual, he did not recognize me; but when I made no effort to make way for him, he gave me a second look.

"Excuse me, sir. Macaroni salad's righteous, I gotta scarf some. Outrageous. Excuse me."

"Why, hello, Mike," I said.

"Hey. Hi." It then occurred to him that since I had addressed him by name I must have reasonable cause to do so. "Hey. Do I know you? You look kinda familiar, but I can't really place it." His arm had now extended itself behind me to extract a dollop of macaroni salad, which he served into his empty champagne glass. "Sorry," he explained, "but when I'm hungry I ain't proud. This food is rully gud."

"Indeed it is, Mike, and I'm so glad you could come. I was afraid I might not see you again."

"For sure," he replied automatically. And then: "Hey, you're not shitting, are you? We really do know each other? What's your name?"

"Well, I don't see how you could forget, after our last encounter. It is something I will always remember, Mike." I had raised my voice deliberately. People around us were watching us closely. Peterson's smile faded.

"Like, whatever your name is, I don't know." He added, with his idea of emphasis, "I cannot *understand* what you are saying, man."

And then I spoke out loud and clear, with an authority fed by the delight of revenge, and the recklessness of champagne: "I am saying, my good man, that you made homosexual advances to me, Mike Peterson—which, however, is not in the least surprising, since it is well known that you are a practicing sodomite." And then I screamed, at the top of my lungs, "Help me, Sergio! I'm being attacked!"

Poor Peterson was thoroughly confused. He looked about him for my attackers. The area immediately around us had suddenly cleared. Then, into the open space came my bodyguard, calmly, inexorably, with an inevitability of pursuit and seizure that is the fundamental operating principle of cops and robbers. But for Sergio it was not a game, it was his job—the realization of which, later on, would have made me feel guilty of irresponsible conduct, had I not known that he felt fulfillment and even a long-awaited pleasure in the practical enactment (which, for that matter, hardly took place often enough for his satisfaction) of his duty.

He walked up to Peterson and placed a grave arm on his shoulder, and Peterson, reasonably enough, I suppose, since he did not know who this bulky stranger was, took offense, and made a provoking motion towards Sergio: half-push, half-fisticuff—which was, at any rate, the wrong thing to do, for in an instant he was down, straining on the floor, his arm in a contorted and painful hold against his neck, which was pinned by Sergio's hand to the floor. This awkward configuration suggested a decisive moment in pro wrestling, but had been reached rather more effortlessly. Then Sergio, looking slightly embarrassed by his seemingly effortless display of force, brought the fated perpetrator to his feet, and ushered him outside.

"What was all that about, anyway?" my uncle said afterwards. "Who was that guy? Did you start a fight with him? How'd he get in here? This is very serious, you know. I'm very concerned." His concern, however, did not prevent him from turning suddenly in the direction of the newlyweds at the end of the room. "Cut the cake, anyway!" he bellowed. "Cut the cake!"

Grandma and her groom were ready to do this, but the photographers kept flashing, and I suppose Grandma thought she ought to pose, out of politeness to them and, above all, a certain decorous observance of tradition. She stood frozen, holding the golden knife; Mr. di Barnaba was uxoriously clasping her hands in his. She gave out a modest smile of acknowledgment—yes, this was the wedding cake; yes indeed, that was her husband standing beside her; but let us not make a great to-do of it. In that faint, persistent smile of hers were exemplified all her years of studied self-effacement and good breeding, the quasi-aristocratic humbleness (derived from an innate conceit of superiority), the subtle but continual, quizzical wonderment of an old lady who has really seen, heard and felt too much, yet suspects at heart that she has not ultimately attained to what she would like to call wisdom—though others might think she has. But others, she knows, are wrong. I now have copies of these photos, and I bring them out occasionally, when thoughts of her grow either too fond or too critical, and I must remind myself of that otherworldly gleam, which, underneath her complaisant wedding smile, like the horseman of Yeats, casts a cold eye on life, on death.

Then Mr. di Barnaba began to cut, or rather to make her cut, working her hands as a puppeteer would handle an ancient, cracked puppet.. There was considerable applause from the guests, whose ranks, I now saw, had swollen to fill the entire dance floor, and much of the sitting room behind the railing upstairs. My uncle was shouting "Bravo! Attaway, Mom!" Others were whistling shrilly. But my grandmother did not look in the least aware of any of these distractions; she was concentrating on the task at hand.

Among the guests, more men had now joined the women, and couples were trying with some difficulty to dance to the music, which was as badly suited for dancing as it was for listening. How such musicians can feel they are accomplishing anything worthwhile is beyond me. Their approach to their music, like the music itself, was annoyingly ambiguous. The singer, with uncomfortable contortions and grimaces, sang as if he really wanted to be dancing; and the dancers danced as if they would rather have been sitting, listening to him singing (or dancing). A couple near the edge of the floor were doing the Bump, so awkwardly that they managed to make their collisions seem accidental. One woman did nothing but shake her hair and wrists, and shift her feet at ninety-degree angles to one another. A man in a shiny red shirt hardly moved at all; he simply snapped his fingers and smiled broadly. His sparse mustache looked like a dirty upper lip.

I moved through the dancers toward my grandparents. As I leaned over to kiss her, Grandma said, "Here, take a piece of cake, do you want a bigger one?"

"No thanks, Grandma. I'm very happy for you. Congratulations again, Tullio. *Auguri*."

Mr. di Barnaba smiled sublimely.

"Now have you eaten enough?" continued Grandma. "I don't think the music is very good, do you? I can't hear anything but noise."

"That's what the young people are listening to these days, Grandma," I explained.

"Young people, well . . . yes, but these people don't look all that young to me," she commented cannily. Then she whispered, "I think they're rather common, don't you?"

"Rather." (I drunkenly enjoyed the opportunity to use this word instead of "yes.")

"Are they all Joseph's friends? I can't think where he meets such people. I don't believe I know anyone at all. Except for Mrs. Marsh and Mrs. Podspur, and I don't know where they have gone."

"That makes two of us. Three of us." I glanced at Mr. di Barnaba, who was surveying the crowd with a disdainful curiosity.

"Yes, no doubt they must be someone's acquaintances," he said. "Or perhaps they are just looking for a celebration—any will do. Look at it this way: we are numerously, if not well, attended." He gave a grudging laugh. "I must say Paul has set everything up very nicely. But I don't see him—where is he?"

"I haven't seen him since we first arrived. He said something about trouble with one of the dishes. Maybe he's gone off to sue the caterers."

"Trouble with the food, eh?" said Mr. di Barnaba. "Perhaps someone is trying to poison me. At least they could wait until *after* the wedding."

"Really, you shouldn't even joke about such things," sniffed my grandmother, adding, with a cryptic allusiveness. "We've had too much trouble with certain people recently. It's terrible, people are wicked—but I don't want to go into it. Who gets this piece of cake? Peter, will you take it?"

"Grandma, you'll kill me with cake." At this, Mr. di Barnaba gave a broad laugh, and patted his little bride on the head; and she desisted for a while.

Grandma married! A newlywed! And I had a new grandfather in the bargain! I needed more champagne to better digest these unfamiliar ideas. I am really not very comfortable with ideas—one of the major reasons I could never be an intellectual, at least not an active one. (But, characteristically, it has taken me some time to be able to approach this idea.) New ideas are especially troublesome, but an old one in endless circulation will do the trick as well. Marxism, Freudianism, Existentialism, Transcendentalism: people expressing themselves in these terms blabber to me in another language. I am aware that some people would call this attitude ignorance. Perhaps it is, but then it is a willful ignorance, learned through arduous contact with stifling ideas, of which I am now convinced there is at least one for every talking person on this earth—including myself.

But perhaps it is more accurate to say that I deal in impressions, in emotions, in the misty bog of intuition; and as soon as I think for any period on the ephemera that visit me—that is, as soon as I imagine them, as soon as they pass for even the briefest moment into ideas—they become distasteful to me, no matter how personal or dear they have been. I don't know why this is so. Perhaps because my dear subjects have now become objects. Or perhaps the mere suggestion of a relationship between my world and the outside world, the annoying and redundant coexistence of *my* objects and *its*, and the various excruciating coincidences that result, is what is so disillusioning. So the marriage of my grandmother, now no longer a private pact, but a public act, and attended by the world, had in this way become distasteful to me.

But of course I recognized that the wedding was no longer

an idea, but a fact. And this fact was most difficult of all to comprehend. What did it mean for me? Had I lost her? And really, wasn't it about time that I got married myself?

These desultory thoughts were interrupted by a voice somewhere below me. The inflection and the words were already quite familiar.

"So hey, what's cooking, you."

No party of ours is ever quite complete without its midget; and I should have known he would turn up today. Latching onto me much as a terrified pet monkey will screw itself onto your neck, he began immediately to interview me.

"So your uncle put on some show here. How he get so many people."

"I don't know. I guess they're friends of his."

"Are you kidding. These people don't look like his friends. I don't know no one here. You seen Ed Richardson."

"No."

"Well, he should be around here somewhere. I know he was invited. No party is ever complete without Ed. How about your uncle—where is he."

"I saw him a while ago. I'm sure he's around somewhere."

"I don't know. I not see him either. I know nobody here," repeated the small alien.

"Well, you know my grandmother and Mr. di Barnaba, don't you?"

"Yeah, but can't talk to them now. Too many people here. How's the food."

"Excellent. Try the *pâté en croute*," I suggested, remembering his penchant, as a Moslem, for forbidden meats.

"What's that."

"Cut-up pork, wrapped in a pastry shell. Delicious."

Achekosa's eyes lit up. "Yeah, maybe I like that. Where is it."

I led him to the *pâté en croute,* which the crowd had left untouched. This delicacy seemed to satisfy his curiosity for the moment. I saw my chance and excused myself, and taking up what I believed at the time to be a glass of champagne from the sideboard, I went off to look for my uncle, whom I suddenly missed. I walked down a path leading from the pool patio, and soon found myself again by the Mariner's Village rivulet as it meandered its way beneath the overhanging balconies of the condominia. Although I was by this time indubitably drunk—I saw that I had a bottle of champagne in my hand, not a glass—I easily recognized that I was headed the right way to my uncle's apartment: over a Japanese-style bridge, past a backwater of the carp pond, over another bridge and then into the courtyard of my uncle's building. As I looked up at his second-story apartment, into the window of the kitchen, where I could see hanging a paper fish-mobile, I felt a painful stab of love for him. I was taken by surprise, and was quite helpless for minutes on end—just standing there in the middle of the sun-drenched courtyard, sweating, crying perhaps, sensing that I was uncomfortable and ridiculous, but unable to move. At the time, in my state of drunkenness, I had no idea what had prompted that sudden access of emotion; but I know now that it all began with the little fish-mobile in the window.

Ever since I was a child, I have been able to cultivate a sentimental empathy with inanimate objects; because I have always known better, I have known that these objects are not at all inanimate, and are really quite sentient. Not only do they feel, but they generally feel sad, useless or ignored—exactly how I would feel in their position. Now objects of an exaggeratedly festive or diversionary nature, or those everyday items whose prosaic purpose would be cosmeticized by an affectionate or humorous label, have, in my mind, been the cause of especially poignant instances of grief. The eager rows of chocolate bunnies waiting in supermarkets at Eastertime; honey that comes in plastic bear-shaped containers; the brightly colored plastic tassels caparisoning the handlebars of children's bicycles; the cereal Lucky Charms; miniature pronged holders in imitation of corncobs, used to eat corn on the cob; magnetic paperholders in the shape of fruit or vegetables, invariably stuck to refrigerators; any type of commercial toy designed for pets, especially birds . . . and the list goes on indefinitely. I'm really not sure what these objects have in common, but whatever it is, if it is anything at all, I seem to respond to it automatically. And it is not merely, as I have sometimes thought, a form of nostalgia for my experience of these objects as a child, for I remember that, even then, I felt for them much as I do now, I saw them then for what they were. My mother was the only one to whom I ever communicated my obscure sense of rapport, and she understood it instinctually. We would call it "feeling sorry for." We used to derive great amusement and reassurance from each other's instant recognition and acceptance of the felt-sorry-for object, which was then set apart from all the rest of its merely inanimate companions by the consciousness we lent and then falsely ascribed to it—a consciousness exclusively our own. It was, I suppose, a sort of "pathetic fallacy" of the banal. "Mom, I feel sorry for the product No Bugs M'Lady" (a household cabinet lining). "I know," she would reply, "and how about these garden clippers?" (stylized to resemble a bird's head and beak). We responded to the corny, the kitsch, the ridiculous; but there was another, more fundamental criterion for the felt-sorry-for object, without which it failed to capture our imagination, and the presence of which we could no better analyze, predict or prepare for than by acknowledging simply that we knew it when we saw it.

Suffice it to say, then, that I knew the fish-mobile when I saw it. That it happened to belong to my uncle, and had been hung there by him, made me feel especially sorry for it, and him. It was an unbearable feeling while it lasted, which was fortunately only a matter of minutes, after which point I composed myself and walked up to his apartment—knowing full well, even in my condition, that he would not be there. I suppose I wanted to get a closer look at the felt-sorry-for object. I walked up the steps to the door and tried to open it; it was already open. I walked across the living room and onto the sun porch, where I looked senselessly for a moment onto the glistening esplanade. I could hear the band playing below and behind me. I then walked back into the living room, where I turned right, walked through a short hallway and up to the door of my uncle's bedroom, which was closed.

I stopped in front of the door, not intending to open it, but unable to walk away from it either—as if it marked a threshold, a sacred boundary that mysteriously compelled my respect, my obeisance—my violation. I opened the door. Inside, crumpled on top of the disarranged waterbed, fully clothed in his yellow seersucker suit, lay my uncle; beside him, the imprint and excruciating perfume of another recent body clung still to the sheets. Half-hidden in the folds I recognized a single paper flower—one of the paper flowers he had brought back from the Orient. The bed still undulated softly, mockingly, and the inanimate body rode with it senselessly, like animal cargo. I put my hands out to stop the hideous posthumous motion, but this only made it move in another direction, and I quickly took my hands away, horrified. I knelt by the bed and waited for him to settle into peace. I don't know how long I stayed there by his side; it must have been hours, for when I eventually returned, hardly sensible, to the party, I found that my grandmother had left on her honeymoon.

Epilogue

"Dearest Peter," writes Grandma on embossed di Barnaba stationery with baronial coronet, "We were thrilled to get your beautiful long letter, which set my mind at ease about so many things that had lately been disturbing me. Joseph's silence, which as we all know is not at all like him, had worried us terribly, as he usually manages to keep in touch one way or another; and I must say I am still quite surprised not to have been informed beforehand of his strange new project. Are you sure he has our address here? It's *Palazzo* di Barnaba, you know, not *Piazza* as Paul once wrote, poor thing—though there is a piazza too by that name, but in another part of town. At any rate I expect to hear from him sometime soon, all about his new position in Ethiopia. It sounds very exciting—though I must say it is a bit remote, still it's a job—his first real job, I'm sorry to say. (I suppose I've been a wicked mother in that respect. Still there is time for everything and I do believe he's taken a step in the right direction.)

"But please tell me what exactly is Sheba Enterprises? It would clear things up a bit if you told me—you know I could never really understand Joseph's explanations, they never seemed quite to the point. I believe it has something to do with yoghurt, if I'm not mistaken. At any rate, once he gets settled down there, whenever that will be, I expect to have it directly from the horse's mouth. (And what a mouth on that horse!)

"Peter darling—I look forward to your upcoming visit with great joy and expectancy. Though I chide you for waiting so long—three months is too much, what can have kept you? But I won't complain now that I know you are coming. I think you will love it here. It is quite traditional and old-fashioned—not at all what a California boy is used to—and the language gives one a bit of a start at first. I am content to let Tullio do most of the talking—an ideal arrangement, and one which he is satisfied with, I'm sure!

"We get along very well with the townspeople and servants here. I must say they are more polite and cultured and really much nicer than people in California. I think you too will find this to be true when you come. I have already told the servants much about you, and they are eagerly awaiting your arrival. 'When is the young gentleman coming? We will make a banquet when he comes,' they say—in their own language of course. (It's a very strange-sounding affair—not at all like the pure Italian. Still, the meaning does get across.)

"Peter darling—though I sometimes worry terribly about you, I do think it is preferable you will be coming alone. The bodyguard is such a nuisance to have around, though he is a nice person, and I know he cares for you greatly. As for Paul, it's much better to have him stay and look after the house. And to be very frank, just between ourselves, I do think he's getting a bit old to do that much traveling, especially with his leg and all. Do give him our love, tell him we are thinking of him, and there is no one here quite like him (fortunately!), and I will write him a long letter very soon.

"I'm trying to think now of anything for you to bring with you that we don't have here. And do you know I can't think of anything. Except for potatoes. It seems they have no potatoes here—at least not the kind I am used to eating. If you could arrange somehow to have some nice American potatoes sent over—of course I don't expect you to carry them, that would be ridiculous. Perhaps you could have them sent ahead. I miss them very much. Several bushels, I would think.

"Give my love to everyone, including the house and the garden, and also Mrs. Marsh and Mrs. Podspur, if you ever see them. (I haven't yet written them—isn't it disgraceful? I think they must not be very pleased with me. I feel very naughty.) And the lawyers too, I suppose, though to tell the truth I don't miss them at all. Also say hello to Mr. Richardson, whom I still don't know. And I was so pleased to hear of Mr. Scroflone's new dessert, the 'Cassata di Barnaba.' Perhaps you might bring the recipe with you when you come.

"Peter dear—I am counting the days until we are together again. Do not forget to cable us your definite arrival time in Rome. We will be there rain or shine, to meet you. Perhaps we will take the boat—at any rate it will probably not rain. Italy is so sunny! Even more than California!

"God bless you, watch over you, keep you from all harm.

"Your loving Grandma.

"P.S. Do not forget the potatoes."